MW00959318

Yaël König

Producer & International Distributor
eBookPro Publishing
www.ebook-pro.com

The Secret Jewish Village
Yaël König
Copyright © 2023 Yaël König

Translation: Seree Zohar
Contact: yael@yaelkonig.com

ISBN 9798872443148

THE SECRET JEWISH VILLAGE

*A historical fiction novel
based on a true story*

YAËL KÖNIG

In memory of *Moise Rahmani*, who first told me
the story of the Jews of San Nicandro.
Without him, there would have been no book.

To Mona, Louise, Chloe, Sam and Isaac,
with all my love.

Friedrich II, King of Prussia:
"Voltaire, prove that God exists!"

Voltaire: *"The Jews, Your Majesty."*

INTRODUCTION

Back in 1999, when my novel "Fresca" was published, I was invited to Brussels to present the book. The host, Moise Rahmani, a humble, wonderful man despite his vast knowledge, impressed me deeply. He had spent his entire life actively involved in preserving Jewish tradition and restoring several truths that had either been distorted or erased.

Our professional friendship grew until one day, he handed me a manuscript titled "Shalom Buana" on which he had just added the words, "The End," although those words in connection with the history of the Jewish community can never be true in the literal sense.

It was barely two days later when I called Moise back and proposed that the book be published in the Tera Hebraica series which I was managing for the Romia publication company.

It didn't take long before Moise came to visit me, manuscript in hand, titled "San Nicandro: The Story of a Mass Conversion." The name "Elena Kassen" was on the manuscript. Ms. Kassen (1909-2011) was an Italian Assyriologist with a Ph.D. in the history of religions, and who managed research for CNRS, the Center for National Scientific Research in Paris.

"Well, I brought you this book too," Moise said, "and it's almost impossible to find these days. But it, too, is a *must-publish*. Beyond the scientific text, there's an amazing story here for you. You should write it. It needs to become known to Jews worldwide and for that matter, to non-Jews too."

"Of course I'll read it, but why don't you write the narrative?"

"I'm busy presenting events. You, on the other hand, know how to empower events and people's stories. Do it, Yael."

Transfixed, I read the manuscript, as well as "Le Compagnons de San Nicandro" by Albin Michel Laid, a novel that was only available in French, and published in 1961. Suddenly nothing seemed more urgent than delving into the story about this village in the district of Foggia. The further I progressed in the research, the more I longed to actually go and meet the Jews of San Nicandro.

That story doesn't belong here in the Introduction, of course. I am merely attempting to convey the thrill I felt toward this new and unique adventure in modern human history in general, and the history of the Jews in particular.

My actions and some of my books express that desire and need to present my Jewish people's annals of history. But this specific narrative not only brought me the greatest of satisfaction, it made me more motivated than ever to ensure that the truth would come to light through quality writing.

Writing the book required a shift in my thinking processes, and the need to physically meet witnesses to the event initiated by Donato Manduzio, whose piercing gaze, reaching us from his photos, clearly expresses how the force of will and deep thinking can move mountains.

The archival materials on San Nicandro and surrounding areas as well as Donato's personal diary, handwritten in Italian, were revealed – once I'd translated them – to be both exciting and pragmatic. Various works in English also enabled me to enrich my own efforts, coaxing my curiosity and chain of thought. Testimonies on the Arte broadcasting network turned out to be highly important, and my thanks to Jozian Sbero for helping me obtain them.

Not so long ago I met Ester Cherona, for which my thanks go to Eli Jimmy, and to Elisheva Sabah, for whom I felt great affection and admiration in her lifetime. Ester is one of the twins mentioned in this book. As we sat in her Acco home, a breeze wafting in from the Mediterranean Sea cooling the four of us, we could feel something else in the air: a wonderful feeling of connectedness and joy. On seeing the documents I brought, Ester simultaneously cried and laughed.

"You've brought information about my father, my family, and that period which I hadn't known! And your book presents everything I witnessed back then."

In a living room loaded with photos, it seemed that time had opened its arms to cradle the adventures of the Jews of San Nicandro, which began at the start of the twentieth century and extended all the way to this unexpected meeting of the four of us, accompanied by a deep sense of belonging.

As is well known, an author's work requires long days, months, of quiet, of pondering, of questioning and answering, and is infused with a desire without which no progress can be made. There are no words to describe the gratification and enthusiasm of an author who learns that a publisher is greatly interested in his or her work, and that the work will be made accessible to the public. it fills the author with serenity and delight.

This delight was further increased by learning that Israel's Ministry of Immigration had bestowed me with the title of "Israeli Francophone Author of Excellence." Suddenly I realized that I needed to make sure the book was published in Hebrew.

Last but not least, my thanks to Isabel Butte who, throughout the years, has been an active partner and has always shared her insightfulness on pagination and production of copy. Here too, because of her involvement, keen eye, and smart approaches, she has my eternal gratitude, respect, and friendship.

Moise Rahmani passed away a mere month before the book had been completed. How fortunate that he'd managed nonetheless to have read it, and reaped pleasure from seeing the story come to fruition.

The Jews of San Nicandro's adventure is not yet complete. It is an ongoing work of advancement and development. As a reader, you too are now an important link in the chain of the continuity.

Yael Konig

Manduzio, the elder, climbs the hillside.

Used to the loose stones that could upset his balance, he avoids any falls that might delay him by kicking them away with a flick of his ankle. The man who, for some inexplicable reason feels connected with his forebears, is known as "caccaba," Italian slang for poop, hurries to reach San Nicandro.

It is still the early days of 1900. A new atmosphere is spreading through the sleepy Foggia region along with the warming weather. A new spring, first of the new century, began infiltrating the sense of time standing still.

Changing seasons are a cause of concern for San Nicandro farmers in their village of thieves and ignoramuses, a village nestled two hundred and fifty meters high, adorning Garganico Mountain's slope.

After their hopes of expanding their plots were dashed some fifty years earlier, it seemed to them that the fresh young century would not last long, that it would self-destruct while simultaneously shattering the world through some kind of magic or evil, or perhaps both, wrought by humans.

In neighboring villages from San Severo to Foggia, folks are sure that the evil is likely to erupt from San Nicandro, where the dangerous Camorra, a crime organization rampant throughout Italy, has not managed to get its foot in the door. Neither aggressiveness nor heroism enabled San Nicandro's residents to resist the organization. They're simply slow, grumpy, and immersed in the boredom of routine everyday life. "Unremarkable people," one of the region's authorities calls them.

Caccaba wonders whether the ominous change of year is what's driving greater attendance in church. Perhaps there's a growing need to connect to God, since the end of the world could occur tomorrow. It's hard to know. Manduzio is a Catholic, body and soul. True, he behaves like any self-respecting villager, and while his wife is busy praying to Jesus and the Holy Virgin to safeguard San Nicandro, he spends a pleasant hour with his peers at the village inn.

And who better to converse with our holy protectors if not the women? They know so much that the men don't, or aren't interested in. They survive births despite the bleeding, they heal illnesses by laying their hands on foreheads, they knead dough and produce the most delicious tortellini and tagliatelle, pliable and light, to the enjoyment of the menfolk returning from their work in the fields and vineyards.

Caccaba walks with a measured gait. His friend Ferrando, from San Severo, with whom he's just held an important business meeting, has given him a ride in his carriage, dropping him off no more than a few kilometers from San Nicandro. Manduzio is unperturbed by the twenty or so kilometers separating the two villages. He walks it frequently. But in light of the excellent deal he struck with his friend, Ferrando insisted on easing Caccaba's long walk back. In fact, on Sunday, Caccaba plans to bring Donato, his youngest son, to the Communion ceremony in church to receive the wine and wafer for the first time, ensuring that his son becomes a devout Catholic.

Manduzio plans to let the wine flow on this festive occasion: not the cheap stuff that burns the throat and is generally sold to the village folk; but the thick, quality wine which he makes and sets aside only for his own use. Ferrando promised to come early on Sunday morning, accompanied by his entire family. Importantly, he will bring the princely suit tailored for Donato. The two men shook hands on the deal and drank a toast.

The Manduzio family members aren't wealthy. Far from it! They have no more than a slip of land that barely keeps them going, and several grape vines that provide them with tradable merchandise in the Foggia market. Nonetheless, the whole village will be invited on Sunday to share the Manduzio family's wine, wafer and celebration in the name of the Lord. Nothing is too much for the Lord Jesus who gives of his blood and body to his disciples.

The festivities for Luigi, the firstborn, left quite the impression in the memories of those who participated. The boy received the body of Christ with such fervor that several women swore they noticed a beam of light gently touching his hair. To some of them, that beam appeared rounded, crystal-like; to others, bright and shaped like a cross. It would seem that the abundance of salamis, dishes made of fresca, that wonderful homemade fresh pasta, and secca, the dry types of pasta, as well as the biscotti filled with nuts and raisins, made everyone cheerful and attentive. Or at least, that's how it was on Luigi's special day.

Now it's Donato's turn to receive the wafer. He's also a good boy, if a little mischievous, though isn't that how most of the children are? And of course he's a total ignoramus, too. But he catches on quickly and is a diligent worker with strong arms. Wonderfully, there's no need to beg him to listen to Don Adriano, the priest, who talks about the lives of saints and Jesus. But Donato never says a word. And when the priest asks questions, Donato stays silent, his eyes downcast. His eyes: they're blacker than black and their gaze is piercing. Their color sometimes speaks, sometimes screams, without anyone understanding what they're saying.

***

The slopes of Mount Garganico, which seem to watch over Dubrovnik on the other side of the Adriatic Sea, look like a painting van Gogh would produce. The shades of blue burst through the red which extend into infinity, and the hues of yellow spatter the abundant foliage in gold dust. This blossoming of flowers erases the stark, gloomy winter that has just passed.

Year after year, century after century, Mount Garganico gazes upon life's flow without being affected by it, without changing, even though layer after layer of culture is building up. The tranquil mountain can never claim to be part of a stormy history. No revolutions ever took place there, nor did the population ever change.

The sight revealed to Caccaba's eyes this morning is precisely the same as that which his forebears saw. Farmers still worked as they had in Roman times. They use old-fashioned plows to till their fields, delineated as narrow oblongs, since that's the easiest shape to work. They advance between the ridges bearing the hope of a rich harvest. Caccaba has no idea, and it interests him about as much as last year's snow, that the Italian word "porca" is also used to mean a very different type of furrow, that which is concealed in every woman's body and where her husband would sow his seed. Had he known, he would surely have grinned lopsidedly, emphasizing the deep creases on each side of his mouth.

Caccaba stops before the stone cross not far from the village. He is almost tempted to remove the cradle held by the statue of San Nicandro, which was heaped with melted candles and withered flowers, but he doesn't. That's not a man's job. Without a doubt, the women are starting to become negligent. The flowers' nectar is seeping out. Scattered about, the flowers seem disappointed, as though asking: please, wait, we're coming!

In San Nicandro, things sometimes ferment between couples. The men fume. The women scold. These force their views on those, those grumble, and frequently end up gaining the upper hand. Only after the village's men cross over the threshold into their homes, do their spirits calm down and their posture becomes cowed. No woman wants a man who's known as a push-over, chicken. Outside the home, the women play their role of humble and happy with their lot.

Caccaba passes the trullo – small, round straw-roofed houses painted in white lime, scattered across the fields. Taking a right into the village's only street, lined on both sides with trullo, he quickly reaches the plaza, marked in its center by a fountain centuries old. A little beyond that is the church.

San Nicandro: a village no one stops in, a village where people are born, live and die as prayers are directed to Jesus, requests for him to watch over the neighbors and make sure they know their place. Woe to the envious who, using the devil's magic, deaden the archaic olive trees marked by

15

branches showing complex twists and turns, or the ancient vine trunks which collapse into dust because of an evil spell. And then, praying, crossing themselves constantly, they dispel the evil eye and curse it in their hearts.

Reaching Garganico Street, Caccaba hastens his steps like a horse breaking into a canter. His home, identical to those surrounding it, awaits him. He glances at the walls which he and his son have just finished whitewashing to destroy bugs and other pests. He remembers that the roof still needs to be done. Until it is, it will be uppermost in his mind.

As the extremely short-cut puntine pasta floats in bowls of aromatic minestrone soup, Manduzio-Caccaba gives a firm push to open the door to the house where his family awaits.

In an instant, his gaze takes in the entire and only room, while mentally praising Carmella, who runs his household. As always, he first looks at their wide double bed which faces the door, and the chest of drawers next to it which only Carmella is allowed to open. To the right, the crank that enables drawing water from the internal well, and which looks like it was just recently in use, its rope still wiggling and its bucket still wet. To the left, the fireplace, unlit and clean, and currently holding a wooden seat for Manduzio's sole use.

Caccaba glances at the mezzanine where an internal storage space takes advantage of the home's three walls, where for decades various metal and wooden objects were jumbled together. One day, that corner must be taken care of, he notes.

Then his satisfied gaze returns to the center of the room, to the table around which his family is seated. He watches

Carmella as he places his hat on the drawers. He will wait for another occasion to protest the neglected statue.

"It's all set," he says, simply. "Sunday, you will bring us great honor, my son."

Donato lowers his gaze and says nothing. The family sits down to dine, speaking very little, but the atmosphere is easygoing. In this house, the family members love each other.

They're typical villagers, but they love each other.

***

Of all San Nicandro's residents present in church, Don Adriano is hands down the best dressed. And the most rotund. His profile can't be discerned for good reason: as he tills, harvests and sows, this overly plump, short-legged and thick-fingered man of God is a stream of calls to heaven, accompanied by constant bowing. Even those unfamiliar with him would immediately identify him as the village priest, thinks Donato as he follows his father.

Donato likes Don Adriano. The latter smiles a lot, hands out countless pictures of saints, and is great at telling stories, even if they aren't all fully understood. Donato has already discovered that it's not worth directing too many questions to the priest. Sometimes his eyebrows draw together and his thick lips purse. That's his 'thinking-hard' look, when begging for an answer won't help: he won't provide one, and it may be that he doesn't even know the answer. But Don Adriano continues being nice as long as you don't contradict him. And if you do, he says you're taking the name of Jesus in vain, a claim he repeats dozens of times each day.

Donato, walking ahead, asks himself: where's God right now? This instant? His Sunday best, the congratulatory wishes of San Nicandro's old women, his father's barrels of wine, his mother's tears held back tightly, at least for now. How does any of it indicate the presence of the Supreme Divine? Nothing indicates a divine entity.

But, bottom line and as a fourteen year old, what should he even expect from this ceremony? To be counted now as an adult? That's already been done. Donato has never been to school: there's nowhere to go and no money for such a waste of time. Very early in his life he was already accompanying his father and his brother Luigi to work in the fields while his mother and Alina took care of the home, busy with the endlessly repetitive chores that are housework. As a child, Donato assisted with the easier jobs: working the small plot, supervising the black goat and the dark-hued sheep unique to the region, collecting firewood, checking the grapes, shooing birds away.

The rest of his time was spent running around the fields with his friends, rummaging around in dens and sneaking chewing gum from the merchant's supplies each time he turned up in the village. But that was a rare event: Sannicandro, as it was still known then, didn't attract many visitors. One day, Focelli, the policeman who hailed originally from northern Italy, expressed his boredom with the place.

"If I could, I'd heap this whole place up and set a match to it! I swear! You're all thieves! What kind of profession is that! Although I must admit that in Calabria, where I was previously, when you arrest someone, you know that as soon as he's out of jail, he'll try to finish you off. Here?

No. At least they're decent. They invite you to coffee once they're released."

Today Focelli is laughing at the whole world, enjoying the thought of the feast he'll soon be attending. He knows the young lad about to undergo the ceremony well: a pilferer, as simple-minded as all his friends. Nonetheless Focelli doesn't chase the *ragazzino*, the little rascal of a boy, because that kid knows the region like the coarse palm of his hand and can run like those African tribesmen known to be as swift as antelopes.

Donato looks straight ahead and steps forward in a somber manner in his new black suit, which Ferrando helped dress him in earlier that morning. He is well aware of his obligation to honor his parents by displaying exemplary behavior.

Even though he's familiar with everyone who'll be there, the lad feels a little anxious. The aromas are familiar, as is the light surrounding him and the priest, who has his mother's admiration and is his father Caccaba's friend. Slowly he follows his father, who leads him to our Lord Jesus. Nothing here is unfamiliar, so why the butterflies?

Facing him, Don Adriano smiles from the dais. Everyone stands as though awaiting the entrance of a bride. Caccaba walks proudly: two sons honoring Jesus, a daughter who can slice a person in two with her tongue, though no one yet knows that, a wife who most of the time is submissive. Today is a day of glory for him. His gaze proudly scans the rows of people, to the left, to the right, and for several moments, Manduzio the elder is ecstatic. Then he bows lightly to the priest and walks to his place, filled with joy at the impressive image his young son is conveying. Here is the priest, swinging the censer. The choirboy follows him.

Donato has no choice – right before the ceremony begins, he has to kiss the priest's plump hand, held out toward him in an easygoing gesture of familiarity. The lad stares at the hand as one gazes at a continent on the map: pores, planted with hairs; thick folds on the finger joints; protruding veins around the knuckles. He imagines that hand's moistness and accompanying odor.

Donato freezes. The congregation smiles forgivingly. Rarely has a child seemed so intently focused on the ceremony. They recall his brother Luigi, who might have become a fairly decent priest had he just agreed to learn how to read. After all, he's from a good family.

Wanting to help the lad, Don Adriano speaks softly. "Welcome, my son, to the house of our Lord Jesus. Today is the most beautiful day of your young life. Come closer."

And the hand is still there.

Donato cannot move. Surprised, the priest takes a step forward: it is a personal invitation to action. Donato appears about to cry. But no: he is battling nausea. And loses the battle, right there, on the church threshold, staining the priest's robe and well-buffed shoes. The devil's work in that retching.

Whispers mention the fable of La Fontaine: a frog wishes to be an ox, and swells and balloons up until, at last, it bursts. Signs of the cross are quickly made by all. Fingers shape triangles in the air. San Nicandro's residents wonder if they're watching the end of the world happen.

Initially, Caccaba is paralyzed. Suddenly he stands, takes his son by the arm, and drags him home. It's hard to guess whether the father is about to give the son a remedy or a beating.

A beating. Hard. And the lad is grounded. To the cowshed, so that he can't defile the family home. He won't be given any meals until he admits to his terrible sin. He won't be given anything to drink until the priest exorcises the devil in the lad.

Donato cannot persuade his father of his innocence: he doesn't understand how it happened, it came up suddenly, it was the smell of something connected with the priest. The slap came as fast as a shell fired from a tank, and stung as badly. Donato's black eyes grew blacker.

Alina and several of the women neighbors hover near the refreshments, uncertain what to do next.

"It will all be wasted," one laments.

"Ah, Madonna, what a waste," cries another.

They wait for a sign from Alina. She is despairing. Her brother's shouting can be heard even if he is trying to restrain himself. The boy's father, apparently, is far from sparing the rod. He shoves Carmella off: she is torn by her fear of being punished by the Lord, on one hand, and her son's cries of pain, on the other.

The village buzzes with unpleasant commentary. Groups form, spread, unravel, and spontaneously reform into other groups. No one thinks of going home. Come to think of it, such an event in this miserable godforsaken village in the district of Foggia is like a heaven-sent gift! The village elders are scrummaging through the Manduzio family's past. First, why is he called Caccaba? As were his father and grandfather before him? Perhaps there was some dirty story. Others raise the idea that a new century brings trouble.

Everyone crosses themselves again. Repeatedly.

Late at night, the sounds of people can be heard walking up and down the street. They carry candles which flash – left, right, up, down – like fireflies in the panes of closed windows. The daily *struccio*, groups of youth prowling the village streets for fun, although under the adults' watchful eyes, just didn't gather any steam that day: no one wants to be seen chattering, gossiping; but everyone wants to hear and voice their views.

Donato, grounded in the cowshed, cannot comprehend what made him bilious, choke and vomit. He'll be taking this up with God, but all this fuss around God, who everyone understands according to personal preference and whose views they state as though they are appointed spokespeople, and their persistent refusal to study His existence, makes Donato shake his head. He feels like he's been turned into some kind of playing piece in a religious game; he can smell that it's based on ignorance. No, he just can't accept that at all.

On the other hand, what could the reason be for such a reaction in the church? For days he worked hard at learning the movements and words needed for the ceremony. He memorized, he repeated, over and over, and he was ready. So what explanation could there possibly be for what happened other than it being the devil's work?

During the day, Donato works nonstop, rarely chatting with anyone. His father indicates the chores that have to get done by signals, and woe to him if he doesn't understand the senior Manduzio. Luigi won't go anywhere near him, perhaps in fear of catching whatever it is that is afflicting Donato. A friend or two, who admire his tranquility and are drawn to his courage, bring him food on the sly so he won't go hungry. They don't know that his mother is also taking care of him from the first day of his punishment. Caccaba is still refusing to cancel that penalty.

In the evening, Donato settles down to sleep alongside the animals. It comforts him to use the donkey as a pillow although he really misses the camaraderie with the other village lads.

Days pass. There is no change. The story of this adventure puffs up, is embellished, passes across the hilltops, heads down to the sea, goes up to San Marco in Lamis, hovers near Apricena, flies all the way to Lecenna and stops for a while in Foggia. Everywhere in the region, the story goes that Caccaba's boy raised witches robed in stinking capes from the depths, and desecrated God's holy house to the point that it must now be destroyed and rebuilt after the demons are driven out.

Even if no one in San Nicandro can forget the incident, life's daily worries quickly return to their place in Sunday conversations.

Donato is not put off by work. During the weeks that his father forced him into isolation, a new threshold of tolerance was born, an ability to successfully persist in every activity he begins, as though he wished to prove that he is not a good-for-nothing, nor a wily devil. He works hard, copying Caccaba and Luigi.

And then, when his father lets him free, he wanders the fields, hunts foxes and fowl, and quickly becomes the leader of his peers.

Yet he never forgets to come to his mother's assistance.

Despite her young age, she is showing growing signs of fatigue by the day. He notices the village women's frequent visits. One brings a pain-killing potion. One brings an ointment to rub into her back. Carmella is exhausted and it's only morning. She is getting increasingly tired early in the day.

Caccaba fumes at these women, who he sees as too delicate, but inside he is very worried. His Carmella had never shown unwillingness, never grumbled about her work. She bore her chores well. Alina helps her mother a good deal. For some time Carmella appears to have something like a matchbox in her left breast, and it keeps growing. She is still unaware that metastases are already spreading into her brain. She lies in bed for a day. Then for two, and then three.

Now Donato is the one who feeds her, to his sister's chagrin. His sister feels that her place has been usurped. As soon as the plate is set down Donato glances at the leftovers of food his mother's friends have brought her. He pokes around and studies what's there. He wants to understand, to learn, and take care of her.

Caccaba and Luigi double their workloads, and doing so means leaving the house that is increasingly looking like it's caving in. This time of waiting is daunting, mocking, hard on each of the Manduzio family members; so they stay quiet, not wanting to scare each other. When families love each other, they absorb the shock quietly.

Carmella understands that she is about to die. Forcefully, she pushes that thought away. She hasn't finished her work yet! She hasn't married Luigi off, nor Alina. Donato still needs her attention, her motherly warmth, because outwardly he comes across as a bit rebellious but inside, he's an angel.

And what will be with her husband? Who will he criticize now? She herself was impervious to his criticisms, because Caccaba was wound around her little finger. I love you, he'd say far too infrequently, but it was true, and he always wanted the best for her. So when he woke her frequently and even rebuked her for getting up in a bad mood, she, Carmella, would smile. But the children? None of their lives are in order yet! And she: is she already so old? Not yet fifty, but with one foot in the grave? *Miseria!* What bad luck! She must hold out!

For six months, day after day, she battled, gave up, battled again, until at last she abandoned the struggle forever.

Everyone crumples. Within several panicked minutes, Caccaba ages by a decade. Luigi leans over the mother who has departed. Alina throws herself over the body. Donato, the youngest, cannot stop stroking his mother's arm. Then he gently takes Carmella's hand in his, and slides her wedding ring off. A simple circle, very slim, made of low-grade gold. No one would ever look at it as an item of value. Not even Alina.

The children arrange the funeral, a simple but respectable affair. The whole village turns out to pay their respects. They are sorrowful, feeling that their everyday rhythm, in which Carmella was central because of her generosity, has come undone.

Bonfito's horse, in its black harness, pulls the modest carriage, which in actuality is more like a wagon. Right behind is Don Adriano, walking somberly. Donato stands straight, knowing that they, Alina, Luigi, his father, and himself, whose treasure and world of affection had just been taken from them, are the ones who should rightly have walked right behind Carmella's coffin on this final path of honor. That's what she would have wanted.

And then, not wanting to offend anyone, but out of his wish to provide Carmella with the respect he knows is her due, he takes hold of his brother and sister's hands, and advances ahead of Don Adriano. It surprises the latter but Don Adriano knows this is not the time or place to cause a ruckus. Donato's black pupils gaze without wavering at Don Adriano. All goes well. Nonetheless, the priest feels he should have been the object of the gathered congregation's gaze in such circumstances. That impudent Donato!

The men, used to acting like masters, gather around the edge of Carmella's grave. A whisper of sweet voices comes from the group of women. Their eyes are red, and some are wearing their scarves back to front as a sign that all is not right in the village. The whisper grows into song, a gently swelling melody. This is their last gift to Carmella: their mournful singing is an act of their steadfast affection.

Our souls will be friends on the gravel in the sky,
We will walk close together, our eyes raised to the sun,
Like bees our sorrow buzzes, our sadness is a swarm,
And tears of farewell flow freely.

You, loathsome time, our enemy, we will curse.
You seep into every corner and quickly possess it,
You run unbridled, you swallow love whole.
In our trembling hearts you always flow.

My hands scratch, and yet again, against your wall,
I slap, I scratch, I cry and bite you,
Your hair shall stand on end, your scales shall jut out,
You are cruelly mocking my aimless passion.

Our companion is dying. Our friend has passed.
May the name of the Lord be at her journey's end.
That is Carmella's desire, Carmella's greatest wish.

The men, in shock, retreat, freeing the space for those who know how to bring life into this world, until the first clod of earth signifying Carmella's departure thuds down.

Surprisingly, Carmella's death brings Donato frequently back to the room in the church where Don Adriano gives his religion classes. He listens, but hears nothing worthy of his attention. The priest describes tales of control and corruption, of negotiations routinely conducted between man and his God from one generation to the next.

Each time the young fellow wishes to talk about God, Don Adriano sets Jesus on the cross in front of him, saying that the Holy Trinity must never be challenged: it is a hierarchy that prohibits gaining knowledge.

Donato has seen Don Adriano going house to house in a flurry, trying to dissuade parents from sending their children to school. A waste of time. Opening the door to the devil. Reciting prayers is above and beyond the call of duty. Despite the priest's views and actions, Donato continues coming to the priest's classes on and off.

Since his mother's death, Donato's bleakness has grown. His certainty that he no longer has anything to lose has made him into a terrifying gang leader. San Nicandro's youngsters flock around him, ready for any challenge he declares against the neighboring villages' youngsters. The indirect damage drives the residents crazy: startled goats, hens that forget to lay eggs, and most of all, the lasses who are left breathless by the good-looking, olive-skinned fellow whose face is delicate, whose gaze is intense, whose lips are sensuous.

Fury accompanies bitterness in one house after another. Donato Manduzio exaggerates, and does not hide it. He stares at the lasses on the church steps, and some do not look away. Two or three of them even express intimacy in their eyes: no one can figure out what drives that.

Donato is too young to marry, too independent to take the advice of those wishing to dole it out, and certainly not crazy enough to decline the girls sending him their smiles. Worried parents are comforted by Don Adriano: despite his nature and the event in the church, Donato is a good boy, who respects others and would never harm a girl's good reputation.

The priest himself is not convinced of his own words, but first the villagers must be kept calm. Since 'the event,' Caccaba has been even more generous with his gifts. So the priest persuades himself that he is keeping an eye on the boy. He even attempted, by means of allaying his own doubts, to have the boy take on responsibility for religious lessons, but the boy's refusal was instantaneous and total. Paradoxically though, the lad is almost always present when Don Adriano instills the word of God.

He's also there when evangelists and members of other cults crisscross the region in search of new populations lacking in faith. Donato listens to them but gets impatient with their standard speeches which hack bluntly at people's minds and offer the standard fare of superstition and threats of Hell.

As for him, he prefers to listen to his inner voice: it carries certainty, though it is unlike any reminiscent of the priest. Rather, it is simple and perfect, alludes to indescribable plans, and awaits recognition.

Donato was always sure that this imperfect world is "an impressive work" by an exceptional entity, although he cannot identify it in outbursts of unshakable Christian faith. He himself feels that a primordial truth exists. He is also aware that he could be wrong. But as time continues to pass, he feels a growing sense of heading toward an encounter. On the other hand, as long as Don Adriano is in charge of teaching the way he does, Donato understands that such an encounter may never take place.

***

In 1909, Donato finds himself fancying one of the village lasses.

She's tall, pretty: Emanuela Vocino has a mischievous look about her. Donato has known her since childhood. She always left him a little breathless. He almost feels as though he needs to ascend a few steps in the village hierarchy in order to approach her. Never once does she stay with her girlfriends when the guys get closer to their group. She's never even glanced at Donato, or any of his friends. She just calmly walks away with a measured step, seemingly oblivious to their existence.

From the distance he sees her acting cheerily, chatting, busy. Then suddenly, when she notices the guys, she says goodbye to her friends and leaves them.

Her black hair is tied back on her nape. Peeking out from her *pacchiana*, the typically multi-layered and belted dress favored by San Nicandro women, are slender ankles. Her arms, hugging a woven straw basket, are firm and gently rounded. Donato is seduced by these images, which bring an end to his career as a local Casanova. The young man is drawn like a moth to a flame, then finds himself bursting with desire, and later, mad with love. But how will he make his love known to Emanuela? Will she let him say what's on his mind? Has she become betrothed to another? Patience is not one of Donato's better traits. Impatience makes him scatterbrained in his work, which angers his father. His brother just shrugs, and his smart little sister calls him *fifone*, coward. When it comes to Emanuela Vocino, indeed he is a chicken!

Because he's very concerned and scared as a *fifone*, he sets himself two days to confess his love. And if he's rejected? He'll move on.

But fate intervenes, shoving him gently in the right direction that very same day. Noticing Emanuela walking toward him, he loses his balance when his wheelbarrow suddenly tips to the side. Emanuela's hand flies to her mouth to hide her laughter and then, because she is good-hearted, she hurries over to help him gather the wood that fell out. They're both strong, and the job's done in minutes. But Donato promised himself, as it all happened, that he wouldn't move on with the barrow without first declaring his feelings to the girl. So he takes advantage of the opportunity and thanks her profusely, then suddenly realizes that she is still there. For the first time, she has not moved away. And they begin discussing anything and everything, although mostly nothing much. In a sudden rush of words, Donato asks if she is *fidanzata*: anyone's fiancée.

Emanuela smiles at him but remains silent.

Donato moves the conversation forward. "Remember last year's grape harvest? I can't explain it, but you're the only one I noticed. You, and no other. I needed to tell you that. Well, I feel better now that I have. You'll probably laugh at me in your heart and run off, but…"

Emanuela holds her hand up to stop him, and points to the fountain, where they can sit. Donato wonders: how many pairs of eyes are now glued to them? How many tongues are conveying reports? A lad and a lass from the village are sitting in the center of the plaza and conversing like brother and sister, or worse, like… He dare not even think that word. The villagers will reach their own conclusions, have a field day, mocking, embellishing and embroidering a tale, until their lips go dry.

Emanuela tightly clutches the heap of clothes she'd set aside on the railing when she'd helped Donato. Suddenly she looks straight into his eyes.

"Everyone says you're strong and agile. And very smart. I'm not at all sure I agree with them."

"What do you mean?"

"During the grape harvest, I passed you a glass of good wine which I specially chose."

"I remember, but…"

"But that Rafaella blinded you, and later I saw you two behind the blacksmith's house."

31

Blushing hard, Donato busies himself with balancing the wheelbarrow's handles even though they're perfectly balanced.

"*La mia Nonna*," Emanuela continues, "always told me, 'Granddaughter, men aren't smarter than babies at birth. When they're in love, they're as noisy and clumsy as babies. If one day you fall in love with a young man, and if he's a good fellow and you want him as your husband, implement the rule that my mother taught me: *seguimi ti fuggo, fuggimi ti seguo*. Follow me and I'll run away. Run from me and I'll follow you! But I... I want you, Donato."

Stunned by joy, Donato could just as easily have returned home with the barrow on his head and he'd never have felt its weight! The youngsters separate: a pact has been cast between them. Or at least, it will be, quite soon.

In these villages set against the mountain slopes, every event, no matter how small, grows to vast proportions and makes daily routines, now hundreds of years old, tremble and shiver. And this is no less so, of course, when it comes to the marriage of the pretty conqueror of hearts.

The very next day, as custom requires, Donato, accompanied by his father, walks over to the Vocino family home. That morning Alina had taken her brother to the well, and handed him an object that touched him deeply.

"*Fratellino*," my little brother, she says, "take this. It's what our mother would have wanted."

"Mother's engagement band? Are you crazy? You're the one who deserves to keep it. I already have her wedding band."

"I'm happy for you to have it, Donato. I can wear her shawl, and when my turn comes, let's hope my future husband's means will allow him to buy me an engagement ring. Luigi also agrees. Take it, our brother."

The ring is in Donato's jacket pocket. Emanuela and her mother have disappeared: what is about to take place is an event meant only for the men. But yesterday, the two women immersed Vocino, husband and father, in such a stream of words that it left no doubt in his mind what his answer to the proposal must be. Donato is from a good family, he's a hard worker, he's nice looking. Yes, he's broken some hearts, but who could possibly compete with Emanuela? Vocino knows from his own experience that marriage is the best medicine to cure wild skirt-chasing.

He accepts Donato's proposal of marriage spoken confidently by Caccaba. They discuss the dowry and the bride's possessions. Then the women join them. With excellent cheer, they share the refreshments, prepared in advance of a successfully concluded proposition.

Donato, at a signal indicating Vocino's agreement, stands, taking Emanuela's hand in his. She stands too. Slipping his other hand into his pocket, he pulls out Carmella's delicate, engraved gold wedding band inset with four pieces of turquoise. Together they make the shape of a clover leaf, its center marked by a tiny, brightly shining pearl. Emanuela is enchanted. She loves the ring! And because her ring finger is so very slim, she moves it to her forefinger. That way it won't slip off.

Anticipation of the forthcoming wedding sets the village buzzing. The parents are thrilled: here's the young Manduzio son back on track with his life, and no one will need to keep their eyes peeled anymore over his shenanigans with their daughters. Carmella is remembered warmly by the village women, who promise to put on a wonderful spread for her sake. The men nod and mutter over the wine that will flow like a river: Manduzio makes some of the best wine the village has ever tasted! Everyone knows that the Manduzios can be depended on when it comes to wine. At last, a breath of life and joy fills the village.

The two families seek Don Adriano's approval for the ceremony's date.

"My children," he answers, "do not choose the time right before Easter or Christmas, the month of May which is dedicated to Maria, or the month of August."

"August? Why not?"

"It is a month of evil and disease."

Donato looks at the priest in surprise, but says nothing. Another baseless assertion. Eventually the wedding is set for February.

Bells in San Nicandro chime, calling the villagers to church for the young couple's special day. It is on February 12th, 1910. Donato arrives, climbing the street's slope and entering the churchyard, already filled with people: family members, friends, witnesses, all smiling broadly, eagerly awaiting the bride.

Donato strokes the bit of metal which Alina had put into his pocket as protection against the evil eye. He looks around: the church is adorned with more flowers than it's ever been, children run around excitedly despite mothers' hands reaching out to control their behavior and hold them back, and the hubbub of anticipation typical of such events dances in the light coming through the round windows.

At last, there she is: Emanuela, almost carried forward by the cheering crowd. Her white dress shines in the sunlight. According to local custom, a scarf covers her face to ward off any evil spirits which might be trying to trap her with their filthy gaze. Her cheeks are rouged lightly, her lips are red: the freshness of being twenty is her most beautiful adornment.

Countless candles paving the path to the pulpit fill the church with light. Alina and her friends have hung four hundred white roses on the walls and the ends of pews. The ceremony is long: to some, grandiloquent. Don Adriano is getting carried away instead of letting the young couple begin their married lives. But does it really matter? The songs and speeches are not given here. They're scheduled for the festivities that will follow.

As they leave the church, the congregation's cheering reaches the very furthest edges of the village. Rice-confetti rains on the couple like a downpour of cupid arrows bearing gladness. Children help Emanuela and Donato hand out sugar-coated almonds in tiny, embroidered sachets to guests, as is the custom. The sachets are white, a symbol of purity. Each holds five almonds: one for fertility and one for health; one for a long life, one for happiness, and the last, for wealth.

The lavish ball accords with San Nicandro custom. In the Foggia district, no self-respecting family would provide guests with less than fourteen courses: freshly caught fish and sea urchins, ear-shaped pasta known as orecchiette, buffalo milk burrata cheese with its unique flavor, braided fried fresh pasta richly dusted in sugar, local wines, but this time richly spiced.

The Donato and Vocino family members are having as good a time as their guests, enjoying the fine foods, the songs, the dances, and of course the distinctly rhythmic tarantella courtship dance.

And the moment everyone's waited for comes at last: the auction! Francesco Cerrone, a friend of the groom, goes up to Donato, pulls off his tie, brings a pair of freshly polished, sparkling scissors from his pocket, brandishes them and sets to work snipping the tie into tiny bits that he heaps on a tray. Mimicking the fishmongers' market calls, he invites guests to buy a piece of cloth. Of course everyone does! No one wants to be caught out as a miser! Coins and smaller denomination banknotes replace the pile of cloth on the tray. Francesco's mother, Ermelina, takes the tray to the bride's purse. Outside, the winter day is cold and dry, but inside the hall, men are removing their jackets, women their scarves. It is wonderfully warm and joyful indoors. Some of the village youngsters are already showing signs that they'll soon be the reason for festivities in the near future.

The evening comes to a close when Emanuela and Donato uphold a long-time San Nicandro tradition: together, they smash a vase onto the floor, the number of pieces it shatters into indicating the number of joyous years they will share. No one in the community knows that this custom originates in Judaism: actually, it is meant to remind everyone that no matter how great their joy, they should never forget the catastrophic event of the Holy Temple and Jerusalem being destroyed.

The meal over, older guests go off to sleep. Now the youngsters can get a little wild. A wedding is the only time that parents, capitulating to their age and the long day, allow their children some unsupervised fun. Emanuela has gone to change into simpler clothing, not wanting to damage the wedding dress. Donato has long since shrugged off his jacket. The band plays louder, livelier. All the young folk of a suitable age are eyeing each other and setting up their futures.

It is two in the morning when Donato finally takes his wife's hand, smiling at her. The message is clear. The hall is filled with cheers and ululations. A crazy, cavorting bunch of youngsters accompanies the young couple to the Manduzio home. Tonight, Caccaba, Alina, and Luigi will sleep over at the Cerrona family's home. The young couple will need their own home, but that will be dealt with in the future.

Meanwhile, the groom carries his bride over the threshold to the crowd's cheers, and gently pushes the door shut.

***

Even though the Manduzio household now included the young lovers, nothing in the home changed much. A sack of flour near the hob is a sure sign that Emanuela was now making the bread. On the wall facing the entrance, Donato has hung two photographs of the couple at their wedding. In one, Emanuela's face is serious as she stands in her white gown. The photo captures something of the mystery and weight of that important occasion. In the other, Emanuela stands in her multicolored pacchiana, beaming as she walks arm in arm with her husband. The tranquility with which the home has always been blessed continues to be felt from the doorway, despite the constant activities around home and farm.

For many long days, the village was animated by the joy

exuded by the young Manduzio couple. They were held different from the rest of the villagers, as though seemingly positioned on a higher rung of the village hierarchy, despite their day being no different to that of any other San Nicandro villager: constant work, often hard, and tiring daily tasks which left very little private time for the couple.

Donato's days went from grape harvest to sowing the land to filling his duties toward his wife. He showed no interest in world events playing out somewhere far away from this poor village. Life just kept carrying on.

***

From its perch high up on the cliff, through occasionally severe winters, San Nicandro continues to exist beyond world events. Leaves on the plane trees and the pines covering Mount Garganico form a thick forest which slowly gives way to an expansive desert rolling all the way down to the Adriatic Sea via Torre Mileto. Here and there, an obstinate cactus or orchid insists on surviving the layer of gravel covering that part of the mountainside. The eye catches sight of them momentarily in the dry, harsh landscape.

San Nicandro's small homes cling to each other along alleys overlooked by the ruins of a castle, the history of which is no longer remembered by anyone. The homes seem anchored in place with the apathy of eons. And yet, no more than a short four hundred kilometers from the village, beyond the Adriatic Sea, a horrifying and tragic event playing out is shocking the world.

From the start of the nineteenth century, the Balkans have been continually in a state of strife, driven by a spate of rebellions. Serbia, Bulgaria, and Bosnia-Herzegovina have allied against the Ottoman Empire. Russia, representing pan-Slavism which seemingly bonds all peoples of Slavic origins, as though that shared identity is sufficient to unify them politically, is increasingly overwhelming the Turks in a sweeping victory, making it possible for Turkish regions known as sanjaks which are located in Bosnia-Herzegovina to be conquered and controlled by the Austro-Hungarian Empire.

In 1903, San Nicandro residents are convinced that wars will no longer erase entire populations, and that the devil is the only danger to humanity. They have no clue that the revolution has set the pro-Russian boundary – extending Pierre Karageorgevitch's role as ruler over Serbia.

In the complexity of land allocations, Austro-Hungary annexes two sanjaks, Bosnia, and Herzegovina. This action raises Russia and Serbia's ire. Waves of rebellions, conquests, and conflicts make everyone increasingly fearful of evil itself, despite persistent efforts and investments by diplomats on all sides to restore equilibrium.

On June 28th, 1914, Austro-Hungarian Archduke Franz Ferdinand, accompanied by his short wife, the Duchess Sophie Chotek, who left the Konopiště Palace in the city of Benešov some thirty-seven kilometers south of Prague some days earlier, reach Sarajevo to attend a congress labeled as vital and attended by a bevy of diplomats.

This visit is indeed viewed as highly important by the royal couple. On that same day, 28 June 1914, they celebrated their fourteenth wedding anniversary. Leaving the royal court for a while was intended to allow Sophie Chotek, as behooves the wife of a prince, to enjoy the full privileges she could not enjoy in the palace court; it was a chance to show her the respect and honor reserved for emperors and royals.

Right before the royal couple sets out, Franz-Ferdinand's personal priest, who also served as his educator when the prince was young, tries to persuade him not to take the trip.

"It exposes you to a violent end that may throw the entire world into perdition," he pleads.

"We will go! That is what I wish!" the prince insists.

***

In Sarajevo, a clan of young Serbian, Croatian, and Muslim anarchists finalize the details of a plan that will eventually kill millions.

Gavrilo Princip, a young Serbian nationalist, is about to become the strong arm of history.

Some days after leaving Belgrade in the company of five friends involved in the struggle to free Serbia, and after detailed preparations, Gavrilo and his accomplices make their first assassination attempt on their way to the city hall. But they are unskilled, and unused to using weapons. All six of them miss their target. They throw their bombs, set to eight seconds before detonation, too early. The Archduke manages to throw the one that reaches his carriage into the distance. Of course it claims victims from among the crowd. Fearing they may be caught, several of the terrorists bite into their cyanide pills and throw themselves into the Miljacka River. Unluckily for them, the river at that point is no more than several dozen centimeters deep, and the dose of poison they've taken is too low to cause anything but horrible damage.

The convoy accelerates. The royals, calmer now in the knowledge that the would-be assassins have been caught, continue waving to the crowd.

Gavrilo Princip flees the disaster.

Convinced that the Archduke is dead, he is busy buying a sandwich in a shop near the Latin Bridge when he suddenly sees the royal carriage approaching. The Archduke and his wife are smiling and waving to their admiring public!

Princip races out of the shop, catches up with the carriage, and shoots two bullets. First to collapse is the duchess. A moment later, her husband the Archduke topples over, lifeless.

"I have avenged the vast suffering that Austria has caused the people! A new dawn shall light the empire of Serbia! Cheers to the victory!" Princip shouts over and over.

The crowd tears his weapon from his hands. The police are too late to stop him swallowing his cyanide capsule. But it is insufficient to do its job and causes nothing worse than repeated bouts of vomiting.

With the Serbian government's admission that it orchestrated arming the youths, Austro-Hungary responds swiftly with a resolute ten-point ultimatum. In indignation, the Russians protest vociferously yet the Serbs, despite their reservations, accede to nine of the ten points in the ultimatum. They adamantly reject clause number six, however: it is a provision that empowers Austro-Hungarian police officers to conduct investigations within the boundaries of Serbian sovereignty.

Treaties between European nations began to literally ignite the barrels of gunpowder. Swiftly, Europe in its entirety was ablaze; alliances shattered, nations clashed, and the conflict spread to the four corners of the earth, even as far as San Nicandro.

Amidst that global turmoil entangling seventy-two nations and destined to claim the lives of twenty million, Italy hesitates before deciding to intervene. Preferring neutrality, Italy observes the unfolding events. Despite public opinion and moral debates, many are aware that the Italian military forces do not rank among the most esteemed. Far more preferable is to delay, to contemplate, and to weigh the prudence of Italy's involvement.

One particular socialistic journalist who heads the *Aventi!* daily paper, and whose nature is a mix of fanaticism and delusions of grandeur, strongly opposes Italy joining the war. Benito Mussolini, on the other hand, loudly protests intervention unless territorial gains are to be had. Since 1912, he has headed the revolutionary faction within his party, promoting Italy's rebuilding as a united society of social equality, one that does not prioritize the future global war. His voice resonates; he is heard, his articles are read.

But toward the end of 1914, he is removed from the Socialist Party. Without anyone noticing, Mussolini goes turncoat and claims that Italy's revival is conditional on entering the war. And because any opportunity is a good one for making himself heard, he slams those whose view is compromising, indecisive, and is not supported by threatening speeches and articles.

Having joined the ranks of the bourgeoisie, he now advocates for Italy's intervention in the war, particularly since the Triple Entente, an alliance between France, Russia, and the United Kingdom, prominently highlights territorial guarantees, particularly in the Balkans and the Trentino region in northern Italy.

Instantly, Italy joins the war.

Italian soldiers appear in increasing number, their equipment deficient, their commanders inept, and their skills virtually non-existent. They are no threat: no sparks will be ignited by them. Their infiltration into Austro-Hungarian territory will extend no more than a few kilometers.

From this boiling cauldron, a solution emerges which catches the attention of San Nicandro's residents concerned for their daughters! Daredevil village boys not yet summoned for conscription are offered the opportunity to join the army by enlisting with recruitment officers covering the breadth and width of Italy. One such, pompous in character, and accompanied by junior aides with an air of self-importance, has set himself up in the village square near the fountain.

Don Adriano quickly comprehends that a golden opportunity has presented itself to him for helping Donato escape the beatings that his father doles out when angry. Yes, he's married four years now, and the couple live very harmoniously together. Often laughter wafts through their home's open door, and Donato has absolutely no interest in any other female in the village. That reassures the villagers. But countless men have left after being called to fight for peace, and young brides of the same number have been left alone, day after day, night after night. Everyone knows that the devil never sleeps for long, and these days, young women even dare to imagine the unthinkable. If Donato were to get it into his head that he might be able to console any of these poor girls, woe! He is a very attractive young man and has a magnetic presence, a kind of inherent charisma that turns heads. Far better to pre-empt his excessive desire than provide it greater opportunities.

In memory of Carmella, devout and of unwavering faith, and in acknowledgment of Caccaba's constant contributions, the priest has always strived to his best ability to redirect the lad's exuberant energy. Current times are no different in that respect. It takes no more than a few cleverly chosen words spoken to Donato, noting moral obligation, and ethical choices. "The mother country… Carmella, who sees all in heaven above… Italy, beloved to the Master of the Universe and protected by Holy Maria… Emanuela, who would be so proud later, even if in the moment she might be despairing and even quite angry with me…"

A long line of youngsters waits patiently. Many come from groups of thugs who initially balk at the idea of a uniform, but are instantly subdued by the recruitment officer's cold glaring eyes. Donato's turn has come. He speaks to the recruitment officer holding his beret, and identifies himself. The corporal jots a few words down on a document, hands it to Donato, and asks. "Might you be the first among the recruits here who knows how to write?"

"Of course I know how to write!" Donato says emphatically.

He takes the pen held out by the corporal, checks its sharpness with his thumb tip, and confidently marks three crosses at the end of the document. He is stationed in Infantry Battalion 94, like so many others of the village youth.

Donato disappears for four long years.

**

Four years pass. Four years of war, of waves of destruction, of intentional dawdling, of persistent savagery. Not a single letter reaches Emanuela: how could one possibly find a letter writer and letter reader in the midst of this hell?

Bit by bit, Emanuela notices that some village women have chosen to wear clothes of mourning even if they haven't heard anything definitive about their husbands, brothers, or sons.

Emanuela adamantly refuses to follow their example. Were I to don black clothes, she thinks, Donato for sure will be sent to his grave! No, on no account will I do this! I will wear the bright colors of life until he returns to me, and will wear even brighter colors when he does come home!

In north-eastern Italy's Friuli-Venezia-Giulia region bordering on Austria, and in the Alps, confrontations are incessant. Initially the Austro-Hungarian army took control due to its well organized defenses, striking hard at Italy's soldiers even though the latter are greater in number.

Slowly but surely the Italians wrest the upper hand from their enemy and seize control of the Piave River, assisted by the allied forces. In the spring of 1918, the Italian army gains a decisive victory in The Piave River Battle, effectively halting the Austrians' advance.

That's when peace talks commence. Although the armistice agreement is signed on November 3, 1918, the Italians manage to stipulate that it will only come into effect the following day, a tactic enabling them to occupy additional territories.

It's during these massive battles over the river that Donato discovers his own fear and fury, but also his courage, his modesty, and the comradeship that makes it possible to withstand the difficulties of life in the trenches.

On a particular day, Donato was sent on a reconnaissance mission with a few other soldiers. An Austrian cavalryman's lance pierced his thigh. Injured, Donato collapsed. He was left stranded in the field. His fellow soldiers have either been killed, or have fled, leaving him lying on the ground wallowing in mud, suffering hellish agony. Thick froth coats his lips. Blood stiffens the fabric of his uniform. Two days after he fell, the Red Cross finds him and transports him to hospital, where an unskilled doctor carries out surgery. The operation is a failure, only serving to damage the soldier's agony even more.

Donato is evacuated to the home front: he finds himself in a hospital in Pisa, where he will spend eight months suffering horribly throughout. Doctors and nurses there do all they can to ensure the young man's leg is saved, wanting to preserve his ability to walk and preventing him from becoming crippled to the point of being wheelchair bound.

But their attempts cause Donato great pain. Several nurses deeply touched by his proud gaze despite his dire suffering give him the kind of care that only a mother or fiancée would. Donato is supported by a shoulder or an arm, a chair, or sheer hope. Each time he falls, he ages a fraction more. The injury is slowly fracturing his faith in his productivity in the future. What kind of farmer would he be, handicapped, watching the days and seasons change without preparing his land, without taking care of the animals, without tending his crops, without pleasuring his wife?

Donato begins to feel increasingly worthless. He sinks into the depths of despair.

He wants to contact his family but fate, or a chain of recurring mishaps, causes messages to never reach the village, as though that place's name has been erased from the map, as though Emanuela has disappeared, as though…

The continent, the world, is in a state of utter chaos. No one can help Donato.

How fortunate, then, that Giorgio, his roommate, a socialist and revolutionary at heart, is such a pleasant and dedicated fellow. Encouraging Donato with his rolling laugh, he gently jibes at Donato as a way of raising the young man's spirits.

"Are you going to keep whining here all day, laddie? I've lost my right arm, and my right eye, and both my legs, and one lung has burst. Have you heard even a sigh from me? Almighty God, life is here, inside us! So take good care of it! You'll still be able to caress your wife and give her children. My wife, on the other hand, will take one look at me and fall off her chair in fright! That's if she's even still waiting for me! I know her inside out… garbage, those Austrians!"

During the time that passes between two fiery speeches and a spate of diplomatic solutions which aim to reassert Italy's position, Giorgio begins teaching his roommate how to read and write. It's a wonderful palliative for them both. Donato is smart and progresses quickly. Suddenly he sees how the marks spread across the page are letters, which make words, which express ideas and thoughts, and manifest culture.

Donato takes it all in: newspapers and the farmer's almanac with its hundreds of wise and knowledgeable tips; the dictionary which they find in the hospital's tiny library. Donato is like a child entering a toy shop and allowed to take anything he wishes: not only has he been given access to the thoughts of others, but he is now also able to write letters home! And he writes for others, too, with the same diligence as he expended while learning, whether those letters relate to administrative matters or matters of the heart.

***

In the autumn of 1919, Luigi receives a letter to collect his injured brother from Pisa. When he arrives, he finds Donato deeply engrossed in a thick tome about Latin syntax.

Luigi is still mourning Caccaba's death, which occurred exactly one month after the war was officially declared over. It makes him afraid that he may not arrive in time to see his brother alive. His thoughts and fears are worrying: what if he is left on his own to handle the entire family's needs, take care of the animals, the vineyards, and Alina? She will be marrying once the period of mourning ends, and there will no doubt be insufficient funds to help her. And if his brother is indeed alive but severely handicapped, how will he provide Donato with financial support?

Luigi is horrified by what he sees: Donato is ashen, skinny as a pole, and seems glued to his chair. Luigi is flooded with pity for his brother. But on seeing Luigi, Donato's face bursts into a huge smile. It takes great effort but he manages to stand, although the pain it causes shows clearly. Instantly Luigi, notices that Donato has not lost his powerful will, still has that same effusive energy. His black eyes shine the way they always did. The two men are not used to outward displays of affection. They gaze at each other with warmth but hug for a bare second.

Luigi wants to know what happened. A doctor explains but loses his patience when Luigi, with the calmness typical of men of the land, asks him to repeat everything he couldn't take in first time around.

"Yes, he will be able to do light work, repair tools, write letters for neighbors, but not much more than that."

"Write letters?" Luigi exclaims. "But my brother doesn't know how to read and write!"

"He most certainly does!" the doctor smiles. "He's actually excellent at formulating letters. He's the correspondent for everyone at the hospital."

"Correspondent?"

Luigi is stunned into silence. He stares, gaping at his brother who was promoted to sergeant in recognition of some action of bravery he had performed, and is still standing despite the injury.

Luigi moves closer to Donato. "Don't worry, my brother. Everything will work out fine. When we get home, Alina will take good care of you. I won't have the time to do that."

"Alina? Why? Has something happened to Emanuela?"

"She's also waiting for you. Even before Alina had readied a food package for the journey, Emanuela cleaned the house from top to bottom. Ahh. Well…"

When Luigi didn't continue, Donato prompted. "Well, what?"

"Ah, no, nothing."

"Luigi, say what you have to say. Your evasion and the thoughts it brings up in my mind hurt me more than this injury."

"No, really, nothing. I was just thinking to myself that the two of you.. I mean, later... when children..."

"Will I give you some nephews? Is that what you're getting at?"

"Yes. Sorry, Donato, I was wondering that."

"Well, I can certainly try. But the outcome of my efforts is in the hands of God."

"Donato, our parents' home was given to your wife while she waited for your return, just as Papa wished. You deserve it. We still have the fields. Alina will live with you until she marries, quite soon. I'm in the house next door, the one I had my eye on for quite a while."

"Wonderful!" Donato grins. "So you managed to buy it?"

"Yes, but in actuality it's now become a burden. It looks like we'll have to sell it. See, Donato, our money's starting to run out.

"No, no, you won't be selling anything. I'll help you. My compensation allowance will help."

"Allowance?"

"They gave me compensation because of the injury."

"They? Who is 'they?'" Luigi asks, not understanding a word his brother is saying.

"The army. Or the government. I don't know exactly how it works and maybe it doesn't matter, but in any event, I've been receiving income for a year now and I haven't needed it. Here I have no financial obligations. It'll help us once we're home. How does 2,880 Lira every month sound?"

Luigi breathes an audible sigh of relief as he quickly realizes life could be developing in ways he'd never expected.

"Well, Donato," Luigi's beginning to let ideas replace worries, "How'd you get through all those months of hospitalization? You of all people! You were always like our goats, here, there, doing more than your workload."

Sadness flashes across Donato's face for a moment as he remembers the agony his injury caused. "For months I was furious. I hated everything simply because hating gave me pleasure. Well, not exactly pleasure, satisfaction, more like. But at some point, I began to accept my miserable body. If I listen carefully, it actually guides me. If not for the hospitalization, my overthinking brain would have been wasted on unimportant things.

"Sometimes, Luigi, we need a disaster to help us break into the mysterious paths of human consciousness. Like gunpowder: no pressure, no explosion. In the same vein: without those years of war and recovery, I wouldn't have discovered my capabilities to the full because until then, I'd never more than glimpsed them. And as you know, when clouds clash, electricity results, and from the electricity comes lightning, and lighting is light!" So Donato also recorded in his diary.

Luigi is amazed. What's happened to his brother? Luigi doesn't understand it all and he is taken aback, even a tad angry. Is that how Donato will also present himself in the village? In the language of the knowledgeable?

***

Donato gets very tired on the way back. He isn't used to so much movement.

Not far from Foggia he can identify the landscape, the stunning hues of autumn which will soon fade; the paths that go here and there, those same paths that some years ago, he'd drawn smiling and easily persuaded lasses along. He is very grateful for always having been able to jump the train on time, which reassures him that he hasn't added any Manduzios to the well-known ones in this tiny village.

Sparkling white, clusters of trullo suddenly remind him of Emanuela's wedding gown. His Emanuela, the white roses in church, and Carmella's donuts with their rich coating of sugar. These traditions pad the paths with the certainty of hundreds of years, infusing Donato with strength, and bringing him comforting childhood memories.

They've just passed the San Nicandro statue when Luigi and Donato notice the villagers coming out to greet them. It seems Alina couldn't keep the news to herself and shared her happiness with the neighbors. In fact, the entire village has shown up to wait for him.

But as they notice the wounded man, smiles leave people's faces. The carriage bringing him back to his home wobbles and shakes its passengers like a boat in a wild storm. What kind of future can this young man possibly have, trapped in his chair, his legs hanging loosely, yet his gaze still challenging? He is like a ruler who forgets to greet the crowd with a practiced wave.

Donato suddenly halts the carriage with a hand movement. Together, the wagoner and Luigi lower the chair to the pebble-strewn path, preparing to push his brother into the house. Donato refuses. Instead, he grips two sticks, and with Luigi's assistance, stands to his full height to acknowledge his friends, his head held high, his smile beaming.

First comes utter silence. Then, tears fall silently. And then a thundering wave of cheering. This is how the village opens its arms to one of its sons, and expresses its gratitude that he is alive; so many others of the village boys never returned, but now is not the time to talk of that.

Donato is accompanied up to his home's front door where his two "lasses," Emanuela and Alina, wait for him with teary eyes and arms held wide.

They help seat him in Caccaba's chair next to the unlit fireplace. This simple wordless act positions the wounded brother as responsible for the family's plight: he has seen life, the world, and no less so, helped save Italy.

Luigi accepts his brother's status with equanimity. Donato's monthly pension is likely to help them smooth out any number of rough spots in the years to come.

Initially, Donato insists on going to the fields to work the land but quickly discovers that his legs cannot bear the pain caused. Having no other choice, Donato decides to resume the use of his old chair. His return has made Emanuela so happy that she sings from morning to night. His wounds, his need to stay at home, do not discourage her – at least she has the man she loves with her, now and forever! She cares for him. She lives and breathes for his sake. They quickly get back into the swing of their interrupted life, a very rare phenomenon in San Nicandro – for long hours they talk together as the day draws to an end, seated alongside the warm fireplace or at the home's entrance, but they fall silent for several minutes after the meal, paying no mind to the burdens that still await them. Sipping coffee together, they share moments of love.

Every day Emanuela seats her husband at the home's

threshold in his wheelchair, constructed by the village shoe-maker, Francesco Cerrone.

There isn't a villager in San Nicandro who doesn't appreciate Francesco Cerrone, even though he's not from San Nicandro, having been born in Cagnano some twenty kilometers away, where he spent his childhood and teen years in much the same fashion as San Nicandro's youngsters did. But after marrying a San Nicandro lass, Angela Persicchetta, a brave young woman and well able to handle hard work and hardships, he moved to San Nicandro.

Nonetheless, something of the immigrant aura has clung to him, something of the non-local, even though for quite some time now he himself has not only felt to be an inseparable part of the San Nicandro population, but also to be among its more elite members.

He's often known as "*Cicillo lo Zoppo*," the limper, due to an old handicap, but Francesco has never complained about needing to take on more work to support his family, which quickly grew to nine children. Patching worn shoes isn't enough to keep his little clan looked after. At a time when no village could even imagine a refrigerator, Cerrone decides to produce ice that can extend the shelf life of food. Every winter he digs a gaping hole in the ground, piles snow up, and covers the ground with earth and straw. When the hot weather comes around, Cerrone uncovers the blocks of ice and quickly sells them.

Despite Cerrone's 1898 birth making him thirteen years younger than Donato, Francesco and Donato become very close. They share a fierce curiosity about life and are often seen immersed in long conversations in which San Nicandro's farmers show no interest.

But curiosity has a way of becoming contagious. Increasing numbers of locals stop to greet Donato and exchange their views about weather and farming tasks that are becoming tougher day by day. The locals are quite surprised by Donato's unexpected and very up-to-date answers and tips, and the grapevine rumor is that Donato's injury has turned him into a seer. Did the medications which were generously doled out to him affect his brain? Luigi thinks so, and the doctor at Pisa said so outright: Donato is a mixture of human and divine.

"A bit like a crossbreed between a horse and a donkey," Bonfito explains.

"So, as a counterbalance to what his brain gained, he lost something that belongs in his pants?" queried Tony, the village clothing repairer, who has a rollicking laugh. "We profit both ways: Donato isn't busy with everyone's daughters, and he's also giving us excellent advice. Did you see how he healed the cattle?"

In actuality, while forced to stay in the northern Italian hospital, Donato carefully observed the latest agricultural methods used there and until then, unknown in San Nicandro. He learns everything, takes it all in.

And now he's sharing tips and advice which greatly assist his farming community. He's also writing letters, whether personal or business related, for anyone who wishes, and doesn't ask for even a single *centesimo* in return. Self-respecting women of greater means bring him hot bowls of minestrone soup. Others bring aromatic fritters as payment for the time he devotes to assisting them. Alina and Emanuela are not enamored by these gifts, which to them have the whiff of charity. Why do they, the Manduzio family members, need other people's food? Their own is far tastier.

"My brother, what do you need these miserable gifts for?" Alina huffs.

Emanuela, on the other hand, disappears into the home as soon as she sees the grateful village women, looking away so that she can't see Donato's amused grin.

"*Picolla sorella,*" he addresses her as my little sister, "they give the best that they can. It makes them feel that they aren't taking charity. Why be cross with them?"

It is a miserable period: Mussolini is rigorous in shaping his regime, evangelists, gung-ho on converting people's beliefs, go from village to village and field to field, and crooks get rich through scandalous schemes worthy of imprisonment. Donato becomes the villagers' recourse to survival as they gnash their teeth and set to work improving their crops. Slowly but steadily this brings Donato to herbology and becoming a healer.

And he is accruing success.

When he was in the army, or more correctly, in hospital, he was drawn to books on astronomy and elixirs which he found scattered about on tables in the small room set aside for resting and relaxing. He was fascinated by any subject he read, endlessly grateful to the world for the unexpected way it raised him from an illiterate unable to pen his own signature, to someone able to read and understand information about so much.

At the time he would read the *Rotilio,* an annual journal containing profound, serious content which included superstitions but also various fanciful medical recommendations. Donato drew a good deal of information from it. He isn't inclined to superstition, but understands how his fellow San Nicandroans view the world. Aiming to draw them into using his products, he adds a bonus: a small metal ring, or a goat-shaped charm, or some other second-hand ornament. In this way he convinces his community of his capabilities. Farmers need demonstrable proof.

Donato has plenty of spare time, and his military pension prevents him from becoming a burden to his family. So he applies his knowledge to expand his knowledge even further, and to becoming increasingly involved in complex situations. He recommends a medication that helps a black goat recover from diarrhea which, if left unchecked, could cause it to die. He blends up a mixture to treat an infection in one of the rams. He explains the phenomena of the moon to the villagers to help them plan their crops. Often he is successful, because he is also blessed with highly perceptive intuition that helps orient his growing body of knowledge.

Using readily available items such as cheese from cows, milk from goats, olive oil, hot water, and sugar, Donato becomes known for bringing relief through his magical infusions or soups made with different kinds of flour. In those days, every village in the region boasted its own healer or person viewed as highly educated, wise with secret formulas. San Nicandro, too, had its own man of broad education, as he was viewed, and better yet…he was extremely useful.

Donato's reputation reaches neighboring villages. One day, Donato decides to visit Foggia where a particular family has asked many times that he come and help their twins who, at three years of age, still cannot walk or talk.

It took quite some time until he reached that decision. Traveling is never easy for someone who has lost control of his muscles. But it pains him to think that these two children could spend their lives dependent, like him, on others. He eventually goes to their home accompanied by Francesco Cerrone.

As they always do, Donato and Francesco talk along the way about the harvest, the vineyards, and the missionaries they recently encountered in San Nicandro who anger them deeply. Then Francesco directs the talk to the war years. Since his return, Donato has described those events thousands of times. Cerrone never tires of hearing what Donato has to say. The world's madness terrifies him. After experiencing it firsthand, Donato must certainly know how to keep away from it.

Bonfito's horse trots along at a brisk pace, and in what seems like no time at all, they reach Foggia, which looms like a giant under the burning summer sun. The closer they come, the louder the sounds typical of a mass of excited people. There's no way they can reach the central plaza: the crowd is large, tightly packed, electrified. Francesco helps Donato down from the wagon and onto his wheelchair, sorry he can't bring Donato closer to his destination.

"On the contrary, my brother. Walk alongside me, but don't push the chair. Watch how people make way and let me through."

"What! Do you think you're the *Duce?*" Francesco asks, using the Italian word for leader by which Mussolini likes to be known. "They'll squash you!"

But they're not trampled. Despite the crowd buzzing at the events playing out in the plaza, they do step aside, a step this way, a step that way, letting the two men, whose gaze is similar and whose manner is genteel, pass untroubled, one walking on his two legs, the other rolling forward in a wheelchair. Donato and Francesco reach the front row of the people in the plaza, which has been recently renovated with broader, smoother flagstones. It looks larger than it did in the past and is split up into sections in a more efficient manner. But today, a writhing river of human beings fill it, looking like an entire battalion setting out for war. In fact, milling among the people, keeping a close eye on them, are men with menacing facial expressions in uniforms.

"Mussolini's *squadristi!*" Francesco calls out to Donato over the din of the crowd. Francesco was referring to a paramilitary organization which violently attacked socialists and communists in Italy. Both men knew that the *squadristi* had formed before fascism, but had since become Mussolini's armed fascist wing.

"Are you kidding me?"

"Can't you hear their leader's braying?" Francesco, fearful now, whispered into Donato's ear.

"Mussolini? Cerrone, how much wine did you have this morning, eh? Do you really think he'd come here to this godforsaken place unknown to ninety-five percent of Italians?"

"Stop being as obstinate as a donkey, Donato. I'm telling you, he's here! No one else talks like that!"

And it was true: the leader of fascism in Italy was on stage, and the representatives of fascism's armed wing strode about, back and forth, and through the swaying crowd. These silent soldiers' faces are stern. In the past they ambushed socialists and communists whose names were on regime lists. Now even the names of people apathetic to fascism had been added. These soldiers are feared for their acts of horror.

They particularly enjoy humiliating their prey. Even their slightest action is meant to demean and cause agony. They rain blows on the victim with batons and force victims to drink large doses of cod liver oil as a way of temporarily incapacitating them. If they're in a jollier mood, they add some petrol to the oil, causing a horrible death lacking any respect of humanity. The whole world knows about this. Some encourage their actions with cheers of *Viva!* accompanied by blatant hand movements, but most people are so afraid that they try to be invisible.

The stage is adorned with a massive symbol of fascism which had been passed down from ancient Rome: a bundle of rods tied together at both ends, and an axe diagonally tied to the bundle.

"Look how Mussolini has finally managed to train them, these squadristi," Cerrone notes.

"And how quickly he did! For six or seven years, he made their lives pretty unbearable, organizing them in wild battalions. They're thugs. Who's their inspiration? Listen to him, that criminal. Can you hear what he's shouting?" exclaims Donato.

Mussolini is indeed screeching non-stop. His delivery is more like marketplace shouts than a considered political speech. The *Duce* recites a poem of praise for fascism: he claims that it bestows nobility of purpose to all who join its ranks.

Mussolini's fisted arm is raised. His chest is flush with the rallying: he looks as though he might topple right over at any moment.

"With regard to domestic policy," he screeches his Trieste speech, "the racial problem is of the utmost relevance.

It is relevant to the conquest of the empire because history teaches us that empires are conquered by weapons but preserved by prestige. And prestige requires a clear and strict racial consciousness that establishes not only differences but also unequivocally asserts superiority! Despite our policies, world Jewry has for many years been an enemy with which we can never reconcile!"

The Duce slams his fist down on the stand as though struck by hysteria before continuing.

"The pursuit of peace is a sick notion! Only war, with its power, can bring human strength to its peak and bestow nobility upon nations. Any other approach to victory is merely a futile substitute. Do not listen to what your ears hear from others! Fascism loves life; it regards life as the obligation to fight and achieve conquests that add beauty to life and an end to conflicts of interests."

"And what about how that gets done!" Francesco whispers.

The Duce screams on. "It is necessary to develop means of production. Fascism will assist you in this endeavor. It believes in, and fights for heroism. It does not waste time on class struggle. Men are mere puppets led by chance, whereas by joining fascism, you will combat the weak ideology of democracy. Fascism denies democracy, behind which the vileness and failures of the system hide from you. Authority guarantees success. The twentieth century must be a century of authority if we desire order and prosperity. We will make this century the century of fascism. With its strength and will, the fascist state is a moral state of unwavering ethics. The dictatorship of socialism, communism, and syndicalism is over! We will once again become a free people with sovereign decision-making after enduring too many humiliations. But for that, we must possess the spirit of sacrifice and accept all the necessarily drastic measures we will take against those who oppose us. Our fascism is our faith!"

The crowd roars in enthusiasm. The ecstasy of happiness entices as though it is just around the corner.

Donato and Francesco exchange wordless glances. They haven't caught all of the speech but the danger to their futures is absolutely clear to them.

Instead of leaving the stage by a set of stairs in the back, the Duce hops down right in front of Donato, pushing the wheelchair away as he passes. Initially his gaze at Donato is all apathy, but noticing that neither Donato nor his companion salute, he stops, turns and comes back to face them.

Donato quickly grabs hold of the walking stick attached to the chair and with extreme effort, manages to stand. The Duce is taken by surprise: this man is as tall as Mussolini himself. In fact, he's taller!

"Hey, you two, why don't you salute?"

Donato fixes his gaze on Mussolini's eyes and says nothing. Francesco steps forward.

"We wish you well, Duce."

Mussolini notes to himself: this one is like a farmer, from his clothes to his accent, but there's something in his eyes, something too personal to simply walk away from. So the Duce ponders. And this second one, thinks the Duce, has the same gaze. What are they, these men?

"Did you not like my speech?" Mussolini asks.

"I didn't understand it all, Duce," Donato answers.

"Are you mocking me? What's your name?"

"I wouldn't dare. But you express things that are some-times difficult to absorb. My name is Donato. Donato Manduzio."

Donato wonders how they'll get out of this sticky spot without any harm done. He can prove the emptiness of Mussolini's speech in just a few words but then he'd be fin-ished off with a single blow. They're surrounded by dozens of squadristi, silent, spittle showing on their lips as they think only one thought: let us loose on this idiotic cripple and give us some fun with his companion.

"Donato, you say? I'm curious about what you didn't un-derstand."

"If I may be permitted, Duce, war does not seem like the preferable and reasonable solution, unless there's a wish to be rid of excess human flesh. War inherently causes sorrow, poverty, and starvation. More than all else, it brings fear. You also claim that fascism is your religion. I respect you, Duce, and your religion is as precious to you as mine is to me. But fascism was shaped by humans. My faith comes from the depth of my soul, from that fragile yet invincible place that allows us to feel truth. And all of it is a gift from God. After all, aren't we his children?"

"You are making a great mix-up of things, and addition-ally, playing the role of priest! Where are you from?"

"From San Nicandro, Duce, the very top of Garganico. I'm not mixing things up. You're talking about power, about acknowledging the superiority of a specific group. You're promising a future dream based on fascism. That's politics. I'm not fully knowledgeable in that sphere. My area is the power of God within us, in the superiority of his laws, in respecting fellow humans as unique individuals, and not treating them like rags. I am grateful to still be seeking Him, seeking and finding God."

Mussolini responds with resounding laughter. He knows nothing of God other than that, God's earthly representatives are ambitious and no less dangerous than the gang accompanying him. For that reason he ratified the Lateran Agreements the previous year – on 11 February 1929, the precise date comes to mind. They granted Pope Pius XI and his successors exclusive rights to Vatican City. And since Catholicism was the state religion, it was an easy step taken into implementing a policy of racial segregation, which was precisely the Duce's wish.

"God, God, God! Let him be, wherever He is, and take into account that I'm your god, the one that King Emanuel chose so that Italy could become the most robust state in Europe. For several decades, everyone's tried to make me believe in God. As far back as 1903, I held a vocal discussion with Father Tagliatella, who was left fuming over my insistence on not believing in God."

"Insistence?"

The Duce studies Francesco. Francesco bothers him less than this chap, the cripple with the fiery gaze. "Not insistence," the Duce continues, "but fact. That's what I answered him, and I'll prove it to you. I blasphemed against God with coarse words as I let loose the full force of my ability to persuade. I ordered God to get rid of me, if He exists. Do you see how brave I am? And what happened? Nothing. Therefore, God does not exist. And as you said, what is mankind but a mere thing, a slip of rag, and another and another. Even that raises mankind's value to more than he is worth. Living, dead: what difference does it make? This person, that one: they're unimportant. The nation is what's important.

"Fascism knows its role in reality, and it's doing that perfectly. Tell your friends and your children, and recommend that they join us. You've got no better choice, be sure of that. Tell me, how do you spend your days if you're stuck in that chair? How'd you get to such a situation? A drunkard's brawl? Over a girl? An accident with the plow?"

"The war, Duce," Donato says, his voice weary. "During the day I work with my hands, much as your father did. They're strong, and I can fix or make various items. I also treat people and cattle, helping to heal them. I read a good deal, just as your respected mother must have." Donato had read up on Mussolini, whose father was a blacksmith and whose mother a teacher when their son Benito was born in 1883.

Francesco was listening intently. From the outset, he was taken by surprise by the Duce's wicked streak and crass language, whereas Donato came across as an intellectual. Despite his handicap, Donato stood nobly face-to-face with the enthused leader.

Their gazes left a strong impression on Francesco. Mussolini's was that of a man-eating giant waiting to satiate his hunger. Donato's was as inky black as a priest's cassock, and as calm as a clear sky.

His face contorting with the pain that syphilis was causing to his joints, the Duce brings his thoughts to a close. "I must leave, but I'll come to visit San Nicandro to check on what you're doing there and how you live. Believe me, I have an excellent memory. And then we'll see if, by then, fascism will succeed in changing you for the better. If not, I'll work harder at making it do so."

Mussolini snapped his heels together. It shook Francesco out of his reverie. Donato simply remained as he was.

"Does he want you to salute him? Is that why he's ruining his shoes?" Francesco asks once Mussolini was out of earshot.

Donato laughs. "I don't think he noticed that we didn't salute That man's so tiresome. He has no backbone. That's a leader? Our miserable king made a dreadful mistake."

"You said you didn't understand everything. You were fibbing, right?"

"Not entirely. But what I did understand was enough to make me deeply disappointed. No good's going to come from that creature. Let's go, Francesco. Let's find the house we're looking for, where they're waiting for us."

The twins' mother beckons them inside. Donato hobbles in, leaning on Francesco, because the wheelchair is too wide for the doorway. Lying in a very old crib that's clearly been repaired several times, the children are wrapped to their necks in rough cloth, looking for all the world like two mummies bound up tightly in cotton wadding.

The mother offers coffee and biscotti to the two men who, to her, are two scientists gracing her home. Her sister-in-law, Sambiana, recommended Donato after her nephew, mute from childhood, began speaking again following Donato Manduzio's treatment. Donato had rubbed the boy's ears for a very long time with tubes coated in a strange ointment. It had seemed to her as though Donato was drawing something from the boy's ears. What a strange sight! Yet how effective, since the child's speech had improved by the day.

The young mother is so unsettled by Donato's very forthright black gaze that her hand trembles as she pours the coffee. He smiles to put her at ease.

"Don't worry, it will be all right," he diagnoses. "Remove this bundle of wraps from them. Throw them away."

She does so, a little fearful and a little insulted.

Donato takes a small container of salve from his pocket. He has blended olive oil, valerian, thyme, and chamomile; as well as traces of other healing herbs, the names of which he guards as his secret. He gives some to Francesco.

"I'll treat this twin and you do exactly what I'm doing to the other," he instructs his friend. The two men slowly massage the two young, miserable bodies which had been cramped and imprisoned, and are showing it. They knead the children's limbs slowly and deeply, particularly their legs, arms, and shoulders. Initially, the children scream but quickly calm down. The bruises of long-term swaddling are fading.

Donato asks the mother if she has watched closely enough to continue repeating his movements on the children's bodies for several days more. Of course she knows what to do! Every morning, before she diapers them, she hugs and caresses them, and only then rolls them over and fixes the diapers tightly around them.

"No diapers," Donato's voice is firm. "Dress them as what they're meant to be: little men."

"But…"

"But what? Legs were meant to move, to walk and run. Arms were meant for hugging, for balance, and to defend

themselves with. Your children aren't worms growing in co-
coons!"

"My mother, my mother-in-law…"

"Two ignorant dangerous women!" Donato brings his
fist down hard on the table. "Do as I say, my dear, and your
children will become the healthiest among the city's children!"

"Do you believe that's enough?" Francesco asks Donato
once they've left.

"If she does as I've shown her, those two will be racing
her off her legs in the very next fair in Foggia! And we'll
likely have a chance to see them chasing each other!"

Donato not only has vast expertise in healing but has also
shown noteworthy skill as a director and producer of theater. No one in the village can imagine life there without Donato taking a focal role. It may come as no surprise but from
the hay harvest to the olive harvest, field work comes top of
the list. Work needed in the fields leaves little time for the
soul: the fields require all hands on board all the time.

And nonetheless, the village buzzes with social life
when these fair weather chores are not necessary during
the long winter days and nights. But who can sleep for so
many hours? This is when the pipe players take up their
ciaramella, a woodwind instrument reminiscent of bagpipes
and used in lively folk music, leave the Abruzzo region, and
wander through the narrow streets. Here and there, unpretentious performances are put on, the villagers playing the
parts taken from folklore. This is a region where unusual
events simply don't occur; it's like an isolated island where
populist literature blossoms and folktales center around the

villagers and their actions, or lack of them, across different stages of the year.

Surprisingly, San Nicandroans frequently perform excerpts from "The Count of Monte Cristo." Admittedly, none of the locals has ever seen the book, but the rich, tense plot around Edmond Dantès and the motifs of friendship and loyalty fascinate the San Nicandro locals. Donato has related it numerous times, drawing the suspense out over several evenings during a week's telling.

Now he's letting his imagination run free and wild, producing the story as a play. He decides on makeup, posture, intonation: sometimes he behaves like a capricious but always confident director. What used to be half-hour shows have lengthened into ninety minutes, occasionally longer. Everyone loves them. These cultural activities, unexpected in this unassuming population, drive Donato's success. In no time, he's enriched the performances with recitations from legends and anecdotes he'd read in the past. With each rendition, he embellishes the narrative with a dash of flair; with every round of applause, his and everyone else's spirits soar.

The results are so good that the village's few members who view themselves as rather more sophisticated and respectable, keeping their distance from the simpletons, open their homes to the future actors and their director, who openly shows his pride in them. Now shows can be put on for a limited audience, Donato always at the ready to make his demands ever more stringent.

One fine day, Concetta de Leo offers Donato her home as a place where "his theater" can be located. She has the means…she has a lavish home in the village center, and her house is far better maintained than that of so many others. Actors will be allocated a room where they can change costumes, and their costumes will be stored in an adjacent room. Donato is thrilled. He imagines himself as Foggia's minor Moliere – he imagines his troupe performing in Foggia, perhaps later in Trieste. Who knows? Maybe even in Pisa!

Concetta's appearance and quick wit impress the villagers: she not only fits the description of Colomba in noted author and archaeologist Mérimée's novella of that name but also resembles the main character in her nobility of manner.

Concetta is thrilled at having found a way to expand her highly restricted lifestyle by connecting to the world of culture which had, until now, been inaccessible to her. She is literate, writes poetry, and Donato sets her work to music.

Concetta de Leo offers Donato her assistance in sewing costumes and designing backdrops. Nothing is left to chance: every detail bubbles up from Donato's busy mind. In "The Count of Monte Cristo," the triple-masted sailing ship known as Le Pharaon is heavily battered as it heads for Marseilles. Edmond Dantès takes over command when the captain is injured. The scene is enacted against a very long piece of blue cloth representing the stormy sea and thrashing winds, and is presented so cleverly that some in the audience begin to feel seasick.

The audience applauds long and loudly.

Donato loves these moments of escape, these tales being retold, the expanded, enriched versions which continue developing from week to week. He breathes new life into a village that for a very long time has been mired in boredom. It is a village where the only type of entertainment had been repeat visits by members of the clergy trying to instill deeper faith in the villagers. Their visits' only purpose is to try and increase the numbers of people in their particular branch of Christianity.

***

The church sacristan frequently comes by to air his views with Donato. Theater interests him less than religion. Donato's opinions on religion are clear-cut.

Working fiercely to convert hearts to their church throughout the rural areas are the Evangelists, chiefly derived from the "Brethren" Christian Church founded in 1864 by Piero Guicciardini of Florence. Their grandiose speeches to laborers vie with those from Adventists, Pentecostals, and Jehovah's Witnesses. They have no problem with persistently and repeatedly knocking on the same doors. They're politely listened to, and some even join them: some experience a strong need for divinity and a religious framework that promises more than the unexplained Catholic faith. These missionaries never tire: they are like a swam of locusts weaving across the fields, not leaving until the field's crop has been razed.

Donato isn't opposed to chatting with them, but their views find no traction in his thoughts. The shallow convictions on which their statements rely, join the pool of information he's acquired after delving into witchcraft and herbalism.

His love and confidante, Emanuela, listens to his explanations. "For a long time now, I've noticed how it's all fabrication, like magic by sorcerers, fraudulent. I'm so very sick of speaking what amounts to lies to convince the public."

"Yet you do help others. Even if what you say isn't entirely true, it helps heal them."

"That's very probable. But I pray deeply that if there is
an entity which created and governs the world, and if that
entity is one of justness, I wish to serve it with integrity.
I don't want to continue teaching my friends about lunar
movements and so on, which I know aren't entirely true so
I teach them reluctantly."

"You've failed to teach them well, you say? But you've
nevertheless healed those who trust you," Emanuela is annoyed, too busy with her own household's real-life matters
to take on those of others.

Donato is not satisfied. He keeps searching, researching,
cannot identify anything that is clearly derived from God,
about whom he's been taught as existing. He finds nothing
in his village's existence other than superstitions and fear of
the devil.

One night, Donato is seated in his home's doorway gazing out at the faraway horizon, content because he'd managed to save the neighbor's sheep and goat the previous day
despite what he'd told Emanuela. Those animals belonged
to his neighbor Tino, a regular villager so far from wealthy
that their loss could have resulted in a huge disaster for the
man's family.

Donato's gaze takes in the immediate surroundings. He
notices someone walking toward him, holding a lamp that
has burnt out as he slowly takes shape in the darkness.

"Look, I am bringing you light," the man says in a soft
voice.

"Light? What light? Why don't you light the lamp you're carrying?"

"I can't. I don't have a match. But you do."

Completely confounded, Donato sees that the man is actually holding a lit match. Taking hold of the lamp, its wick already damp with oil, Donato lights it up. Instantly the man and darkness disappear. In their stead remains a brilliant beam of light.

Breathlessly, Donato records the odd phenomenon in his diary, much like a dreamer capturing the details of a dream. He ends as follows: "On the night between the 10th and 11th of August 1930, I saw an incredibly powerful vision… its meaning is unclear to me, but I am storing it in my heart with reverence."

Donato is still deeply astonished. He joins Emanuela, who is asleep in bed. He has a burning desire to tell her what he's just experienced. He knows it's a vision, but he's also convinced that he really did speak with the man, and that every word of the conversation will remain etched in his memory forever.

Gently, he wakes his wife and describes the event. Emanuela believes him right away. She knows Donato's nature well: not easily enthused, not easily deceived. This stunning event is so far beyond her comprehension that she crosses herself repeatedly, calling on Jesus Christ. That restores her confidence, calms her, and then she remembers that one of her roles as a woman is to keep her husband calm. And she must also rest if she is to deal with the livestock at sunrise, which gives rise to her practical suggestion.

"*Mio marito Donato,*" my husband Donato, she says, "go

to sleep now with that beautiful image in your mind, and surely tomorrow God will provide us with an explanation. Place your trust in his hands. I see that you're exhausted. Let sleep bring you serenity and strength."

And that is precisely what happened.

The next day, at the end of a busy morning which left no time for chatting, Emanuela and Donato sit down to sip coffee together and share their precious daily moments of intimacy which keep them bound more tightly than any other couple in San Nicandro. They are about to discuss the previous night's event when a knock sounds on the door and someone walks in without waiting for an answer. Leonardo, Emanuela's cousin, greets them. Large-boned, strong, diligent, a lively fellow who like his glass or two of wine, he smiles broadly above a belly wrapped in wide, brown cloth. He's never been seen without it. A scar running from the corner of his mouth to his left temple shows on his pleasant face. It's testimony to his hot-headedness.

"Greetings to the lovers! Here I am, *Babbe Natale*," he says, calling himself by the name with which Italy's version of Santa Claus is known, "about to start his usual rounds!"

"And where would he start if not at his cousin, of course! The one who treats him to the hot wine that he loves. I understand that a criminal like you isn't interested in coffee, right?" Emanuela teases playfully.

Leonardo bursts into laughter. If there'd have been a book of records in Italy, he'd have been *numero uno* for the amount of hot wine he could put away, even at the height of summer. It's an odd custom but he won't forego it.

"Donato, I helped Cerrone fix the peddler's wagon this morning. Both send their regards."

74

"And that's why you neglect your own work? To come and convey greetings?"

Donato is not happy to see him right now when he wanted to enjoy espresso with his wife. He's especially displeased to see Leonardo today when he's bursting to discuss his vision's details to Emanuela, particularly because she always has such keen insights and advice. But Leonardo isn't perceptive enough to realize he's barged in on private time. His grin broadens as he answers.

"No, not at all. The peddler paid Cerrone, and gave me this. He said that since he doesn't know how to read, and because I'm in the same boat, he thought you might enjoy it."

Leonardo pulls out a thick tome from his rucksack. Although wrapped in a shabby rag, its cover is beautifully worked, made of carved leather engraved with arabesques and flowers and as soft to the touch as a newborn's skin.

Emanuela is awed but, as always, practical. "*Madonna, come e bello!*" In the name of Holy Maria, it is beautiful! "Why not sell it? You could get an excellent price!"

"And who, tell me, would buy a book from me? What would that person do with it? Who has money for such a thing? And anyhow, I am truly happy to bring this gift to my cousin!" Leonardo exclaims.

Leonardo is speaking the truth: he is a good-hearted chap who loves to celebrate and enjoy life. He is far from wealthy but has always sought a way to show Donato his deep gratitude for saving his vineyard after aphids had spread throughout it, causing severe damage. For Leonardo, this is an opportunity to repay Donato's kindness.

Donato's nose is already in the book. Pages on the right

are in an incomprehensible language, and on the left, in Italian. The book's title: TORAH.

First Donato quickly thumbs through it, then goes back to the start and begins reading a section or two with intense concentration. He can feel a wave of powerful potential coursing through these pages. It's as though their voices are familiar; it reveals the concealed.

Indifferent to Donato's internal turmoil, which causes him to sit so silently that he could just as well be absent, Leonardo plonks down at the table, enjoying a glass of wine and prosciutto, while chatting with Emanuela. That lets Donato lean back in his armchair near the fireplace and focus on reading.

"Look how his back has straightened! If this carries on, he'll be up on his legs any second now! What's the book about?" asks Emanuela.

"How should I know?" Leonardo shrugs. "In any event, he always behaves like that when he's reading."

"No, Nardo. Something's different this time. I know my man too well not to see the difference."

Yes something's very different: Donato is struck by an inner peal of thunder, shaken by a silent earthquake, gripped by a revolution.

Later Donato will jot this down in his diary.

I picked the book up and turned to the first section. With great wonder, I saw the creation, the existence of a God before creation of the earth, and how this God created everything. And then a beam of light burst forth in my heart and after remembering the previous night's vision, I came to an awareness that in the vision, the Torah was the light.

*Instantly I declared to all the peoples that there is one God,
that his Torah was given on Mount Sinai, and that the
Creator rested on Shabbat.*

*And I confirmed the unity of this Creator who takes advice
from none, since he alone is God. And I praised the Creator's
holiness in the heavens.*

For a week Donato never leaves the chair in the doorway.
He does not hear Emanuela losing her patience because the
minestrone is getting cold. He sleeps in fits between bouts
of reading which unsettle his soul. In his father's old armchair he sits engrossed, he reads, absorbs, identifies, learns
how the world came to be and continues to be.

Donato, as though driven by a long dormant urge, wakes
suddenly, realizing that these pages contain the truth. He
has found the Divine! The divine entity known as the Lord,
the omnipotent One, who Donato will eventually call,
should he have such a need, God.

Before this book came into his hands, Donato had constantly searched for an explanation for the world's creation.
Here, at last, he has it, gleaming, in the form of a just God,
a Creator, a divine who gives direction to what He created.

At last reality has been infused with meaning. This
book, this Torah, provides proof that both man and God
have a part to play in the universe that God designed.
Reading the Bible, Donato sees how divine enlightenment
emphasizes the existence and continuation of a relationship with every person on earth; Donato finds in the Torah
an explanation for the entirety of existence, which is accessible to everyone, yet so many choose to ignore it. That's
what Donato has discovered.

As soon as he began reading the fascinating creation narrative, Donato began trembling: had his vision of the previous night been sent by God or one of God's messengers?

Yes, it's all very clear now. The remarkable man had held a lamp, but Donato had held the match for it. Imagine penning an article stating that the Mass was no longer relevant! Is it incumbent on Donato to spread Judaism, and perhaps do more than that?

Her husband's vision repeatedly pops into Emanuela's thoughts, and as often as it does, she exclaims. "What a coincidence! At night, the vision. The very next day, the Holy Book!"

"Coincidence? No, my dear wife. God's actions are purposeful!" Donato's response comes from his heart; he cannot know that elsewhere in the world, a scientist by the name of Einstein would, at some future point, reach the same conclusion and state so. Here is a God who acts infinitely yet remains hidden in the background…hidden from those who do not want to see, but evident to those who do.

The Torah presents ancient events. As he reads, Donato follows the wars, conquests, the flood, the destruction and killing of the nations from the face of the earth thousands of years ago. And among them were the Jewish people.

Thus, not only does Jewish tradition need to be reinstated, but the Jewish people themselves, concludes Donato.

But why would God choose this tiny village of Foggia as the place for reinstatement? And why Donato? The message from the previous night's vision, and the arrival of the Torah today, are sufficient for Donato. He can feel God; he sees and hears God in these events.

For the first time, every question he can think of has its

answer in the Torah, answers that bear the clarity of a path that has existed forever.

For the first time, Donato feels a joyful connection with the world, thrilled at being in the present, and not fearful or put off by superstition. Now he understands his past perplexity, the helplessness of a skeptical Catholic: he could not fathom being in a world in which one is led to believe that the messiah already came, having given his life for humanity's sake, yet this messiah died without bringing any change to the world. For Donato, it's clear that the label of messiah was nothing but deception which served the clergy to tighten their control over the illiterate populace.

That Jesus is claimed to be the son of God does not bother Donato, but his arrival improved nothing in the world. Perhaps he was a prophet and certain people took advantage of him for their own personal gain.

In light of the misery and suffering which have not passed from the world, however, no! Donato simply cannot accept that Jesus was the messiah.

And so today, he is flooded by gladness. The Torah has provided an explanation for every question that Donato had pondered. It clears doubt and provides revealed truth.

He hurries off to tell others. Donato is not driven by altruistic love, but he has perceived what God expects of him: to encourage as many people as possible to adopt this one and only revealed religion. He feels able to precisely express what has to be said as a way of helping others also find God, without ploys such as saints arguing with God, or priests and clergy manipulating people for the sake of their own greedy need of control.

"From that day on," Donato later records, "I began to

spread the Oneness of the Creator among my friends, this God who created the world from nothing in six days, and sanctified the seventh, and later called on Moses to bring his people the Israelites to revelation."

As he reads, Donato is aware of an absolute, intimate recognition that builds between himself and God, and predicts that his life will be conducted according to the commandments in the Torah.

Donato isn't seeking explications: human intervention doesn't interest him. He is smart enough to understand that anyone might err until that person also encounters the holy God, the Only One who has any value.

Having read the book cover to cover, the Torah indeed seems to Donato to be the match from his vision. All that remains is to help bring light to his surroundings. And later, to the whole world. How simple! How encompassing!

Without delay he sets off on his mission: to bring this light to others. On Sunday, some twenty of the village folk are there listening intently to his words.

Although they're simple farmers, those listening to Donato begin to sense an ancient vibration. They come in increasing numbers day by day to listen to him, to let him bring them tranquility, to have him firmly drive out superstition from their religious belief. And some women underline Donato's message with a flurry of signs of the cross.

On one particular day, Donato was sitting at his doorway working on unraveling a chapter of Torah in the original Hebrew text. As his finger runs across one page after the next, he notices a man slowly approaching, a Protestant in search of new souls to convert to the Protestant church. He'd heard about Donato and wanted to meet him. Moving closer while trying to act as though this were none other than a chance encounter, the man caught Donato's eye. In a flash Donato realized the man's covert goal.

After enjoying the glass of wine that local custom dictated, Donato addressed the man courteously.

"Have you come to visit a relative?"

"We're all relatives through God. In fact, that's what I'd like to remind the village residents because I was told that they have wandered a little off the path. What are you reading?"

"The Torah."

"The Old Testament? Why? Its time has passed. Only belief based on the Gospels will save you," the man answered.

"From what?"

"From hell! Do not choose the way of desecration!"

"From this book, which I will not allow you to belittle, I have learned that God created the world in six days from nothing, that he sanctified the seventh day, and that he later called on Moses to bring God's people out of slavery. All that is, to you, meaningless?" Donato challenged.

"The ancient Israelites were an important people indeed, but in the past. Jesus, though…"

"What does 'Jesus' mean? What has God ever done to you for you to offhandedly reject God himself?"

"But Jesus is God, and God is Jesus!" the man exclaims, roused.

"Extrapolate."

"There's nothing to explain. That's the way it is. You must humbly accept that which you can't understand, and trust us to lead you."

"That's precisely what I won't do, and what I've never been able to do. The Torah provides an answer to every question that insightful people might raise. That's why I'm providing these answers to my friends who you want to convert. I'm helping them shake off their ignorance and connect to God the way he has commanded us to, and that is my mission. Would you like me to explain Torah to you too?" Donato continues. His tone of voice carries a challenge.

The man is taken aback, too prideful to accept. "I'm the one who explains religion and divine requirements! I don't think you're suited to matters of the church."

"Who was speaking of the church?"

"From the church you must accept the word of God, and only from it. Return to Jesus!"

"I didn't receive the word of God from any man. God himself revealed his ways to me, as he did to the forefather Abraham."

Donato explains his beliefs, as he's been doing for some time now to his friends. "God revealed his existence and his will through three creations: the world, the Sabbath, and choosing mankind to be the mediator between him and that most ancient of all people on earth. If you diverge from this understanding, you make the most terrible, irreconcilable error."

The protestant gave a cocky laugh at Donato's insolence and tried once more to make Donato withdraw from his dangerous insistence. Later, lacking any convincing counterarguments, he opted to quietly leave, his face twisted in scorn.

***

Many San Nicandroans have begun showing an interest in Judaism, drawn to and convinced by its authenticity. Surprisingly, Tino, the church sacristan, is one of the first to bring about change. His chores aren't too time consuming, which leaves him plenty of time for lengthy and frequent talks with Donato, whose explications often oppose the Catholic church's rulings. The sacristan is not the type to reject Catholic views. Not him! Of course not! But Don Adriano, fearful of his authority being usurped, often makes things tough for Tino, so much so that Tino eventually decides to push that form of worship and his cleric into a back drawer. As for Donato, Tino senses that his friend truly has a special relationship with God, a closeness that appears to him utterly impossible within Catholicism.

When Tino listens to Donato, Tino is infused with a wish to smash Don Adriano's air of superiority. That thought fills Tino with joy. For that reason, a little for the sake of teasing, a little for the sake of politics, he tells Don Adriano about Donato's book.

"What are you rambling on about? What book?"

"I don't know, padre. Donato usually keeps it closed on his lap, and places his hands over it."

"And why did no one tell me about this? I'm going over there to shake him up good and proper, those fake church members! What's he told you from that book?"

"He talks about God," the sacristan says in a wistful tone. "Always, about God. 'Elohim' is the word he uses for God."

"How dreadful! Did you see any pictures in the book? Any, let's say, bothersome images?"

"I just told you: I've never seen the book open."

"Another act of sorcery!"

Suddenly acting worried, Tino knits his brows. "Padre, do you think it's a satanic book?"

"I'm very much afraid so. Go quickly to finish your church chores, and don't waste your time on blasphemy. Your broom hasn't seen the light of day since the month of May devoted to holy Maria!"

Don Adriano trusts Donato. But now he's concerned that something may pitch them against each other and cause mutual anger. Will he perhaps find out today why young Donato recoiled so evidently at the ceremony some years earlier?

Wanting to keep things calm, he never accused Donato of sorcery or magic-making. On the other hand, he'd been very surprised at how the boy had been unable to control himself, vomiting violently. The bishop had praised his subordinate's compassion toward the lad, but never followed up on the rebellious young Manduzio's life. Who knows what might have occurred meanwhile? Yes, caution would be wise.

"From rebellion matters move to shooting with a sling shot, and from the sling shot, to blasphemy, and from that to devil worship, my dear priest," the bishop says. "Keep an eye out for that chap, or you could one day be seeing him publicly revealing his improper tendencies. When that happens, we must be ready to react."

Had the time come?

It was certainly time to check on what was happening in the Manduzio household.

Don Adriano finds Donato seated by his doorway, as

always, reading a thick, leather-bound tome. He cannot make out any other details because Donato, having noticed him, instantly closed the book and positioned both his palms on it.

Don Adriano settles himself into Emanuela's armchair. Emanuela brings two glasses and a bottle of the better quality wine. The priest enquires about the grape harvest, and the Manduzio couple's health. And this is where he finds the thread that allows him to touch on the subject he wants to question.

"My dear Donato, forgive me if I ask about your personal lives, but as you know, God is everywhere, and especially stands with those who long to give birth to Catholic children. I know how much you both, Emanuela and Donato, want a child. Are you treading firmly along this path, or perhaps you need to divulge something that will help bring you your wish?"

A spark of mischief lights up Donato's eyes. Now the purpose of the priest's visit is as clear as the light of day. But Donato has no intention of making matters easy for Don Adriano.

"Drink, Don Adriano. This is the wine my father set aside for special occasions and important people. It's the same one you almost got to taste on the day of my ceremony," he adds with a wink.

The sounds of swallowing, the sweep of a tongue across lips, eyebrows raised in appreciation of the fine wine, embellished the home with a sense of glowing warmth and hospitality, yet with the undercurrent of life-altering discussions about to take place.

"Drink up, Don Adriano, drink up! Taste these *fritelle*

which are hot and fresh, straight from the frying pan!" Emanuela invites the priest. *May Emanuela be blessed! Because of her clever thinking, this meeting will end far sooner than had been planned.*

Five cups of wine later, Don Adriano is beyond logic and comprehension. In any event, Donato thinks, smiling to himself, what I'm about to tell him will be like a bomb going off!

Don Adriano drains his glass, glances at the bottle, but doesn't dare to ask for more. He picks up the last fritter and decides he's really no more than God's representative on earth.

"So I started to ask, Donato: is no child expected yet?"

"No."

"You know… how shall I put this… sometimes the child is begging to come into the world. God has already decided which one it will be. Shall we say, designated the child, but there's a barrier."

"What do you mean, padre? Emanuela is prepared to buy any charm in the village if it helps her become pregnant!" Donato jokes with him. "And I, well, I'm not put off by the work needed to bring a child into the world, believe me!"

"Sometimes people think they're doing the right thing, but in fact they're opening gateways to the devil. And certain means, that are beyond doubt, can sometimes help, such as holy writings."

"Holy Mother of God!" Emanuela exclaims, making three successive signs of the cross.

Donato flashes a gaze that signals her to stop. He then studies the priest. "I understand your intent. The word is out in full force in the village. I've read the holy texts, of course. Have I not behaved appropriately?"

"Did I say that? But to understand them well, without being harmed by them and to be sure you retell them correctly later, you must be clergy. No one but they can do such a job. Everyone else is forbidden from doing so. Would you mind pouring me a glass of wine, Emanuela? It is so very good for my health. It fortifies my blood. Do you understand, Donato, that you are prohibited from opening that book? Only we are able to comprehend its contents."

"How odd! This book of Moses describes ignoramuses just like us who understood everything, and conveyed it all without a single mistake. Abraham, Isaac, Jacob: do you think they ever went to school? And this is the book that must not be spoken about once it's been discovered? I don't understand, Don Adriano."

"My dear Donato, I am listening to you, and I'm convinced that you surely wish no harm to all which we hold sacred when you lecture to Concetta, Cerrone, Leonardo, Tino, and all the other villagers about the holy saints God appointed. Those saints were able to forego study because they were chosen. Regular folk do not have the ability to understand God. Only the religious authorities do. We must put our trust in them, and let them think on our behalf, and accept what they teach us with full faith. See, it's so simple."

"Don Adriano," Donato's response is ready, "You know me well. How could you possibly think your words are appropriate to who I am? Are we not as brittle as garlic skins, as lowly as a floor rag? As for me, what I see and what moves me is the need to know, the passion to become closer to our

Creator. This vibrant, immersive passion is not something that only I can feel. Everyone who comes here to talk with me asks questions, and for the first time in their lives, they get answers. I don't ask any of them to commit to anything. Often I even prefer that they leave me to my thoughts and let me continue discovering the divine glory which illuminates me."

"But I'm here, Donato!"

"So you are, and that's the whole point! Your belief requires you to believe that God's message will not be revealed again. That is a lie, and lacks all logic. Anyone who says that the Holy One won't return and reveal Himself is lying. He seems not to reveal himself because we've stopped looking for Him. We don't look in the Torah, nor in prophecy. But if we conduct ourselves according to Torah, God will keep watch over us, because He's holy. Adonai is the Creator, who created me from nothing and made me into a man and then presented me with the vision of his kingdom. In his light which shines onto anyone seeking him, he makes his voice heard and states the name of his holy people in that very place that is all darkness."

"You are speaking baseless nonsense! Every word you've uttered is blasphemy. The book you're holding must surely have been written by those deviants who infest these regions: Evangelists, Pentecostals, and other deceivers. That book needs to be destroyed. Hand it over to me and turn your thoughts in a different direction, for example by uniting plentifully with your wife. I'm sure your wishes will be answered once you've given me that book."

"Enough, Don Adriano. And if we're already on the subject, don't worry so much about my offspring. It's not respectful to say, in front of Emanuela, that no child has come because of the devil. It's more reasonable that the war is the cause of our disappointment. There's nothing wrong with reading the Torah. I'm even learning Hebrew by virtue of the translation, and in that way I'll become even closer to Elohim."

"Elohim?"

Donato can't hold back his chuckle. "Yes. That's the Hebrew word for God. Perhaps you'd prefer that name. Did you know that God has many names, some of which must never be stated?"

"In Hebrew? Are you out of your mind? Why do you need to learn Hebrew? That's forbidden!"

"And essential. Moreover, I think I'm receiving help with my studies. Having read the text in Italian, I look at the facing page containing the original text, and without too much difficulty I can identity the sounds. I understand the holy language a little better as each day passes. I want to understand Hebrew's nuances, the meaning of what God revealed to Moses. And of course you know so well, Don Adriano, that *"Tradurre, questo è tradire sempre,"* Donato ends, reminding the priest that a translation is only ever a betrayal of sorts.

"Superstition! The work of the devil, I tell you! You are not entitled to keep this book with you, let alone read it! You have already been tainted by intolerance and impatience! I was told that you forced Concetta to call her son by a Jewish name, without the child being baptized! Are you aware of how great your blasphemy is? Why not circumcise him too, then?"

"The church is what preserves empty statements, Don

Adriano. I don't force anything on anyone, and certainly not on Concetta, who has a heart and mind of her own and knows how to use both very well. Her husband wanted to call their son Vincenzo. She refused and of her own will chose Giuseppe. I wasn't involved at all. And as for circumcision, the day will yet come, with God's help."

"Give me that book, Donato!"

"Never."

"How can you possibly believe in a God who has multiple names? Here, that's another proof of Judaism's fraudulence, not so?"

Fury flashed in Donato's eyes. "And those trying to persuade the world of the unity of the father and the son, and his miraculous birth to a virgin who never knew a man, isn't running afoul of delusion and in fact lauding forbidden relationships? And those who tyrannize entire populations using illogical claims whereas everything that derives from God is based on pure logic which will yet be proven by science: is that not the epitome of deception?"

Don Adriano rose in anger, his chair tipping over behind him as he stepped away, shouting. "I will tell the Bishop everything. He remembers your ceremony's scandalous day! Let's see if you dare withstand him! *Scomunica, scomunica!*" You should be excommunicated, the priest shouted over and over as he scurried away.

Turning to Emanuela, Donato noticed she was pale and fearful. "Don't worry, *mia cara*. My dear wife, you know what he's like. He'll be back and then we can at last chat together."

"From your mouth to God's ears," she said, crossing herself repeatedly. The movement reminded Donato of shaking out a dusty cloth.

Donato knew that the priest felt threatened by a possible conflict with the village folk, many of whom were now turning to the Torah for guidance on how to live their lives. Would Don Adriano dread being moved to a new parish and having to start over? Would he need to then pinpoint the affluent members of the community, mingle with them to establish relations that would allow him to obtain their assistance toward benefitting the poor, requesting support for the feasts that follow Mass, teaching catechism to their children, saying nothing undiplomatic but by using sweet words, gradually secure his grip on them and carve out a cozy spot for himself?

"Donato?" Emanuela whispers.

"Your face is as white as snow, my sweet. Nothing's happened. Don Adriano…"

"Donato… I wanted to tell you… Donato, I'm pregnant."

Donato wakes the heavens with his whoop of joy!

***

Every time Donato opens the Torah to read, he is thrilled by the closeness he feels and which so fully corresponds with that of the ancient, erased nation of Israel. The Hebrews fought for centuries, escaping one foe after the next, and Pharaoh was hardly the worst of them! They left Egypt, returned to the Promised Land, and at some point afterwards, disappeared.

Donato knows he won't be able to rest until he revives

Judaism. God's reason for wanting this revival to take place in San Nicandro of all places, a tiny forgotten spot on the heights of Mount Garganico, and right here at the doorway to his home, is incomprehensible, and makes him shake his head in amazement. But the reason is unimportant. God says, and Donato does.

He starts by burning the pictures of saints and destroying the figurines of the Holy Virgin and of Saint Michael which he finds scattered around his home. This brings to mind how startled he'd been as a child by the guilt-inducing speeches over Jesus' death to atone for the sins of humanity. He remembers having the idea drummed into him: a person is born guilty and must constantly earn salvation. Donato always rejected this approach: the label was a disgrace to humanity, and reflected terribly on God. Donato understands from Torah that a person is born innocent, and that the Sabbath elevates us spiritually. To Donato, Torah is clear proof that God presides over the Sabbath and speaks of it with love. God would never kill his son.

Flakes of plaster, a snippet of a blue cape, and a broken hand have fallen onto the floor. Emanuela starts at every sound of ripped cloth and smashed figurine, and instinctively crosses herself. Donato calms her.

"You know me, *mia cara*. Do you think my actions are bad, that I've been taken over by an evil spirit the way Don Adriano, who knows no better, claims? Think about it: could Maria have given birth yet remain a virgin? There's no such thing in Torah. What God has granted humanity is not in the realm of torment or mystery. He gave us the Ten Commandments. You know them well. Did you find any satanic or harmful aspects to them?"

Donato collects and removes more objects related to Christianity. Emanuela follows him around, unable to stop herself from collecting the shards and stuffing them in her apron pocket. Maybe she should burn them instead of throwing them away? Burning seems less of a dishonorable fate.

Being well versed in the Torah text now, it suddenly occurs to Donato that his actions parallel those of Abraham, who smashed the clay idols which his father, Terah, made and sold. The enormity of his action makes him suddenly aware that if not for the vision and the way he perceives his future, he himself would have wondered if he hadn't gone mad.

He translates the Ten Commandments faithfully into Italian, spending several weeks teaching them and examining his own behavior against their guidelines.

1. **I am the Lord your God**, who brought you out of the land of Egypt, out of the house of bondage. You shall have no other gods before me.
2. **You shall not make a graven image for yourself,** nor any manner of likeness, of anything that is in heaven above or on the earth below or that is in the water or under the earth.
3. **You shall not bow down to them or serve them,** for I, the Lord your God, am a zealous God, visiting the iniquity of the fathers upon the children up to the third and fourth generation of those who hate me; yet show mercy even to a thousand generations of those who love me and keep my commandments. **You shall not take the name of the Lord your God in vain** for the Lord will not hold one who takes his name in vain as guiltless.

4. **Remember the Sabbath day to keep it holy.** Six days you shall labor and do all your work but the seventh day is a day of rest unto the Lord your God: you shall not do any manner of work in it, neither you nor your son nor your daughter nor your manservant nor your maidservant nor your cattle nor the stranger who dwells within your gates. **For in six days the Lord made heaven and earth, the sea and all that it contains, and rested on the seventh day**, and the Lord blessed this Shabbat day and hallowed it.

5. **Honor your father and your mother, that your days be long on the land** that the Lord your God gives you.

6. **You shall not murder.**

7. **You shall not commit adultery.**

8. **You shall not steal.**

9. **You shall not bear false witness against your fellowman.**

10. **You shall not covet your fellowman's house; you shall not covet your fellowman's wife**, nor his manservant, nor his maidservant, nor his ox nor his ass, nor anything that belongs to your fellowman.

Donato thinks about Emanuela's panicked reaction as he shattered the idols in their home. He must find a way to encourage and soothe villagers who will call out to the heavens when he says they must do the same. Even for Abraham, Donato recalls, it was no easy matter.

He decides that the best way to go about it is by encapsulating the Ten Commandments in a simpler, more easily comprehensible way for the villagers. He adds one more line as a way of ensuring that they will stay firmly lodged in the minds of those who come to learn from him.

1. Elevate me as your one God and I will elevate you as my People.
2. Do not make idols.
3. Do not use my name in vain.
4. Sanctify the Sabbath.
5. Love your father and your mother.
6. Do not shed blood.
7. Guard your self-respect.
8. Do not cheat.
9. Respect the innocent.
10. Do not covet.
11. And I will betroth you with eternal love.

Once he's finished, he calls Emanuela over. "Copy these letters the way you see them, and if you wish, embroider them on cloth and ask other women to do the same. The more we repeat these words and look at them gracing San Nicandro homes, the better we'll get at keeping God's instructions and honoring God."

Despite their lack of education, the women in every home compete with each other to produce the most beautiful sampler, using their skills, their imagination, and their faith. But the discomfort roused by destroying the figurines, especially that of Saint Michael, does not dissipate.

Concetta de Leo wonders. "Donato, maybe you rushed. I know the Ten Commandments, but Saint Michael is the most venerated saint in our region, along with San Nicandro. Perhaps you should've waited and given the public a better explanation for your actions."

"What reason could be clearer than the second commandment? 'Do not make a graven image.' Isn't that sufficient?"

"Oh yes, of course, but as you know, the sanctuary near Foggia has attracted hordes of people for centuries. I went there too, to pray to the Angel Michael. They say he revealed himself several times to the bishop of Sipontum next to a cave which he insisted should be dedicated to God in return for protecting the city against idol worshippers. These were Saint Michael's first recorded appearances in Europe. Maybe that's the reason why the church which was later built there is never empty."

Donato ponders for a moment. Has he acted too rashly? No, not possible. The work of God cannot be postponed. "You may be right, Concetta, but what's been said can't be taken back, and what needed to be done was done. Let's progress and if a rebellion flares, we'll offer explanations."

***

Donato, an educator at heart, is always looking for ways to improve his teaching skills. He's fascinated by his mission and is not prepared to see it trivialized.

And what action has been made his lot to fulfill if not that cast on Moses, the greatest of prophets? Redeeming his people the Israelites and bringing them to the Promised Land! That's Manduzio's mission now.

He is deep in thought, and repeatedly studies sections of Torah, concluding that he must add two more injunctions to the eleven he has already formulated.

That brings him to a total of thirteen, concisely and

precisely worded, which can be easily learned by heart and are easy to remember, so that no one is enticed to breach them. This time, Donato decides to directly link his simplified form of the commandments to his mission and authority, because San Nicandroans are all so incredibly obstinate, nor do they show anything but the rarest gratitude, let alone discipline. Yes, one needs to know how to handle them correctly.

After thinking the matter over thoroughly, Donato words his thirteen principles.

1. God was and will be for eternity.
2. There is none other than one God.
3. God does not have a body nor is he embodied in any specific form.
4. God created everything.
5. Prayers should only be directed to God.
6. Prophets receive their prophetic inspiration from God.
7. Moses was the greatest of all prophets.
8. The Torah was given to Moses.
9. The Torah can never be altered.
10. God knows our thoughts.
11. God punishes the wicked.
12. God will grant us a Messiah.
13. The soul is eternal, and righteous people will come back to life.

In this way everyone will discover, if they haven't yet, that Donato is the Prophet of the new era, the representative of God, who showed Donato the true path without deviation. He is the Moses of God, and is vital.

Sometime later, a wondrous vision is revealed, as though meant to encourage Donato's faith.

Somewhere between sleep and wakefulness, Donato suddenly sees his house shining in the light of a vast square lamp holding twenty-eight lit candles. Seven large, long candles in the four corners of the house give off an unnatural light. His gaze takes in the finest details.

Donato pauses, then understands that this is the avenue through which Elohim commands him to convey his commandments, even guide through prophesy, in order to restore Judaism to the world. From his humble home, the truth must spread until it floods the universe.

The vision seems etched into his retinas. It is a direct link between him and God. It encourages Donato in his role as leader and infuses joy and gladness.

Donato goes back to reading the section where God makes a pact with Abram, soon to be renamed Abraham, through a vision, promising Abram that he will be the head of a great nation even though his wife is currently infertile. God reveals that Abram's progeny will serve as slaves for four hundred years before returning to the land of Canaan, which is the land promised to them and stretches from the Nile to the Euphrates.

Donato's visions are frequent and clear, always relevant to an issue of concern in his life. He understands these visions as divine signs, personal messages, and none of them mislead him nor remain indecipherable to him. Eventually he states that, "We are born to receive visions, and through them we can bring the Torah into practice. Whoever denies the vision will end up cut off from us and from eternal life."

But everyone trusts him.

A long time has passed since he functioned as Donato-the-healer and Donato-the-theater-producer.

Donato is now an active prophet of integrity. No matter the price, he will revive Judaism and lead his people. The promised land has never ceased waiting for its children to return. Wild barbarians exiled the land's true children, but he will lead them back once Judaism has been restored to its rightful place.

Whatever activities had filled his earlier years were now relegated to dust.

***

Nonetheless, one day, two women quickly cross the plaza on their way to consult with Donato about Silvio, the café's owner. Silvio has been suffering for a long while with some fierce but undefined sickness.

"It's as though some never-ending force is ripping through his back and digging around in his flesh to leave him chopped into pieces," the younger of the two describes.

Despite being a devout Catholic, Silvio, capitulating to the pain, had just made a second suicide attempt. In light of the horrors that such an unforgivable sin, which was prevented at the last second, brings, Silvio's mother and wife suddenly remembered Donato's renown for healing.

"I appreciate your trust but I ceased practicing my healing activities some time ago," Donato says, then adding "and in any event the term 'healing' was really a misnomer, my dears."

The two women seem not to understand. Nor do they ask for further explanation. Instead, they present an odd plea. "If you refuse to help him live, then at least help him die. If he commits suicide, what will the villagers say? Do you realize the priest probably won't agree to handle the burial? And what will happen to our children? Would you want them to be treated as lepers?"

Donato seems to be studying them although his gaze is not focused on them. Instantly a vision flashes before his eyes: A she-ass carrying three barrels of oil. The oil…the anointing…life. He looks directly at them and speaks to the women, who are on the verge of breaking down. "Return home. Do not give him any medication. None at all, do you hear? God will heal Silvio."

Donato writes the name of God on a slip of paper and hands it to the mother. "Place this beneath your son's pillow. Every morning he must swallow one hundred grams of oil, and the same amount of sugar and of water. But nothing else, you hear?"

Without expressing any doubt or concern, the two women bow to Donato. This gesture of honor fills him with satisfaction.

Three days later, Silvio is improving. The pain has gone. He describes a dream to his wife: he watched his brother hold up a glass of oil and drink it in one go. That, for him, validates Donato's advice.

Three more days later, Silvio is healed.

Coming from the patient's body, he saw a secretion that looked like a snake so hardened that not even a hammer could break it – that's the description Donato later recorded in his diary.

And since the café owner's recovery, Donato has had no trouble emphasizing God's greatness. Despite being a devoted Catholic, Silvio was blessed by God's compassion.

***

Donato moves ahead with his commitments without simultaneously rejecting other religions. Each person must be allowed to live according to their own views. If the Christians leave him alone as he goes about his mission, then one day they, too, will come to Judaism on their own, after seeing how it is revived.

But not everyone says amen to his activities. As usual, the Protestants, driven by an iron will to convert as many people as possible to their branch of Christianity, are showing keen interest in Donato and events in San Nicandro. On a particular Sunday, they invite Donato to a neighboring village to meet the man they call their leader.

Donato listens to the conversation closely and participates where possible. With a degree of patience not typical of his nature, he takes careful note of the well-worn speeches to which, so far, he'd never had an opportunity to respond.

Realizing that he hasn't learned a single new or convincing point, he butts into the conversation and asks the Protestant to let him see the latter's Bible.

He begins by reading out the Ten Commandments and continues to the verses in chapter twenty of Ezekiel which relate to resting on the Sabbath.

"And I have also given them my Sabbaths, to be a sign between me and them, that they might know that I am the Lord who sanctifies them. [...] I am the Lord your God,

and you shall follow my statutes, and keep my ordinances,
and do them; and they shall be a sign between me and you,
that you may know that I am the Lord your God."

"What's all this about, Manduzio? That's the Old Testament! Saint Paul changed all that!"

Donato expected protest. Having obtained the Gospels, much to Don Adriano's dismay, he read several lines from the Epistle to the Hebrews, chapter 4, verses 1-9, quoting Paul: "So there remains a day of rest for the people of God."

"Of course! Today! Sunday!"

"Do you have the authority to decide, despite God himself, determining which day is to be the Sabbath? Is it not the seventh day from the start of the six days of creation? Shall we abide by miscalculations when God himself already made matters perfectly clear? I refuse," Donato states.

The Protestant says nothing. He'd never really pondered the matter before. Did Saint Paul err when he changed the calendar? That couldn't be possible! Could this arrogant cripple be intending to uproot the Evangelists from their very foundation? Minimalize their significance?

"It would seem that your suffering in the war has injured your nerve ends and your concentration. Stay with us. We'll support you."

Donato quietly stands, wishes them well, and leaves. He has also taken a firm decision: never again to waste his time in such a fashion. As he walks home, the insights from his vision clarify further: he must spread the word of God across the entire universe.

In that instant, Donato severs his ties to Christianity.

Manduzio continues his study of Torah, learning Hebrew well. The entire village has become aware of his ability to quote the scriptures and teach the laws of Judaism. He is God's appointed. Not his representative on earth, but his right-hand man, his enlightened servant.

An incredible event is taking place in that end-of-no-where village: more and more villagers feel that Donato's teachings speak to them.

This evening, the discussion centers, to some degree, on mobility and the Children of Israel's movements from place to place.

Donato has the details of the Holy Ark's description lodged perfectly in his memory. Did it ever occur to him to set out in search of the Ark? Or perhaps reconstruct it?

He sits on his rocker, noticing how his friends' faces show they're waiting for him to speak. He loves how attentive they are, how thirsty for knowledge they are, how pleased they often are once they've adopted Judaism's beliefs. Every listener's face is a mirror of that person's nature.

Antonio Bonfito: gentle, with a great love for God, though sometimes he can get heated up. He is aware, and enjoys, the fact that his lot in life has improved since adopting Donato's teachings.

Leonardo nods his head eagerly. He loves attention. Being Donato's cousin, even if by marriage, he enjoys some of the aura of honor bestowed on Donato. He feels himself also to be a messenger of God.

Vittoria Vicidomini serves as the community's beadle. He sets up chairs, makes sure there's a supply of Shabbat candles, cleans the table where the Holy Book of Torah will be placed but is not allowed to actually touch it. He dashes about the village reminding people what time prayers are being held.

Francesco Cerrone, a good listener, frequently repeats Donato's expressions as a way of understanding them better. Cerrone's family has been keeping the laws relating to kosher food since the first day that Donato began teaching Torah. But the authoritarian trait in "the Master" raises his ire. He recognizes Donato's skills as a teacher but since everyone's joining Judaism at pretty much the same time, he feels that Donato errs by considering himself their leader.

This lesson, about the Holy Ark of the Covenant, fascinates Francesco. As he does every time before he begins to speak, Donato whispers several words of praise to God for the unbelievable: having chosen this group of farmers through whom Judaism will be restored to the world.

"The Italian translation does not accord with the original," Donato shakes his head. "In fact, the Hebrew in Exodus 15:22 refers to "the ark of testimony." The description of this edifice intended to bear the Tablets of Stone which God conveyed to Moses is stunningly detailed. The Holy One, blessed be He, was quick to settle himself among his people. Imagine how quickly that could happen these days!"

"The ark was made entirely of gold. That's what my father told me."

Ottavio Vicidomini, at fifteen, would often stroll over and spend time with Donato. Sometimes he'd get through his chores at the speed of light to free up time for his two great loves: girls, and Torah. He's small, but robust. His face and eyebrows still show a little softness and femininity. Ottavio shows increasing keenness to learn Torah, especially the way Donato Manduzio teaches it. This new way of viewing reality allows him to withstand life's tough trials and tribulations more easily. But Donato also relates tales that are no less wondrous when it comes to reality.

"Entirely of gold?" Bonfito asks, raising his shoulders in amazement. "Another legend! If gold is considered by the Jews to be as precious as it is by Catholics, what's the point of converting to Judaism? We folk don't have anything made of gold. Reviving Judaism so that the new Jews will be respected only by their accumulation of wealth or their clothes woven with expensive embellishments… is that what our efforts are for? No, no and no. That's not why we're learning to read and pray!"

Donato becomes impatient. He wants to teach the Jewish way of living for the sake of its essence: the direct connection to God. He cannot accept that a person would convert simply as a way of breaking from the infuriating actions of the church and its scandalous wealth. Fortunately, Donato doesn't know how far some of the church's less favorable acts go.

Donato wants to get Bonfito back on the straight and narrow, but because he's a new cadet, so to speak, Donato eventually opts for directing him to the scripture itself. "The Ark of Testimony is a long box. Its width is greater than its height. It was precisely planned for the purpose of protecting the Tablets on which the Ten Commandments were engraved. Here, Bonfito, and all of you, listen to how the Holy One of Blessed Name gave instructions to build it.

"And they shall make an ark of acacia wood: two cubits and a half is its length, and a cubit and half its breadth, and a cubit and a half its height. And you shall overlay it with pure gold, inside and out, and make a crown of gold around it. And you shall cast four rings of gold for it, and put them in the four feet: two rings shall be on one side, and two rings on the other side. And you shall make staves of acacia wood and overlay them with gold. And you shall put the staves into the rings on the ark's sides, in order to carry it; and the staves shall never be removed. And you shall place the testimony which I shall give you into the ark. And you shall make a cover for the ark of pure gold….. And you shall make two gold cherubs, of beaten gold, at either end of the ark-cover… of one piece with the ark-cover you shall make the cherubs of the two ends. And the cherubs will spread their wings, screening the ark-cover with them, their faces turned to each other: the cherubs' faces shall be turned toward the ark-cover. And you shall place the ark-cover on the ark, and in the ark you shall place the testimony which I will give you."

Not all the details are clear to the listeners. The concentration on their faces show them working hard at trying to imagine it.

Then Donato continues somewhat impatiently.

"Let me summarize. The Ark of Testimony is where the Tablets of Stone will be stored. The ark's made of wood, blanketed in pure gold. The wood is worked along its direction of growth, as a way of acknowledging nature. The ark's cover is like God's throne. The Levites carried the ark by holding the staves. The Levites marched before the other tribes at a distance of precisely three days ahead."

"King David brought the ark to Shiloh and then to Jerusalem, readying for it to be later inserted into the First Temple which his son Solomon would build. No one knows what happened to the Ark when that Temple was destroyed. I didn't find that mentioned anywhere in the Bible."

Now the group's grip on the idea and image clarifies. Lively discussion ensues.

"I'd happily go and hunt for it," Cerrone declares.

"Really? And exactly how do you propose to go about that?"

"I'll go with you!" Giovanni Leone calls out.

Cerrone and Leone have never been apart since they were babies. Their mothers are sisters; their fathers are twins. At family dinners, which are frequently joined by almost all the villagers, everyone's amused by the six family members who raise glass after glass of wine in toasts, raise their voices in joyful song, and then slowly sink into sleep.

Donato's watching them closely. This, he thinks, is where the component of initiative lies. For a while now, some have been talking about the idea of moving to the land of Canaan. If Judaism needs to be restored, so must its possessions. We have no idea who might now be living on the ancient land of the Jews, or if by some miracle any survived their people's extinction, whether progeny were born, whether...

San Nicandroans listen to Donato in wonder as he continues.

"We must not merely dream, my friends. We face a great deal of work. We are the first Jews of a new era, and never forget what an incredible privilege that is!"

"Nonetheless, Donato, if God wants us live Judaism, can

it be that the rest of the world is living mistakenly? When you tore the picture of baby Jesus in my house, it took a week for my wife to recover! And I'm not altogether certain that she didn't stick the bits together and is hiding it from me in her apron!' Bonfito looks around with a satisfied grin at being able to speak openly. He remembers his wife's panicked reaction clearly.

Noticing that he's receiving support from others there, Bonfito carries on. "Me, personally, I'm not against baby Jesus. Even though he can't produce any more miracles, I like the little chap."

Donato readies to answer but a female voice cuts in first. Concetta, who's lost her patience. "Donato's talked about this often enough. Why repeat it all? Bonfito, have you gone deaf from screaming so much to your goats? Jesus isn't our enemy. He was born to Miriam and Joseph. He was circumcised. He lived like a Jew, just as we're doing. He ate kosher food his whole life. He died and was buried in his Tallit," she said, referring to the large shawl Jewish men use in morning prayers.

"Aha! But pardon me, Concetta, how could you possibly know that?"

"Are you calling me a liar? Do you need a sharp slap, *zo-ti-coni?*" she pulls him into line by calling him crass.

Égidia Bonfito steps in at this point, humorously answering in his stead. "No and no, Concetta. That's *my* area of authority!"

"Remind your husband, then, that Donato and I study together every day, in case he's forgotten. Tell him that I have spoken based on knowledge. Is he the only one who hasn't heard Don Adriano's shouted retorts when I asked him for the scriptures? Has he forgotten how I convinced him?"

Cerrone rolls about laughing. "If I live to a hundred, I will still remember, Dona Concetta. You threatened him that you wouldn't let him dine at your home twice a week anymore, and you'd forbid us from filling the collection box for the poor, which means he couldn't buy his favorite style of shoe anymore! Let him not forget the goodness of heart that we Jews still show by helping him!"

While Concetta explains the futility of superstition to those present, Donato closes his eyes. Sometimes he feels weary, torn in two. He never loses his grip on the mission he needs to bring to fruition, nor does he fear failure in achieving it. It's the madness of human actions that he experienced in the war that's left its poison inside him.

Opening the Torah again at the section they're discussing, he imagines the tired Levites carrying the Holy Ark's weight, wading through the desert dust, on through the slow rhythm of endless days. As spiritual leaders of this Israelite people, the Levites bear immeasurable responsibility and evoke his deep admiration.

Donato, wanting to be like them, and simultaneously validate his mission, decided some months earlier to change his name to Levi. No one voiced opposition. His little girl Rachel hasn't gotten used to the name "Manduzio" anyhow. She's never far from her father. She seems to listen as intently as anyone else, her eyes showing how focused she is, as though she's in another world. She absorbs, she smiles to her father, her eyes as happy as can be. She senses that he's different.

The villagers accept that Donato has access to the knowledge they lack. In any event, that's true for now, Francesco Cerrone thinks to himself.

Francesco faithfully believes in, and prays to, God. Anyone with willing ears will hear him say that Judaism is a religion that sanctifies life, no matter what. His enthusiasm impassions listeners no less than Donato's teaching. But it makes Donato feel uncomfortable. How can his young friend who works hours on end to sustain his large family, increased by his wife's very recent birth of twin girls, find so much time for lessons on Judaism? He's definitely smart; he always was, but now Donato listens to the way he speaks to others, his words imbued with intense faith, and realizes that he, Donato, might find himself pushed to the periphery. Francesco, however, still hasn't mastered reading. That's where Donato's advantage lies.

Donato turns to look at Francesco, still talking. "...and that's why I love our Judaism. No one's preferred. Everyone's equal. The Torah's essence is what's important. Listening only to God is what's important. And also, who would ever have thought that there could be so much joy in being connected with the Omnipotent One? In the church, fear always reigned. No one dared to look directly at Don Adriano! Of course, the Holy One of Blessed Name, must be held in awe, but not because we've forgotten to put flowers on the altar and didn't bow to the Monsignor who keeps repeating the same thing about us living in the valley of tears. From the day we discovered the Torah..."

Donato winces. *We* discovered the Torah? Time to put Cerrone in his place.

Cerrone talks on. "...we learned that love of God means loving life blessed by God. The joy of Shabbat deflects the sorrow of mourning. Singing and praising life, and the freedom granted on Passover. We can eat and drink without ever feeling guilty. We're required to bring pleasure to our wives. That, my friends, is truly something!"

Laughter all around. Donato takes advantage of the break in Francesco's monologue to quietly take the reins again. "I'm so proud of you for showing how far you've come, my friend. Allow me to say how pleased I am for the part I played in enhancing your faith and knowledge. Your love of Torah is almost as great as mine and that really warms my heart, but also worries it, because some of your actions make me sad."

Tension pervades the atmosphere. The villagers are familiar with Donato's sudden anger. Cerrone lacks for nothing in that department either. Sparks may well yet fly.

Francesco's gray eyes narrow. That doesn't faze Donato. Or perhaps he didn't notice the gesture.

"Are you certain you're fulfilling God's word?" Donato continues.

Cerrone quickly runs through the commandments encapsulated by Donato, not catching Donato's meaning.

"I know the prayers well. My wife cooks according to the rules of keeping kosher. I support my fellow community members. We are all familiar with the difficulties I encountered when trying to register my twins as Sarah and Ester with the local authorities. Little wonder the Jews became extinct. The clerk refused to register them under Jewish names. I almost let his face taste my fist, that utter idiot! And I told him that! He was shocked but now my daughters are called Sarah and Ester. Just as you insist on being called Levi. And since the twins' birth, Angela brings them

111

to Shabbat prayers. What, doesn't all that count? If not, what does?"

"*È inutile pigliare il fungo, Francesco.*" Don't take it to heart, Donato tells his friend. But each week you ignore the fourth commandment, the one that connects you more than anything else to God."

Instinctively Francesco blurts. "*Per la Madonna!*" By the Holy Virgin!

Several of the people there burst into laughter at this most Christian of all phrases coming from Cerrone. But he's furious. He's already crossed the short distance between himself and Donato.

What will happen next? No one believes he'll actually strike a crippled man, and his longtime friend to boot!

Donato, his voice controlled and calm, continues. "Let me refresh your memory. The fourth commandment instructs us this. '*Remember the Sabbath day to sanctify it. Six days you shall labor and do all your work but the seventh day is a day of rest unto the Lord your God: you shall not do any manner of work in it, neither you nor your son nor your daughter nor your manservant nor your maidservant nor your cattle nor the stranger who dwells within your gates. For in six days the Lord made heaven and earth, the sea and all that it contains, and rested on the seventh day, and the Lord blessed this Sabbath day and hallowed it.*' Yet you, Francesco, what do you do on Shabbat morning after prayers? Week after week, you remove your blocks of ice from their underground cache and run about trying to sell them. What an example to us Jews, and anyone interested in converting to Judaism!"

Cerrone draws in a deep breath but chooses not to answer. His mind is busy seeking the ultimate retort. He comes up with verse 22 in chapter 29 of Isaiah.

"But we know that Isaiah says this: '*Therefore thus says the Lord who redeemed Abrahem concerning the house of Jacob: Jacob shall not now be ashamed, nor his face become pale.*' But you, Donato, do you feel your strength as greater than that of God to the point that you would shame me in front of everyone? I now have nine children. Should they die of starvation? You know that I'm in the workshop from dawn to dark. God can't pass judgment on one who works to feed his family. How dare you insult me like that? I can't buy Shabbat candles because I'm too poor, so I sell ice on Shabbat. That doesn't prevent me from being Jewish, and praying fervently every day."

Cerrone pushes his way through the gathering, takes Angela's arm firmly, and shouts. "Those who love me, leave with me!"

No one moves.

"He'll be back," Donato reassures.

Not everyone's sure of that. Although Cerrone and Angela are among the more constant adherents, those present feel certain that a long dispute has just begun. They notice that the authority which Donato wields over Cerrone is becoming increasingly hard for the latter to stomach. But has a prophet ever been acknowledged in his hometown?

***

As Concetta de Leo discovered in the days when she was the only one incorporating Donato's teachings into her life, the San Nicandroans find that their friend's God is a superior force of integrity and righteousness, who listens and is ever-present: a God of a kind they've never yet encountered. Their and others' reactions do not prevent the adherents of this new way of living from getting together around the miracle in which they're all participating. It thrills them to hear their children saying their prayers. They smile at Antonio Bonfito, a cheery fellow with a mustache that makes people giggle, his hat pulled down tight on his head, taking Manduzio's words in eagerly: they are also relieved to see his response, since he's always very wary when it comes to the Pentecostals' speeches.

Bonfito gives missionaries a wide berth when they show up. And to help ensure that they leave him alone, he adorns his donkey with delicate embroidery which his wife has crafted on a cloth banner: two Stars of David, one inside the other. Antonio's well aware of his volatile nature and doesn't want to embroil himself in a fist fight should any of those missionaries criticize God, with whom he feels so close. This God cannot be called by name, unlike the custom of so many who call on Jesus left and right as a way of guarding themselves from a cruel fate.

Donato talks a good deal, explaining and teaching. For a long time now, these new Jews have been strict about keeping Shabbat, putting their work tools and aprons aside to celebrate the day God dedicated for rest from the work of creating the world. Francesco Cerrone's attitude about selling blocks of ice on Shabbat shook them up a bit, but no one other than a couple of Cerrone's closest buddies dared protest.

Donato's work in instilling this new approach is no bed of roses. He never forgets the forceful opposition from these new Jews while convincing them to destroy the figures and pictures of Christian entities.

Luigi, who'd followed in his brother's footsteps up to that point, was a prime example. He'd been riled to boiling point despite the sin being described as punishable by death. Late into the night, the two men had been heard heatedly arguing.

"You're cursing our Mamma's memory by destroying her holy artefacts!"

"She was my mother too, Luigi, and when Papa punished me for not completing the ceremony, she didn't judge me. She would come to me secretly. I explained to her as best I could at the time what was in my thoughts, and she answered that she doesn't understand it all but she trusts me. Have I said anything so far that can be construed as offending you or God?"

"You destroyed God. Do you realize that? You'll never be forgiven!"

"I tore up the pictures and smashed the figurines because representations of God are forbidden by God himself. I was just complying with God's ordinances."

"Why should a plaster figure of the Virgin on our parents' mantelpiece bother you so much? You heretic, you…!"

"Plaster? No issue with plaster. But as a representation of God who created all things, I can't accept it. Let me remind you of the second commandment: 'You shall not make a graven image for yourself, nor any manner of likeness, of anything that is in heaven above or on the earth below or that is in the water or under the earth. You shall neither bow down to them nor worship them for I am the Lord your God, a zealous God visiting the iniquity of the fathers upon the children up to the third and fourth generation of those who hate me.' How many times have you heard me quote this?"

"It lacks all logic! Do you presume to think that worldwide, the church is lying? Or that there are holy scriptures unknown to it?"

"Judge for yourself, my brother. I'll just share the revelations with you and you'll judge for yourself."

Like a modern-day St. Paul, Luigi slams his brother's door as he leaves, shouting. "If you don't stop demanding that we smash these holy figures, I'll never see you again! You hear? Never!"

But Luigi never had trouble accepting Catholicism while simultaneously focusing on the important aspects from his brother's teachings: observing Shabbat; keeping the laws of Niddah which guide conduct of purity between man and wife; maintaining a kosher kitchen. And recently Donato began discussing circumcision!

"One day you'll understand what God is, my brother. And if not, go to hell, you idiot!"

Alina will despairingly work at mending the family rift, but to no avail. While their paths will often cross in the future, they'll never be seen together again.

***

And now Cerrone is stepping away. Donato wonders aloud about that. "How will he live as a Jew when everything he still has to learn comes from me?"

"Go and meet with him and make up," Emanuela suggests, certain that on the other side, Angela's saying exactly the same to Francesco.

"*Non ne è domanda!*" Absolutely not, Donato almost shouts. "Am I not doing enough as it is?"

"*Stele due montoni idioti...*" The two of you are stupid and stubborn as sheep! Emanuela retorts. "This is going to delay your work so much, Donato! Are you entitled to hold God's work back?"

Bull's eye! Donato refuses to admit the sorrow he feels, but decides to ponder it further. It all makes him so very tired.

***

"I'll stuff his pride down his throat yet, that peacock!"

"Francesco! Have you gone crazy? Your friend, your brother, the one who went out to fight for you while we lived here calmly and quietly and had our children!"

"Each of us contributes to the country in a different way. Nine children: isn't that a beautiful gift to the homeland?"

"*Stupido!*" she sputters under her breath.

Angela tries in vain to calm her husband but Francesco cannot forgive Donato for his pompous patronizing tone in front of everyone about his actions on Shabbat.

"We'll show him what we can do. Come, let's plan on going to the Promised Land! And to bring our plan to fruition, we'll set up another community. There's room for everyone at San Nicandro, no? Marochella and Tritto are just as fed up as I am by this 'Moses-without-roses' attitude. I'm sure they'll help us."

"Costentino Tritto? But Donato saved his son Samuel. He'd never betray Donato!"

"Are you kidding me? Samuel Tritto is a robust chap who got well on his own, of that I'm sure.

"*Miscredente!*" You disbeliever, his wife calls him. And that Marochella wants to follow suit?! Do you know what his wife told me?"

"What?"

"Marochella is a good Jew, I agree, and he's dying to go to the Promised Land, firstly because in his view, things couldn't be worse there than they are here. But yesterday, he had dreamt a terrifying nightmare: that his leg was being chopped off, and he was in agonizing suffering. Blood, open flesh – a horrifying sight! He woke up in a sweat. I said to his wife: I think he's afraid of circumcision. Donato's the one talking about it… and he's the one you're going to establish Judaism with?"

"Actually, I think God was showing him what would happen if he left our community. He'd be cut off from his source of guidance. As for circumcision, we haven't gotten to that point yet. Anyhow, who would do it? It must be someone who's learned how." Angela paused, contemplating the next problem. "And let's say we do break away. Where'd you set up a synagogue? Not in our house here, right? We're already eleven people in one room! Let me remind you of that loud and clear!"

"The Hebrews were nomads, and we can be like them. I'll fix whatever's needed in the shed in our field. I'll uphold the Torah of Moses, but continue working on Shabbat in order to feed my family. It's easy to talk when you spend all day sitting and watching the money rain down on you every month!"

Cerrone, enthused, arranges a second community. For better or worse, some ten people join him.

The community's members do what they can to breathe life into this new "Klal Yisrael" congregation. But it's not easy. Without Donato's voice reciting the words of prayers loudly and clearly, without his daily lessons, and most of all, without the Torah, the actual text, physically present among them as the material source of God's instructions as they understand them, they feel a little helpless. Complaints are directed to Cerrone.

"Time. It'll take time, my brothers, to get Klal Yisrael up and running," Cerrone says. For good reason they've chosen that name for their community: it means "All Israel."

"It didn't take so long when we were with Donato, thank you very much! Weeks are going by, we're gathering here repeatedly but can't find our rhythm, let alone connection. It's impossible to build up from a state of rivalry. And as for readying for our journey, that's a figment of your imagination!"

Angelo Marochella is determined to emigrate to the Holy Land with his family. He's talked about it so much with his family that he's tired of hearing himself say the same thing.

"We'll go, Angelo, we'll go. But going right now is like betraying God's plan. Before that, we need to reinforce the community, increase it, discover who can assist us once the ship docks in the Holy Land, and bring us to the Tomb of the Patriarchs where the forefathers are buried. Then we can pray and live on the Holy Land and receive other, new immigrants every day, please God."

But Marochella doesn't want to wait. Cerrone and Tritto must free up a good deal of time for organizing such a venture because their families are so large. The three of them go on and on about their trip to anyone willing to listen. They've got nothing to lose: life here is tough, poverty is rampant, the work is exhausting.

Even though he lives some distance from the village, Marochella has attained a status of special member in the community, perhaps due to his profession: a gem polisher. Or at least that's how he comes across to others. But his life's tough, too. He isn't consistent about joining the ceremonies and lessons with Donato, yet his faith never wanes and actually strengthens as part of his practical belief and perception of life. Hope is a rare thing in that region. One needs to work hard to earn a bit of food, and cumulative difficulties accelerate feelings of exhaustion and despair.

In a short period of time, he considers sailing to the Holy Land as the only feasible solution, both because it will take him to his newly adopted forefathers, and because he's convinced that his life will improve anywhere he may go, but never in San Nicandro. It'd be preferable to make an effort for God's sake on the land he designated for his people. That action would at least be rewarding and refreshing. And that's the drive behind Marochella and Tritto joining forces with Cerrone.

At this point, the three men, put off by Donato's adoption of authority, continue shaping their community just a few hundred meters from the Prophet's synagogue.

Their ceremonies are also filled with interesting classes and enthusiasm, but their community size is minimal even though Francesco Cerrone is no less charismatic than Donato. Cerrone is pleasant looking, holds his head high, and when he looks at you, his eyes twinkle. His broad forehead conveys wisdom. His thick black hair marks him as having a charming personality. And his limp infringes on none of this.

"He looks like a movie star," Angela repeats even though she's never seen a movie. But she's also pretty, with well-shaped lips and a perfectly proportioned face, even though her eyelids droop a fraction. She loves her husband, and sees each new child as a blessing to their relationship even if her work is piled sky high.

The three men work hard at expanding their community, and it does over time, even though the pioneers in Donato's community make an exerted effort to bring Cerrone's group back into Donato's fold.

But the inconvenience of the converted shed, the lack of clear organization and leadership, and a tendency to rigidity, disappoint the adherents. They aren't finding what they came seeking. They wonder about Donato, whose skills vastly outshine those of anyone else when it comes to organizing, knowledge, imbuing confidence, and in promoting a more flexible and happier form of Judaism despite its stringencies. Donato admittedly seems zealous about his authority, but at some point it becomes clear to them that this characteristic is only for the sake of advancing them in their Judaic practices.

Cerrone's community inherently understands how

deeply Donato is nourished by Torah, which has led him to the truth and guides him daily on fulfilling God's commandments.

Yet the trio of Marochella, Cerrone and Tritto obstinately persists. A convincing community is required, but one that is more flexible than Donato's. Should one who needs to work on the Sabbath be expected to make his family suffer from hunger in order to follow God's ways? Does God expect him to deprive his children in preference to serving God? And moreover, what does Donato do other than pray, study, and teach?

A community should be allowed to discuss any topic. Donato always brings the world of Torah into things when asked a question. When he's asked if books which have been written by people who read the Five Books of Moses, should be obtained to expand the community's knowledge, Donato loses his temper. What need is there of interpretations? He's here, outlining for them.

Ever since first opening the book of the Torah, no type of commentary interests Donato as he learns it by rote. Shaping his internal link to God is the revelation the individual can achieve – a non-mediated connection directly to God. Nothing clouds the Jew's view, no excuses, no obstructions to the Jew's perspective. God is here, and he spoke in the past, and has now recommenced speaking.

Therefore, Donato and the community must walk with God, as the Bible puts it. This is why he keenly adopts Judaism, which perfectly aligns with his earlier set of thoughts. Those following in Donato's footsteps have also been deeply disappointed by Christianity. They are unwilling to capitulate to the superficial speeches of wandering prophets and missionaries. More people join Donato's community, adhering to Jewish principles.

The figure who, in Donato's view, would anger over Cerrone's move is Moses himself. Donato feels a unique closeness to the Israelite leader for having had to deal with the countless trials and tribulations which the Hebrews put him through.

But like Moses, Donato continues to advance, linked in the depths of his soul to this newfound faith, answering those who ask out of hope, and his own keen wish to connect them to Judaism. He actually does that very well. Initially the community numbered fifty persons, and is growing.

***

The rebellion by Donato's three friends has riled and upset him so much that he reaches a level of exhaustion which sees him take to his bed. He shows evident fatigue. As he lies there, his bones aching and his gut churning, a vision comes to him: a man riding a bicycle, a gray beret on his head, moving toward him and calling out "Levi, Levi!"

Donato believes he can identify this man and asks for his name. But the man only answers in a single word. "Eat!"

"What should I eat?"

"The product of the cow."

Donato barely has time to think of a response when the man leaves on his bike through the window!

Donato opens his eyes. Emanuela comes into the room holding cheese made from cow's milk, wrapped in cheesecloth. It's a food known in the region as having healing properties. The cheese Donato eats has a healing effect.

The vision allows him to understand that his power has been restored, thank God, supporting him through his mission: reviving the Jewish people on the slopes of Garganico, an unknown location in the world.

That evening, he resumes his activities, seated by his doorway. He summarizes the story of Jephthah's daughter.

"Jephthah was a judge in Israel. After the Hebrews sinned yet again, God made them fight the Philistines and the Ammonites. Jephthah was made to leave his birthplace because his brother was born to his father Gilad's legal wife, whereas he was born to a woman with whom his father had encountered out of wedlock. His brother never stopped verbally attacking him. 'You shall not dwell in our father's house for you are the son of a different woman.' Nonetheless Jephthah was elected by God to protect the Hebrews from the Ammonites.

"Before signaling that the war had begun, Jephthah vowed to offer a sacrifice to God of the first thing that comes out of his door if they return safely. Jephthah was victorious and returned home. He had one daughter among several sons. She came joyously out of the house to greet him, dancing and playing the timbrel. Jephthah's world came crashing around him: he told his daughter of the vow, and she asked for two months' reprieve to mourn her unmarried status. He agreed, and two months later, he sacrificed his daughter."

"How dreadful! Are you sure you read that right? Is that your religion? Never since joining your group have I heard such a cruel story. I think that…" Michel Soccio reddens in fury. Even though his friend Costentino Tritto did all he

124

could to persuade Soccio that the breakaway community was preferable, Soccio remained loyal to the original group. He and his wife Lucia even began preparing a corner in their one-room home as a place for prayers. They're confused by the fact that they cannot hang holy pictures on the wall. Lucia stitched a large white Tallit, the prayer shawl, for Soccio, with two broad bands of blue and a blue Magen David in the center.

Donato stops explaining. He's also exasperated. But despite his impatient nature, he always lets people express their thoughts before continuing.

"How can you possibly believe that God, who in Deuteronomy 18:18 stated 'Let none of you offer your son or daughter by fire,' this same God who loathes human sacrifice, would allow Jephthah to carry the act out?" Donato pauses. "Have you forgotten the angel that caught Abraham's hand when he was about to sacrifice his son Yitzhak? And so Jephthah asked his daughter to transpose that vow into her dedication to God. That's why he agreed to allow her two months to mourn her continued virginity, because nothing is more important than bringing children into the world to become heirs not only to material items but to faith in God of Blessed Name. As for Jephthah, those two months also gave him time to enjoy his dear daughter's presence. Then she joined the women who devoted themselves to God's work."

The community's relief is palpable. "So why isn't that stated at the outset?" Michel persists, his voice edgy.

Concetta, as always, responds with a firm tone. "To activate the brains of stupid folk like you, Soccio. If you were to come daily, and now that you've started it's worth continuing, you'd understand our holy Torah and just how well it guides us in every moment of life."

Far in the distance from beneath the ancient, twisted olive tree in the village plaza, a voice can be heard. "Soccio, trust Donato. He reads and explains to us, but above all he's our Moshe Rabbeinu," the voice says, using the Hebraic term for Moses our Teacher. "Let's cause him less suffering than the Israelites caused the first."

Donato's surprised to identify Marochella's voice. Concetta exchanges a glance with Donato. "Success!" it wordlessly notes. So Marochella wasn't lost. If one of the more aggressive rebels is expressing regret in such a respectable manner, there's hope that they'll all eventually acknowledge their mistake and return to the fold.

***

Corlone the postman, who's usually more occupied having a drink with mates than bringing the rare bits of mail that make it to San Nicandro to their addressees, knocks on Manduzio's door one morning.

Emanuela puts the bucket down on the well's edge as her eyes fly open at the sight of a disheveled envelope.

"That's for us?"

"No! For the pope! Of course it's for you, Emanuela. What, don't I know my job well enough?"

"Yes, yes, of course. Come in," Emanuela huffs. "I was just finishing baking my matzah. Here, taste some," Emanuela gestures to the unleavened bread.

"I wouldn't refuse but they're always a bit dry."

"The wine's on the table, you boozer!" she smiles.

Donato examines the mud-stained envelope. Opening it, he draws out a page and begins to read, tears rolling down his cheeks. The letter is in Hebrew and bears the signature of Marochella's firstborn.

Could it be that he's driven by regret and wishes to ask his father's veteran friend for forgiveness? Let us hope, thinks Donato, that there's nothing dramatic here, such as a death or an accident! That stubborn ass, together with his wife Lucia, can just as equally cause bad or good, but if his father returned to the community, why didn't they also show up with the rest of the family?

"Read it out! What does it say?"

Donato glances at his wife and Corlone, but says nothing. He has that look in his eye that makes others attentive, obedient. Perfect silence fills the house.

And Donato begins.

"Donato, did you think I had gotten lost? Here I am!
Do you think I'm writing because I'm about to retrace my father's footsteps? Not at all.
Do you think I'm about to ask you for money? We do indeed need it, but we have much more than that here!
I'm writing to you, Donato, because without you nothing would have been possible, and our lives would have just rumbled along from grape picking to tilling and repeat, without ever having turned our thoughts to God. For that, may you be blessed.
The journey took forever and was nerve-racking. We had no idea when we'd arrive, and our mother Gracia's belly swelled up as we watched, unable to help. We were tossed in a heap

127

on the deck of an old, rotting boat. We landed on a burningly hot sandy beach near some shacks scattered across the dunes. Some distance from there is Tel Aviv. A lovely name, but the swamps are insufferable.

We're now settled in Tel Hai in the northern Galilee, on Kibbutz Kfar Giladi. Life's really tough, we work from morning to night, there's no money, nor weapons for self-defense. Our legs constantly sink into pools of mud, but we're so happy being so close to God and our forefathers. We breathe the air that Avraham breathed, we work the land that Yaakov worked, and tell stories about Yitzhak," he wrote, using the forefathers' Hebrew names for Abraham, Jacob, and Isaac respectively.

"The most veteran kibbutz member, who came to the Land of our forefathers, around 1892, told us that in 1920 he was positioned not far off and watched a terrible battle take place here, during which Yossef Trumpeldor, one of the first Zionist soldiers, was killed along with seven of his friends. This event gave rise to the name of the town established in their honor: Kiryat Shmonah, literally 'the town of eight.' Do you understand what this means, my dear friend? His life was wholly devoted to reviving Judaism!

"But you'll discover this when you come. Donato, my letter is written to convince you to leave Italy, bring everyone with you, bring my parents back too, as I never understood why they left, and complete what the Biblical Moses was not able to – that is, to accompany our community to the land where we belong. Lucia has meanwhile given birth to two more children who have Hebrew names: Gadi and Meni, like the two tribes Gad and Menasheh, sons of Yaakov-Israel.

But I've kept the best for last. Read it carefully, because you won't believe your eyes! Be certain that God loves us more than we ever imagined when we lived in San Nicandro. Remember: we thought that we were the only J…"

Donato looks up, annoyed: the letter is difficult to make out, some of the ink had faded, and in some places, entire sections had suffused into the page, leaving only a smattering of legible words. The result is an unintelligible jumble.

Corlone drains his glass. "Listen, going there doesn't sound like such a great idea from what I've heard in that letter. What will they eat, our greedy pigs, in those swamps?"

"Our pigs? Which pigs? Get out already, go finish your work before you're so drunk you lose consciousness!" Donato shoos him out.

"Young Marochella is even more obstinate than his flock of goats, if he still has a flock. He's even more narrow-minded than his father. We can't revive our people if we go and live in desolate swamps! The day will come when we'll go. We'll be as numerous as the seeds of a thousand pomegranates when we rejoin our land and turn it into what God wanted: a sweet welcoming place. But, for now, who'll arouse Judaism among the people if we leave?"

Emanuela, hands on her hips, looks at her husband. "Are you still mad at him?"

"In this case, I'd be considered as one who desecrates the sacred. The Holy One of Blessed Name creates us, fills us with joy, punishes us for our erroneous ways, raises our spirits up, forgives us once again, instills faith in us, then withdraws and leaves us room to live and breathe. So do you think I have any interest in carrying on an argument with the Marochella family? But the truth is that he's a hard nut to crack!"

***

Even though he knows the Torah by heart, he's still unable to recite from the end to the start, but every day he approaches it with wonder. From the time he first read them, the holy scriptures have never stopped providing him with the strength to fulfill his new religion's requirements and finding answers for all his concerns. His recurring visions prove to Manduzio that he's progressing with his work.

That brightly lit morning, Donato abandons the armchair designed by an amateur and begins using one that the blacksmith made for him, with springs and more flexible wheels. He rolls himself out to the neighboring hill where the old, deserted sheep pen is on the verge of collapse. He needs closeness to God. Scanning the landscape where the revival of his people will take place gladdens his heart. He imagines the happiness, the music that will play when Judaism will be reborn in great splendor.

Suddenly he notices a massive flock of sheep grazing in the valley. Whose are they? Excitement floods his veins as the flock climbs toward him. No shepherd can be seen anywhere, nor a sheepdog, which leaves him amazed. Very close by a voice speaks. "I'm here," it says.

Indeed, the shepherd is right next to him, announcing: "Today, they're returning because they've been re-acquired."

Donato's eyes open wide. Until that moment he hadn't

even been aware that they were closed. The sheep have gone.

He ponders for a while. "Amazing!" he exclaims. "God is renewing his faith in me! The blessed day is not far off when the people chosen by God will return to serving him! The miracle of the Torah will manifest when that extinct people is rejuvenated. I must carry on, learn more, explain, and set the path!"

It was the first time that Donato erred in interpreting a vision.

***

Six months later, in the Foggia marketplace which he visited with several other San Nicandroans, Donato finally understood his vision. It was siesta, the traditional early afternoon rest time. The sun burned down and people hid from its rays after herding their cattle into shade. Sometimes, coincidence has a humorous streak: the location allocated for the San Nicandroans' siesta was adjacent to the pen where countless pigs loudly panted.

Men who in the past had raised the now forbidden animal scrunched their faces up in disgust, causing other San Nicandroans to break into laughter. Donato laughed too. The only thing that shocked him was the apathy toward God. He takes advantage of siesta to tell the wonderful story of Ruth the Moabite. It's a tale his followers love to hear, since it proves that Judaism can be attained and is not just the right of those born into the faith. Ruth could have been their sister, no doubt of that.

"People who like Ruth's story must behave with insightfulness since it's of great importance, and especially us, having been born as gobblers of those same stinky pigs nearby. King David, of blessed memory, is Ruth's progeny. She was not born Jewish, but adopted her husband Mahlon's religion, which she grew to appreciate. When he died, she refused to abandon her mother-in-law Naomi, and set out with her back to Naomi's homeland of Judea, Yehuda, all the way to Bethlehem. They were dirt poor. For food, they had no choice but to collect what fell in the fields as the harvesters worked."

As a good educator does, Donato pauses and looks at his pupils. "Which of you remembers the meaning of the name 'Ruth?'"

Passersby surrounding the group Donato is teaching are startled when several shout out. "Compassion, compassion!"

Donato smiles. "Yes, compassion, or compassionate. And she showed compassion toward the elderly Naomi when she was fatigued, forcing her to rest while she kept gathering for the two of them. She met her husband Boaz in his fields. He fell in love with her. She took Naomi's advice, becoming closer to the man until he was charmed enough to take her as his wife. And that was her destiny's realization. Years later, their great-grandson King David would be born."

"So, are we not like Ruth, coming from nowhere, becoming Jewish with all our hearts and souls, and destined to revive the Jewish people? We will spread this wonderful Torah once again, until we see people doing God's will. Then we will have revived Judaism! Today, we're just a handful of people but tomorrow there'll be millions of us, amen!"

"Amen! Amen!" his happy followers respond.

A rolling, loud laugh is heard. It comes from a short dairy farmer. No one believes that such a small fellow could let out such a bellow! The man swaggers forward.

"Where are you from, mister? What are you talking about? Are you living on the moon? Jews. They're everywhere. I know tons of Jews. In Trieste. In Torino. In Napoli. You can even get the address of one from me if you like."

Gaping, Donato and the community stare at him in silence.

"Surprised, huh?"

Donato straightens in his seat. Disbelievingly he studies the farmer's face. The young man is very sure of himself.

Foggia residents are circling around with surprised faces. But how could that be? And then, what of his mission?

Despite knowing he could come across as ridiculous, Donato wants to know more. "We haven't had such good fortune as to live in a city, like you. Explain what you're talking about."

"There's nothing to add. There are tons of Jews. There's even a Jewish leader in Rome."

"A leader in Rome? Do you know where? Or his name?"

"Now you're asking too much of me. I'm a devout Catholic. I don't mingle too much with the murderers of our Lord Jesus."

Donato's group shifts about, annoyed. Antonio Bonfito grabs the man by his neck and is ready to give him a pounding, but Donato holds him back. "Leave him, Bonfito. Once we were as ignorant as he is, and not so long ago, either. Tell me," he says to the young guy, "what's your name?"

"Pietro Beltrano. Did I say something wrong? That's the truth, isn't it?"

"The truth of those who want to preserve their control over you and trample the good minds of believers. Come, visit us at San Nicandro and I'll explain to you. If I lie to you, God will strike me down with lightning and you'll inherit everything I own. But luckily for me, my wife's not around to hear that!" Donato adds, laughing, though he feels uncomfortable using ploys similar to those wielded by Mussolini, even if their goals are vastly different. "Now, tell me what you know about their leader."

"He's known by the title of Rabbi. He's not a leader like a priest, because he's married. They're allowed to. A Jew explained it to me when I was working in his house. I must admit that he was a good man. He never brought me to work for him without offering me food and drink. He asked me to put up bookshelves on all the walls of his house! What a strange idea! And when I…"

No one was listening anymore. The community was agog. Despite needing to sell the calves, the fowl, the vegetables, and the cloth, the Jews decide to return home immediately and take some decisions about what to do right now!

"Donato? Why are you dreaming? Don't just stand there!"

Donato isn't dreaming. He suddenly remembers the unfinished letter, or more correctly, the illegible end of Marochella Junior's letter. He must have been on the verge of saying that there are Jews in the Holy Land! And Trumpeldor, the Zionist… Zionist… of Zion! How had he missed connecting those two words until now?

The vision with the sheep quickly takes on a different significance. Not all the Jews have become extinct. God left some alive. Hallelujah! The Jews' fate was not the same as that of other peoples mentioned in Torah. All ceased to exist but them! What more could be needed than to believe in the Holy One and praise him daily?

"I was lost in thought," Donato answers. "We'll stay and continue working, and tonight we'll get together. That's how it should be done. And you, Pietro, are a man of good tidings. Yes, give me the address of the Jew you know."

"I'll bring it from my home. Don't go away."

From a distance, Pietro looks like a kid racing the wind.

Donato keeps his thoughts to himself. No one dares break the silence. To them it seems like the Prophet is deep in conversation with God.

Donato's pleased when Pietro returns, panting, smiling. "Here it is! Yaakov Fitoussi, Via Campobasso 26, Napoli."

"May God bless you and bestow upon you a desire to join us."

Pietro laughs. "Well, I'll join you in San Nicandro but only to hear what you've got to tell me and if our Lord Jesus contradicts you."

None of the San Nicandroans in the marketplace are thinking about selling their goods, attracting passersby, or praising the freshness of their vegetables and the quality of their meat in calls earmarked for shoppers. They're returning to the village carrying unsold items. They're far too tense to think about anything except what they've just learned. Conversations bubble.

"Can you imagine that, Matteo? If there are other Jews in this world, then there are other synagogues, other Torahs, in multiple places...so Pietro claims."

"And each of them, even if they don't know how to read,

can obtain a copy of the Holy Book. We've hoped so desperately for this!'

"And we can pray together with Klal Yisrael. I'm trembling with joy just thinking about it!"

Pietro Beltrano cannot imagine the splash he's caused among the San Nicandroan Jews. What dizzying news! What tremendous implications! The time has come to face a truth. Who knows, but perhaps Pietro is nothing but a filthy jester overly proud of his silly statements? Perhaps he's making a mockery of them in public?

The men toss the vegetables and chickens into their stunned wives' arms and rush to Donato's house.

In San Nicandro, the women do as they please. The vegetables are dropped on the floor, the chickens shunted aside, and they too hurry to Donato's house, lifting their skirt hems away from the dust lining the alleys.

Concetta de Leo is seated to Donato's left, concentrating. Emanuela is, as usual, carrying on with her work but her ears are following the discussion closely.

Today is a great day. Anticipation over entering the covenant with God is about to become a reality. The men know that Donato will raise the issue of circumcision. Not all of them react similarly. Not all have the same amount of courage.

"My dear friends," Donato begins, "Let's start with a blessing to God for having sent us this special gift today. Let me take this opportunity to admit that I incorrectly interpreted the vision of the flock of sheep. In fact, the Holy One of Blessed Name was conveying to me that the people of Israel do exist, and that we need to join them, whereas I'd thought it was another message of reviving the Israelite people without further delay. So let us praise God first."

Quiet tones of softly uttered prayer quickly become shouts of joy and praise. San Nicandroans know how to express themselves when they feel uplifted!

"Here's what we'll do. We'll write to this fellow Jew and ask him for the Rabbi's address. And then we'll write and ask him to register us among our brothers, and complete our conversion with circumcision."

And that's exactly what happened.

Almost.

***

Donato, with Concetta's help, is busy repeatedly drafting a letter to Jacob Fitoussi. They pore over the correct words for approaching someone unknown to them who may not understand the nature of their request.

"Keep it simple and direct," Concetta suggests. "Just say that we're converting and waiting for the blessing of the Chief Rabbi, the leader that Pietro mentioned and whose address he said he'd send to you. Write that we want to be recognized as Jews. Tell him how God healed me and how he made that knowledge accessible to you. I'm sure that will convince him."

"Are you serious? He won't believe us."

"Donato, I was on the verge of dying from that illness. Have you forgotten how worried everyone was? They were all praying, they gave me the traditional medicines of yogurt and cornmeal in oil, and nothing helped. Then God sent you a vision: a dead animal. A fox that had no gaze. Remember?"

"And how! I watched the fox for a long time and then suddenly it began to move, to stretch out and energetically jump about, turning into a cute pup. I realized then that you'd get well and I told everyone to stop giving you that mixture of food because I could see that God himself would eradicate the illness. And that's exactly what happened."

"So tell that to the Rabbi, Donato. In a toned down way, so that he can reach his own conclusions. Come on. Start writing."

Donato follows Concetta's outline. His writing is awkward. He doesn't like to sound as though he's praising himself.

The completed letter was handed over publicly and with great ceremony to Corlone the postman, who felt ill at ease at being suddenly granted such importance.

Many days passed. Corlone had never before been awaited with such anticipation. Never had such disappointment been felt as when each day passed with no response.

Finally a letter arrived. On Shabbat! Of all days, on the day when all activity is prohibited except for the study of Torah. The holiest day of the week, devoted to enhancing the closeness with God. The community waited until darkness descended on San Nicandro's ancient stones, signaling that the Shabbat had ended. Crowded around Donato, the community waited to learn of the message in the letter he held up high.

Conscious of this moment's importance, Donato takes hold of his walking stick and with exertion, stands up under his daughter's watchful gaze.

Dear Mr. Manduzio,

Your letter arrived on the day that my late husband passed away. It arrived as though it was the angel sent to accompany my late husband Yaakov on his lone journey. But I did not immediately read it. Firstly, I needed to complete the 'shivah,' the seven days of mourning. Then, and please do not mock me, I was troubled by the thought of opening a letter addressed to my husband. Perhaps the contents were not meant for my eyes? I needed time to ponder the matter.

I am not entirely certain that I have understood your explanation about conversion, but I was charmed to hear that a community eagerly wishes to join us, and that miracles still take place. I am pleased at Mrs. Concetta's happiness, and that her devotion moved God to act.

I do have the details of the Chief Rabbi in Rome. I'm not sure where he lives, but this is the address of the Great Synagogue there: 5 Lungotever de Cenci, 00186, Rome. The Chief Rabbi's name is Angelo Sacerdoti. He is a brave man, an intellectual, who fought in the front as a volunteer in 1915 and received an award for bravery in action, so my husband told me. Following the ceasefire, the entire community, guided by Rabbi Sacerdoti, wrote to the king to congratulate him on his victory and express their joy. That is the man who can best guide you.

May you be blessed with good fortune.

May God accompany you all in this endeavor you have initiated.

Please accept my warm wishes for your success.

Ester Fitoussi.

Donato sits. He places the letter on his lap and gazes at the community. It is a determining moment in their lives.

"My friends, ever since we were given the Torah, we've gone through so many events in our lives and withstood so many trials. Some have left us. Others have joined us. Children have been born. Some members have passed away and been buried in the Tallit that their wives had woven. We've learned prayers, the history of our people, and upheld God's commandments, teaching them to our children. We planned on spreading throughout the world but God has made our work easier. We will come together and approach the Chief Rabbi, who apparently is God's leader here, and request that he record us in his lists of Jews after we've been circumcised. We will continue with our Torah studies in larger groups. Rest tonight, and tomorrow we will write to Chief Rabbi Sacerdoti."

At that moment, the crystal voice of little Rivka Rossetti, twelve years old and named for the wife of biblical Yitzhak, was heard. She never missed any of Manduzio's wonderful tales. She sat at his feet, quickly absorbing his statements, then conveying them to the younger village children.

"Donato, what is 'shivah?'"

"Yes, Papa, what does 'shivah' mean?"

"Not now. Our community is exhausted. Tomorrow is another day," Bonfito says.

Donato's voice is loud. "Tomorrow? Should we postpone until tomorrow an answer to a question asked by the daughters of Israel? What scorn you show for the Holy One! No, we'll stay together for a few moments longer and hear the answer. Samuel, would you like to answer Rivka and Rachel?"

A little embarrassed yet absolutely thrilled, Samuel doesn't hesitate. "The word 'shivah' means seven. Donato read the letter and understood that these are the seven days of mourning observed after burying a Jew."

"For women too?"

"Of course. We mourn women too."

"When does the Torah talk about death?" Donato asks, proud of his pupil's answers.

"When Sarah dies?" Samuel half asks, half states.

"Precisely! You answered well, my son. You're a good Jew. Avraham buys a plot of land in Hebron for a high price, which he designates as Sarah's burial place. He also eulogizes his wife. That's what everyone afterwards did: a eulogy before the burial. It says, as I've taught you, that Yaakov cried over Yossef," Donato explained, using the Hebrew names of Jacob and Joseph respectively, "for 'many days' but on the other hand, when news came of Yossef's supposed death, Reuven tore his robe, and Yaakov tore 'his garments.' This was also done after Miriam died, after Aharon died, and even after Moshe died, over whom the people mourned for thirty days."

"So I have understood that after the person is buried, the mourners go home, and make a tear in their clothing, and spend seven days not talking. They sit as close to the ground as possible where the deceased last was, and are brought food by neighbors to prevent disruption to their prayers and internal thoughts."

"And why seven days? This is what I've realized. An entire week is a full cycle of our life, a final cycle. It's a bit like the food that neighbors bring, enriched by eggs and olives. Deep pain cannot be expressed, it goes on and on, just as the roundness of an egg or olive has no start or end. Nonetheless, the pain needs to be contained so that life's needs can be looked after."

"After Rivka and Rachel now have their answer, and we've spoken about joy too, and life, and the future, and mourning, let's say a prayer. Then we'll go home. May God bless you all and watch over you in your sleep. And tomorrow we'll write to our Chief Rabbi."

"Our God, Lord of the universe, bring us a peaceful night's sleep and let us awaken, our King, to life and peace. Shelter us and guard us. Let us live in the way you wish us to follow. Save us through your merciful name. Distance our enemies, illnesses, the sword, hunger, anxiety, and poverty from us. Break down any obstacles we face. Spread your wings over us and protect our comings and our goings. From now and forever you are blessed, our God, who guards Israel eternally, amen."

**

That night Donato doesn't sleep much. He ponders, rearranges sentences, erases errors. In which manner should one write to a chief rabbi? And what should he actually ask? What's the difference between him and a regular rabbi? Would he postpone setting the time for circumcision? Why isn't his name Levi like all the priests in the Torah? The names Levi or Cohen would have reinforced Donato's trust in the man's position, but Sacerdoti?

Finally Donato puts together a note to the Chief Rabbi of Italy on… a postcard! Donato in his integrity feels that the postcard appropriately conveys the warmth of his community because it shows a couple holding hands as they gaze at the horizon.

"I gave it a lot of thought. He's no doubt an extremely busy man. Who are we to bother him with a full length letter? When he responds to this card, which signals our existence and conveys respect, I'll detail our history for him."

Not everyone agrees but no one dares voice a contradicting opinion.

Corlone, patiently waiting while sipping his third glass of wine, cannot restrain himself and airs a thought based on simple wisdom. "All of this is lovely, of course, but without an address, how will the postcard be delivered?"

"What do you mean? It has the synagogue's address!"

"It does, yes, but what if someone there doesn't pass the postcard on? I'd imagine there would be a lot of people there. So if it doesn't actually get to the hands of the Chief Rabbi…"

"Hmm. I hadn't thought of that. But we'll get the address quite soon."

"Perfect. And from whom?" Corlone asks, noticing that the bottle is emptying into Bonfito's glass.

"From you, Corlone. It's your job to deal with mail, is it not?"

"*Che nervi!*" What a cheek! Corlone exclaims. "I collect letters, I deliver letters, and that's all. How do you expect me…"

"Corlone, you're too modest. You're king there, at the Foggia Post Office. Whatever you ask for, you get. So, ask for the Chief Rabbi's address. We'll compensate you for your work, with Dona Concetta's approval."

"Well, in that case…"

143

Corlone raises his glass toward Concetta. The deal is done.

"Come to my house and we'll have a drink before you set out, Corlone. I have something to send to your manager. You can give him the package," Cerrone adds.

And the Jews of San Nicandro begin a period of waiting.

A long period.

An interminable period.

***

In Rome, Chief Rabbi Sacerdoti is busy with far more important matters than responding to an odd group of people who have sent him, in these disturbing times, a naïve and courteous yet decisive postcard. Jews in San Nicandro! Do they think he's so gullible?

Nevertheless he doesn't toss the card out, but slips it into a drawer as he ponders about the meeting convened for that evening to review how fascist Italy is affecting the country's Jews. Then he continues to sit at his organized desk. A multi-colored abstract painting hung on the wall usually brings him great pleasure but today it doesn't. In fact, he doesn't even notice it. The sound of heavy breathing, picked up so far only by Jewish ears, it would seem, can be heard at their napes, threatening to crush them.

The Rabbi worriedly recalls the chaos affecting the community in 1921 when, at the peak of the political and social instability which contaminated Italy, Benito Mussolini established the PNF, the Partito Nazionale Fascista. Now, because of the nationalistic, racist, and antisocial agenda negating the rights of workers to unionize, Mussolini was successfully turning the middle class into his adherents.

The march to Rome, aided by the physical force employed by the squadristi, placed full control of the regime in his hands. Although the Jews were persecuted less than their eastern European brethren, the atmosphere was tense and threatening. Angelo Sacerdoti has not erred in his perception of the dangers that a fascist government could arouse. He has warned his community, but on the other hand, does not want to sow excessive fear. In any event, the community's president does not believe for a moment that Italy's Jews are endangered in any way. The Rabbi and the president's oppositional views do not make the relationship between them any easier.

"Respectfully, Rabbi, some of our community have actually joined the fascist party, so why are you suspicious?"

"One bud does not herald the start of spring, Hugo. And if two or three err, should we put the rest of the community at risk?"

"Really! The Duce loathes Hitler. The Duce is our friend. He won't capitulate to history's whims!"

"Our dear President, you cannot ignore the fact that sworn enemies have frequently united in the past for the sake of eradicating the Jews. Is that not so? Have you listened closely to the fascists' fury-driven declarations?"

And very quickly the speeches get rougher, like sandpaper, and coarsely aggressive. From May 1936 on, when Hitler visits Rome, they become insistent convictions.

The situation has become harsh and riddled with risk.

On September 18th, 1938, Trieste's Piazza Unità d'Italia is once again black with swarms of people. This time the large Jewish community opts to stay home. It is a well-considered decision: energetically raised arms and chins thrust forward, like furious rhinoceroses, emphasize every declaration as the Duce stands on the city hall balcony and fires up the crowd before enumerating the newly-passed laws of race.

The words strike and sear like rounds of gunshot on the battleground. "We must harness our efforts toward protecting the Aryan race. Enroll your children into fascist schools! It is mandatory to read 'The Racial Laws.' Our leading race scientists have worked tirelessly so that you can understand the urgency of preserving the Italian Aryan race, identifiable by the shape of the ear and skull. Here are the ten main points of The Racial Laws. Each of you must commit these to memory for the rest of your lives.

Human races exist.

Superior and inferior races exist.

'Race' is a purely biological term.

Italy's current population is predominantly of Aryan origin, and its culture is Aryan.

The claim that a significant foreign population has been included in Italy's history is myth.

From now on, a pure Italian race exists.

Italians must openly embrace their racial identity.

European Mediterranean peoples must be clearly differentiated from Easterners and Africans.

Jews do not belong to the Italian race.

There should be no alteration to any of the physical and psychological characteristics of Italians."

"Therefore, we must adopt drastic measures toward the foreigner Jews, with rigid rules relative to professions which we will allow Italian Jews to fulfill, the schools designated for them..."

The Duce is inexhaustible. He concludes with a resounding "Viva l'Italia pura!" Long live Italy the pure!" he shouts, which unleashes deafening applause.

Like any dictator, Mussolini supports his views based on the ten well-chosen Italian scientists who signed the Manifesto of Race, as well as thousands of Italian intellectuals and academics who openly support the racial laws.

To a lesser degree, but no less surprising, is Mussolini's inclusion of a clause relating to Pentecostals: practice of this form of Christianity is now prohibited in the kingdom. His argument against it is that it conducts practices which contradict the social order, and are harmful to the physical and spiritual integrity of the Italian Aryan race.

The Chief Rabbi, deeply troubled by these disturbing events and anticipating the disastrous decisions the government will adopt in order to enact them, rises sorrowfully, crossing the corridor that leads to the synagogue. Inside, the congregation is waiting for him to commence the midday prayers.

The eccentrics of the postcard are completely erased from his mind.

***

In San Nicandro, the community wonders what's taking the Italian Chief Rabbi so long to respond. They wait. Nothing comes. Nothing comes. Nothing.

Bonfito leads his horse to the stable, passing Donato's

house. "Donato, do you think that we somehow angered the Chief Rabbi with that postcard? We simply wrote that there are Jews here. But do you think it can really matter to him, if indeed there are Jews everywhere? It's not exactly earth-shattering news."

After thinking briefly, Donato acknowledges Bonfito's comment. Concetta studies Bonfito with renewed admiration. How surprising that the most logical explanation comes from Antonio!

"I hadn't thought of that, Antonio. I believed we acted correctly. I tried not to bother the Chief Rabbi too much. But no one thought of what you've just said. Now that you've put the idea into words, I wonder how I could have been so mistaken. You must certainly be right. I'll write a more detailed letter, and read it out tomorrow before we decide to send it."

Toward evening of the next day, the community gathers in the synagogue. A greater than usual turnout has come. Concetta pulls Donato's draft from her pocket and begins slowly reading. The letter starts by noting Donato's dismay at the silence from Rome.

"Perhaps I offended you by not providing a list of the San Nicandroan converts. If so, my apologies. It is now included. Some 150 people comprise the community. Is this an insufficient number? But God created humanity in entirety from one man and one woman! We wish for nothing but to return to the Israelite faith, and be recognized by our fellow Jews. We also wish to receive, as far as possible, several books toward improving our study of Torah and our ability to

properly pray. Here in San Nicandro we all uphold the Ten
Commandments with great respect, and believe that the Holy
One has blessed our souls. But we lack a synagogue worthy
of the title, and we ceaselessly refresh our Torah learning, so
that we neither forget the word of God nor regress into our
past beliefs. Thus, it is vital to assist us.

Silence pervades the synagogue: the community is listening
attentively. The letter simultaneously expresses modesty and
pride. It is as clear as the water of mountain creeks. It requests so very little.

Hearing the community's history sends a shiver of excitement down the listeners' spines. How surprised they
are, and joyful, at how far they've progressed. Admittedly,
Donato holds the primary role, but without him nothing
would have eventuated. God would hardly have brought
such joy and faith to this end-of-the-earth village without
Donato, let alone imbue them with the motivation to restore the Jewish people. Donato is the man worthy of hon-
or, despite his controlling nature and despite his forthright
manner of speech which over time has angered many.

Donato concludes the letter by respectfully encouraging
the Chief Rabbi of Rome to visit the community, grant it
his blessing, and "bring all the menfolk into the covenant
of Avraham our forefather, for in our hearts we have been
circumcised long ago," he poetically adds.

He explains that it is the community's burning desire to
merge with that of the Chief Rabbi, and with Italian Jewry.
The community's members wish to see their names included among those of their brethren.

Donato has read the document. Silence reigns supreme.

And then Emanuela and her childhood friends, Roza and Palmiero, bring out bottles of wine and their calm faces show smiles of contentment.

***

Once again the community waits for a response from the Chief Rabbi.

And it arrives some weeks later. Chief Rabbi Sacerdoti knows that mail should not be left unanswered, and at last he has taken up his pen.

"Dear Mr. Donato Manduzio,
San Nicandro, Garganico

I have noted your name as the addressee of my letter even though the missive I received was signed by 'Francesco Cerrone & co.' The envelope, however, bears your name as addressor. It is unclear to me why you are known by one name on the envelope, and another on the letter itself, but that is not important for now.

I did not answer the postcard sent toward the end of August for two reasons:

To the best of my knowledge, a matter of such great importance could not have been fully encompassed on the space of a return postcard.

I did not realize this was indeed a very serious matter and was sure the contents were none other than a more or less successful prank. But your insistence via additional correspondence requires that I relate to your letter of 29th September in kind. Your letter does not fully and clearly

*define your request and that of your friends. I do discern a
crisis of conscience and a passion to join Judaism, but that
is not sufficiently characterized. Yet how can your wish be
authenticated in a region having no Jews and where a Jewish
lifestyle is unfamiliar? What do you and your community
know of the Jewish way of life? To what degree are you
knowledgeable of Jewish thought, and the principles of
Jewish faith? I need to know these things before I can offer a
committed response, since my response may alter relative to
the circumstances. Do you know if you are the descendants
of Jews forced in the past to convert to Christianity?
Information on this matter would be extremely helpful.*

*What I can state is that Judaism prohibits attempts by people
to convert into the faith and does not accept such people as
co-religionists except in exceedingly extraordinary cases.
This is because Jews do not believe that only they can merit
the world to come, but believe that redemption encompasses
all people, no matter their religion.*

The Chief Rabbi has correctly fulfilled his duty by referencing the prohibition against converting, and the misunderstanding around the concept of choice, but Donato is not the intellectual conversationalist Sacerdoti had hoped for.

Donato doesn't need an explanation about how belonging to the chosen people is not a simple matter. He knows that. What does the Chief Rabbi take him for? God gave his Torah to Moshe who was instructed to transmit it to the nations, not to patronize them but to be sure the nations as well as the Israelites would fulfill their obligations to God despite the dangers of bringing Torah to others.

Furious, he audibly responds with a single, clear sentence.

"I have not heard the Holy Word from a person but received it directly from God, as our forefather Avraham did. We will manage without these pretentious, arrogant Jews… Where's Cerrone? Move aside. I'm going to see him. I have a few things to tell that man."

"Donato, stop! Listen to me!"

"Let me be, Emanuela. This time he's gone way beyond the acceptable. That's why he asked Corlone to come to his house. He signs instead of me, he impersonates the leader of the community, he lies shamelessly!"

Donato enters Cerrone's house with a sharp metallic twang. The wheelchair has never moved so fast as it does now.

"*Ipocrita!*" You hypocrite, Donato accuses Cerrone. "You took the letter to the Chief Rabbi! You'd better have a really good reason for that, otherwise I'm going to leave you headless despite my disability!"

"Did I erase your name?"

"You added yours next to it in larger letters. Of that I'm certain. Why?"

"You're asking why? Who joins you in services? Who handles educating the newcomers? Who reads the scriptures when you're unable? Who makes sure to collect some money for the synagogue's needs? And I've barely gotten started! But had I asked to have my name specifically noted in the letter, you'd have refused."

"Of course I'd have refused. On the other hand, I'd have noted Concetta, Palmiero, Yanono… I listed everyone's names in the letter! Would you prevent me from receiving the recognition I deserve? Who receives the visions? Who's taught Torah for nine years now, day after day? Who composed the prayers? And more than all that, who did God approach in order to instill Judaism in the world?"

"Stop it, Donato. It's not that terrible."

"What do you mean, 'not that terrible?' You cheated. You lied. Had you stuck with Don Adriano, he'd have given you some weeks of atonements to do. I wish I could take a similar course of action, but God himself will be the judge. Just know that from now on I'll be suspicious of you, Francesco. And this time, forever!"

The two men's conflict bears an ancient bestial hue. They restrain themselves from deteriorating into fisticuffs.

Donato sees that his rival is on the verge of literally throwing his wheelchair out of the house. He turns, heading for the door as he tosses out a departing jibe. "Stinks here."

***

Slowly a limited and inconsistent exchange of correspondence between Donato and Angelo Sacerdoti is established. Manduzio longs for Rome's acknowledgment of the community and a plan to circumcise the men. He tells the Chief Rabbi of even the smallest events in the lives of San Nicandro's Jews. One day, a letter accompanied by a small sum of money for the community's newborns arrives.

On a separate page is a response to one of Donato's questions. "What might I answer to a community which asks when the messiah will come?" The Chief Rabbi offers a surprising and far from expected answer about an unusual trial held in the Middle Ages: The Trial of God. Even before reading it, Donato is thrilled, and turns to his wife.

"Emanuela, a rabbi who devotes time to answering my questions can hardly be indifferent to our community or think we're not Jewish because if he did, answering us would be such a waste of his time. In other words, we are becoming increasingly important to him. Look! Money for the children, and a lesson for us to learn! Probably not too long now before he registers us as Jews."

"You are the champion of all gullible folk! He probably dictated the letter and sent money as a way of shutting us up," Emanuela answers.

Donato's gaze pierces her.

***

The "Prophet" continues giving his daily class, and frequently repeats the story that the Chief Rabbi had written to him. The community loves the plot, finding encouragement in waiting for the Redeemer.

Donato looks at the people gathered there, smiling warmly, and because he now knows the story by heart, he begins. "Here's what our dear Chief Rabbi Angelo Sacerdoti wrote to me."

"This story takes place in the Middle Ages, in Poland. Jews were persecuted throughout Europe and outside Europe. They lived in separate areas called ghettos and suffered terrible hardships. Things were terrible everywhere: wars, superstition, enslavement, death wrought by evil people.

"An old rabbi was incensed and in despair over seeing the 'shtetl,' the little township where the Jews lived in close quarters, destroyed and rebuilt innumerable times because

of pogroms, because of the harsh poverty, and because of the constant dangers to the community, and especially the smell of murdered children. Not receiving any response other than silence from God, he decided to sue the Holy One.

"The old rabbi accused God of apathy, cruelty, and not providing assistance to humans in danger.

"An extraordinary Rabbinic Court was called specifically for this case.

"The three 'dayanim,' the judges, were smart and wise, and well aware of the severity of the case they were about to discuss. They too, were hurt by the events of the times. They sat for a lengthy period of time, giving God every opportunity to explain his stunning silence.

"True, in the past, their ancestors had been required to judge far more complex cases. Often they were required to deal with false messiahs. They even declared entire cities as impure because the residents worshipped idols. And they gave verdicts concerning the destruction of contaminated places. But to date, no court of law had ever handled a case where God himself was being taken to court.

"Based on the severity of the described actions occurring over the course of millennia, one might have expected the harshest of verdicts, being excommunication: that is, exiling God from his community. And yet, despite everything, he was endlessly revered.

"The Rabbi appointed as God's advocate did his best, suggesting a trial period. But the much more senior prosecuting rabbi presented the gravest of arguments: Jewish communities wander from attack to attack; fall victim to ignorance and envy; are marked worldwide as scapegoats; their suffering tests the boundaries of their ability to withstand the hatred; they are annihilated in riots and still they call to God as they die.

"God conducts cruel practices. He is obligated to provide his adherents with an explanation, correct his ways, or at the very least, prevent freedom of choice to brainless gangs of wild men. 'I demand God be excommunicated until we see significant change in the lives of our fellow Jews!' the prosecutor cried out.

"The agonizing old rabbi won the case!

"God was found guilty and ordered to correct whatever could be corrected. But it was too late. Distress continued to plague the world with the same obstinance, accompanied by violence and suffering.

"And then the rabbis went back to praying, because there is no ambiguity in the position taken by the Holy One who is clear and precise at all times. Understanding humanity's incomprehensible deficiency was the key. Presuming the warped human interpretation, which blames God for abandoning humanity because he was so sick and tired of them, was not a feasible option.

"The reason for it all was suddenly discovered, like a dark object against a white background. The Messiah had not come! He was the one who was meant to rectify, or destroy the world!

"Scientific research was conducted. Kabbalistic calculations were carried out. All of it led to a single unequivocal conclusion – that we are approaching Messianic times. And while waiting, it was necessary for each person to do what he'd been designed to do in this life. Or in short, each one must participate in acts of rectifying the world, known as Tikkun Olam.

"Know, dear Donato, that this concept is an inseparable

part of the Holy One's commandments, and derives from the perception of social justice in Judaism. Rectifying the world, which Jews are involved in no matter where they are, aims to accelerate the Messiah's arrival. It is so important that it is given an important place in our rites, as you will soon discover.

"Even some of the world's greatest scientists have acknowledged that the creation of the world by God was imperfect in that it was incomplete, and every time someone carries out an act of rectification, or as we may say, assists in enabling it to attain completeness and perfection, that person advances the universe toward the final outcome which God wanted in the first place. In this way, God directs us toward becoming his partners.

"And so I have found it appropriate to direct your attention to this amazing and true tale. We will soon reach Messianic times. Tell that to your community.

"I am deeply hopeful, my dear friend, that everyone in San Nicandro is well. Please convey my best wishes to each and every member of your community."

As with every other time that Donato relates this tale, it raises questions and drives interest. San Nicandro's converts find it a compelling reason to put their trust in Judaism since it explicitly states that the Messiah has yet to come and fulfill his mission.

At the simplest level, a San Nicandroan would have been considered a believer by obeying church authority, which clearly dictates what to do and how to do it. But for a long time now, the San Nicandro Jewish community has refused the passivity required by the church. San Nicandro's Jews have come to understand and appreciate the value of this unique partnership with God. The community's responsibility is to God and the need to be actively involved in rectifying the world.

In Donato's makeshift synagogue, each person airs her or his own explanation.

The community's members aspire to improvement in light of Judaism which has at last lit up their lives and homes.

Like their leader, they haven't felt any irreversible internal change take place to a degree that might make any of them unrecognizable to another. Although their faith has changed, they are inherently the same people.

They have absorbed a basic principle: each has a personal relationship with God. It radiates from them as a light which they hope to spread further.

Manduzio's reputation has spread far and wide. Not everyone approves of the group's conversion, especially those wandering priests whose efforts to convert Christians from one form of practice to another were often miserable failures. Donato never refuses to debate them but his hot-headed nature quickly makes him fume when he is repeatedly accosted by dogmas based on lies, and on instilling fear meant to intimidate.

A passerby present at one of Donato's lessons tells him that in Lesina, a small city nestled alongside a lake of the same name no further than thirty kilometers from San Nicandro, there's another group of people who observe the holy Sabbath, or Shabbat in its Hebraic pronunciation.

Donato is as excited as someone meeting his twin for the

first time. He writes to them, wanting to know if they are Jewish. Their positive response thrills him. Without waiting to call the community together that evening, he crosses San Nicandro's only street and wheels himself down the paved alley at the end of which Lucinda can be found working. She was one of the first to accept Judaism. Lucinda weaves colorful threads which are used to make the skirts, the *pacchiane*, that brighten every young girl's wardrobe as gaily as peonies in bloom.

She began weaving not as a hobby, which it is for some other San Nicandro women, but as a way of helping provide for her children. Her evident talent brought great success to her endeavors.

Lucinda now sells *pacchiane* not only to San Nicandroans but to other villages. Once a month she travels to sell her wares in Lesina, and always returns in high spirits.

Donato asks if, on her next visit, she'd take a close look and keep her ears peeled to ascertain what lies behind the passerby's claim.

"Who are these people living so close to us and claiming to be Jews? Try to find out," he encourages.

Lucinda is a cheerfully natured person. She has no problem chatting with the husbands whose wives slip behind a screen of thickly woven cloth to try clothes on. The women love these moments of jest and pleasure which give them respite from their never-ending work. They're in no hurry to dash out of Lucinda's place. And with Lucinda's weight approaching a hundred kilos, they don't view her as a threat when it comes to their men.

While she chats with Lesina's residents, Donato's busy carving a log of wood next to his home's fireplace. A vision comes to him which he later enters in his diary. He is marching along a steep slope and notices two shepherds' huts. A man and woman stand there, pale and in tattered clothes. Donato asks how they are. They say they're ill with malaria. The vision dissipates.

Donato quickly understands that something is wrong with the Lesina story: better to keep a distance from these people.

But it's too late. They've already promised to visit San Nicandro.

Lucinda's face on returning home is radiant. He listens attentively to her report about how warmly several of the community's members received her, and that they would soon come to see how their brethren were doing. Donato thinks of the two people in his vision, their faces long and sorrowful.

Barely three days pass when a man presents himself to Donato, asking for the location of the "Shabbat House."

"Right here."

"I'm Jewish. I'm from Lesina, where I met the loveliest *pacchiane* maker, and Jewish too! I've come to pray in your synagogue to hasten the arrival of Jesus."

Donato's blood boils. He rises from the wheelchair, his screams bringing neighbors at a run and making Emanuela rush out of the house, worrying that her husband might be having an attack.

"Out! Out, you Satan! Get lost, now! There are no Jews in Lesina, nor anywhere else! You and your Pentecostal friends have come up with this plot to convert us to your warped faith!"

"Warped? You're warped yourself! Not only your legs but your brain, too!"

Ciro di Salvia, generally reticent but always present at Donato's classes, dashes to Donato's side to assist him, brandishing his carpentry sledgehammer. But the Pentecostal is not alarmed and carries on while Donato tries calming Ciro. "You don't own the Bible. We respect it as much as you do and also have a personal approach that differentiates us from the Catholics who follow their Pope. The Bible is filled with the Holy Spirit, it is our highest authority. It supports each of us as we grow and turn to Jesus through faith."

"For us Jews the Bible is an encounter with God."

"But that's exactly what I'm telling you!"

"Not at all! You're talking about Jesus. He isn't God. He isn't the son of God. Your manipulations of Torah are insufferable. I'm fed up with your lies meant to convert us. And now, scram! If any of you dare come here again, I'll call for my people. Look around carefully!"

And who'd feel at ease when facing determined San Nicandroans armed with hammers and cast iron frypans?

The man spun on his heels and raced off.

And no one from Lesina ever again came to try and talk to San Nicandro's Jewish community.

"Why don't they just let us live in peace as Jews?" Ciro wonders aloud. "What have Jews ever done to anyone else?"

***

In Rome, Rabbi Sacerdoti receives Donato's letter, reads it with some amazement, but doesn't reply.

Some six months later he receives the same letter with the addition of a note requesting that its receipt be confirmed. He smiles, softening.

But doesn't reply.

Donato isn't the kind of person to give up. He wants to be acknowledged as Jewish. All the converts do, eagerly. And they deserve it, in Donato's view.

A fourth letter is sent to the Chief Rabbi. It contains numerous quotes from the Torah, and all are correct.

Sacerdoti remembers the simple postcard he received two years earlier and takes it out of his drawer. He compares the two documents. There is no doubt that something's developing on the Garganico slopes.

It'd be interesting to send a messenger there, if only to close the file on this incident.

But he won't do that.

He has a good reason for that decision.

Furthermore, elections to choose his replacement are coming up. He won't need to be concerned with matters of conversion after that.

***

San Nicandro's Jews simultaneously wonder about the Chief Rabbi, fashioning all manner of reasons for the continued silence following their most recent, friendly letter. What could have happened? They wait. A long time passes, and they begin to get angry.

Let it be that way, then! Donato and Concetta draft a

new letter advising of their plan to visit Sacerdoti, since for a long time now his honorable Chief Rabbi, who must be extremely busy, cannot leave his post long enough to answer them. Donato stresses how odd they find this extended silence. Emphasizing the practical aspect, he asks if they may receive prayer books, if a teacher could be sent to guide them, and whether they might receive some financial support for obtaining a larger prayer house than the room in his home where it all began.

"Who could possibly resist such enthusiastic commitment?" Concetta remarks.

Not long afterwards they receive a letter. Their faith is praised, their commitment is admired, and attached is a small sum to help them advance in their study of Torah. The letter is signed by Chief Rabbi David Prato.

What can this mean?

The San Nicandroans understand nothing of how the Rome community operates. They have a leader, Donato, and anyone challenging that role is quite unceremoniously shunted aside. Who is this new rabbi, then? Why did Sacerdoti leave? Did he die but the community in San Nicandro was not informed? Who decides on appointments?

Corlone the postman provides an answer. "I called Rome from the post office's telephone. Elections were held and David Prato was elected on September 4th last year. He is from Alexandria."

Do they hold elections to appoint a Jewish leader? Even if any of them are entertaining dreams following this announcement, no one would dare reveal such thoughts!

"Can a rabbi from a different country be chosen? Perhaps that's good news, because this new rabbi is answering us," Donato shrugs, his eyebrows raised in hope.

Following Rabbi Prato's response, correspondence is renewed. True, this new rabbi is not committing himself when it comes to circumcision, nor does he mention it, but one day he writes that a colleague is about to travel to San Nicandro specifically to meet the community and evaluate its needs. What rejoicing in the village! The women roll up their sleeves and start cleaning; the men repeat their prayers to get them word-perfect.

For the first time in their lives, they're about to meet a practicing Jew! The year 1938 ends as a year blessed with light.

***

Rafael Cantoni, a member of the Rabbinic Council of Rome, runs through the Chief Rabbi's instructions as he makes his way to San Nicandro.

"You must thoroughly review their level of faith, how they came to it, and what they actually do. If in your view, they truly wish to be Jews, then we will also view them accordingly and work toward circumcising them one day. But if they try to insist that they will come to Rome, you must firmly deflect their wish. It should be clear why, nor is that up for discussion."

The "why" of which the San Nicandroans have no knowledge is a very weighty matter and cannot be circumvented.

The tax collector's carriage makes a twice-yearly appearance in each village to ensure that no one, not even a handicapped person, avoids paying their dues. Today it brings Rafael Cantoni to San Nicandro.

Cantoni hands Donato a packet of twenty-two Tallit prayer shawls and various items to inaugurate the new synagogue which the San Nicandroans eventually rented when no external source of assistance was forthcoming. From his leather suitcase, Cantoni draws out a silver Menorah, the eight branched candelabrum used for Chanukah, and another smaller seven-branched candelabrum for the synagogue. It sparkles in the sun. He also has several additional items for ritual use, including pocket-sized editions of the Siddur, the Jewish daily prayer book, which he now hands out to the converts welcoming him. He is deeply moved by their happiness. No one dares touch the menorahs, but each clutches a new Siddur tightly to their chests.

The community is overjoyed, and awed. Cantoni is received like a prince. That Friday evening, marking the start of Shabbat, a special meal is held according to the Jewish tradition. Nothing is absent: a lavish white tablecloth was specially woven by Lucinda and her friends. Plates and casseroles from various serving sets, although mismatched, shine brightly.

Prayers, all of which have been composed by Donato, are said loudly and enthusiastically. Faces shine. First courses are colorful: sweet peppers, tomatoes, eggplants, egg salad, shelled almonds, all meant to indicate a future rich with abundance.

As is customary, the serving of fish seasoned with lemon and oregano is followed by delicious meat slaughtered according to the laws of kosher ritual.

Rafael Cantoni is surprised. Clearly all aspects relating to kosher foods as noted in the Torah are well understood by these unusual people.

Shabbat passes without any mishaps; these Jews are deeply proud of who they have become.

Rafael notes that the community recites the prayers which Donato has formulated. Indeed, the prayers closely follow Torah principles. But part of the ritual is incomplete. The element of rabbinical guidance, the practices developed by the sages over the course of centuries, and which aim to sanctify the customs while ensuring they are not forgotten or that the correct dates are not missed, will need to be discussed with Donato. How fortunate! The prayer books have arrived with perfect timing to help set the community on its way!

Before the community gathers on Shabbat afternoon, Rafael and Donato sit down to talk.

Donato explains that from his knowledge of Torah, which he's learned by heart, he worked out the festival times and the rituals which must be observed. He quotes the verses. He is proud of his fellow Jews who direct their prayers of praise to God as he, Donato, formulated. He is certain that he's honored the spirit of the Torah's instructions.

"You've done well, my dear Manduzio, but please note that Jews worldwide recite a uniform service and sing the same tunes, which you must also follow."

"Why?"

"The greatest of our sages put these prayers together based on the specific words and their unique meanings."

"Yet I… discovered Judaism."

A smile comes to Rafael's face. What arrogance! Nonetheless, Donato impresses him with everything he's achieved here, practiced on a daily basis, on an hourly basis, for love of God. And yet Rafael must ensure he is viewed by this bubbling, critical community as the authority in matters of Judaism.

"Let me give you an example, Mr. Cantoni. We learn the Ten Commandments over and over, and because I worded a mandatory text, everyone knows them by heart."

"Mandatory text?"

"Yes. Well, a prayer, if you prefer."

"I prefer, most certainly. A mandatory text alludes to a dictatorial approach, my friend!"

"But…" taken momentarily aback and aware of several smirks in the audience, Donato responds, relying on common sense. "There needed to be a text common to everyone, to allow us to come together, understand each other, and practice these laws correctly. Right? And so I penned 'The Twelve Paths of the Children of Light,' which the entire congregation can repeat. Isn't that right, Cerrone?"

Cerrone, annoyed at having to reference a text he didn't write, turns to Cantoni as a pupil would stand before a teacher, and recites the twelve principles without hesitation or errors.

"Yes," Cerrone says, "and here they are:

A Jew must believe that only the Holy One of Blessed Name created the world.

A Jew must believe that we must fulfill the statements provided by God in heaven on the day of purification in the fire of Sinai.

A Jew must believe that the prophets are the children of God and are intended to inherit the world of peace where life is eternal.

Whoever does not fulfill justice as set out by the prophets cannot inherit the world of peace where life is eternal.

Whoever lacks faith in the Creator is not worthy of saying God's name but is the inheritor of death.

Those who uphold Torah are equal in God's view and are the only children or people.

One who does not believe in the prophets cannot be linked to God and will not be rewarded with eternal life

One who does not discern a true prophet from a false prophet is blind. God will negate that one's eternal light.

A true prophet hears the voice of God but a false prophet hides the truth.

One who hates his brother or sister, or betrays them, will not become part of the Holy People.

One who reveals holy secrets to Satan is a friend of Satan.

On the day that the holy ones inherit God's peace, the liars spewing falsehoods and those who hate their brothers and sisters will burn in the valley's fire, as a sign of their sin and God's wrath."

Rafael listens silently. While Francesco recites these twelve principles, his face looking grumpy because he feels, correctly to some degree, that they were written to laud Donato. Cantoni takes note of Manduzio's total focus on converting to Judaism and his aspiration to lead the community to God. Admittedly this invented form of prayer is insufficient for conversion, but relative to people who feel Judaism's relevance has passed from this world, this community shows extraordinary commitment. Rafael's face shows neither enthusiasm nor disappointment: it is not his job to take the final decisions.

Donato, aware of Rafael's silence, continues. "Shabbat, Pesach, Shavuot, Yom Kippur, Succot," he names the various festivals using the Hebrew words as they are known in Torah. "We religiously observe all the festivals. One room in my house is used as the synagogue and is decorated with flowers, and I can assure you that the entire village rejoices, other than on Yom Kippur," he said, referring to the Fast of Atonement, "which of course we must use for soul-searching and reckoning.

"Just think, Mr. Cantoni! Even those who haven't converted come to watch what we do, and nod in approval. In any event, that's what the community thinks. We Jews know that on these festivals no work is done, and a gift of thanks is brought to God. We would never disobey these requirements, from building the Succah to baking the matzah."

Wishing to emphasize Donato's statement, Bonfito tells Rafael that when Samuel Tritto was ill, Donato offered the kidneys, spleen, and tail of a lamb as a sacrifice, to beseech the Holy One's mercy in restoring the child's good health. And that is exactly what happened. In gratitude to God, the community brought fruit and celebrated, offering thanks following the child's recovery.

"We also observe the festival of young lasses in the vineyards, to ensure they are looked upon favorably by God," Donato adds.

Cantoni couldn't remember exactly what vineyard festival Donato was relating to – clearly it had been abandoned in Jewish practice long ago. But he praised Donato, and then began to detail the elements still missing in order to become practitioners of Orthodox Judaism.

"That's why we waited for you!" Donato reminded Cantoni. "We keenly desire to learn, to assimilate into the Jewish people, to be acknowledged as Jews. You were born Jewish, but are we not admirable for whatever long path we've taken to date which, due to your inherent closeness to Torah, you weren't required to unravel from scratch. Of course, our practices are incomplete, deficient. But the main thing which we hold onto, which we worship, is the Holy One. We humbly request that you assist our progress, and that us males may be circumcised. We are happy to come to Rome to meet the Chief Rabbi, and receive the documents from his own hand confirming that we have formally and legally converted, and are thus acknowledged as Jewish."

Cantoni ignores Donato's last sentence and instead relates to the issue of learning more about religious practices. "Yes, you're still missing quite a bit, and the synagogue isn't the least of the problem spots. Why haven't you moved yet to the location you hired?"

"The Ministry of Religion hasn't authorized its use as a place of worship, even though we lodged our request more than a year ago," Donato explains, turning to look at the *podesta*, the senior officer in charge of such matters, who swears that he wrote to the district's management to have the request approved.

In actuality, that never happened: no one thought to hurry the process along by slipping the official a few banknotes.

But in the presence of the messenger from Rome's Chief Rabbi, the *podesta* is deeply embarrassed. He promises to shake the dust off the request held up by the clerks, and reassures Manduzio and Cantoni that the matter will be handled within eight days. No one's banking on his promise, but this isn't the time to show the Jew from Rome what a furious San Nicandroan can look and sound like.

It is a very special Shabbat for the community. Cantoni comes to understand that these "oddball" Jews are completely authentic and serious. But he also notices several who aren't fully observant of Shabbat practices: some do light up cigarettes even though lighting fire is not allowed; some work, another activity not permitted on the day of rest; and none of those transgressors seem bothered by their actions.

"Those few are our, let's say, dropouts," Donato smiles patiently, fearing that the entire community will be invalidated because of them. "But we're hoping they'll fully join us one day," he says.

"Rafael, my brother," Donato adds, later remembering to record this plea in his diary, "When you go back to Rome, please make sure this little congregation doesn't end up as prey for the wolves."

Cantoni returns to the city and the offices of the Chief Rabbi of Italy with mixed emotions. "They can't be defined as Jews," he explains to Rabbi Prato. "On the other hand, they're certainly on the right path. They've conducted themselves as Jews for a long time now. Almost a decade! They need us, there's no doubt of that. They're definitely interested in receiving certificates of conversion. They want to be accepted in a formal ceremony."

"We'll help them in a different way. But they absolutely must not come here."

"Yes, I understand. And no, absolutely not."

***

Donato despairs: Cantoni returned to Rome leaving no promises.

Time passes. Once again, nothing happens.

Donato resumes teaching, an activity which he sees as tying himself to his beliefs, to God. He will never renege on those. But he's so very tired. Sometimes he's also frustrated. His health is worrying. He's been fighting for years. It feels as though he's needed to reassert his goal of spreading Judaism thousands of times. Rebellions are incessant; eventually, the rebels return to the community's embrace, just as Cerrone, Tritto and Marochella have returned. They go stormily, they come back quietly, they criticize, they opt for silence. When their mood gets them, they're the best of the worst, smart, cunning. At least, that's true of Cerrone. But they're in constant need of being kept under a watchful eye.

One evening when he's particularly furious, Donato's sharp tone erupts around Emanuela. "When Marochella dreamt that famous nightmare of his, shall I tell you its true meaning? He was afraid of circumcision. Without a doubt. But he didn't catch on to the real issue. It's the *capo membro*, the head of the member, which must be removed because of its negative influence, but as far as the community is concerned, he is the *capo membro*, he needs to be removed for being a negative influence on some of us. That's what the dream was telling him."

172

The community wonders about its future. Some members are increasingly weighing a move to the Promised Land, while others, aware that because their story began in San Nicandro, believe they must continue in San Nicandro, or at the very least for several more years. Donato is among that second group.

Of course, Francesco Cerrone takes the oppositional stance. Their exchanges are heated. Two honest men, both convinced, more often than not, that each is right. And the ruckus they raise is deafening. Donato is very comfortable with speaking off the cuff, resulting from his theater days and his period of healing others, when people listened and did what he said. But deep inside, he agrees that moving to Israel is God's will. He shakes his head. Maybe it's time to hand the reins over to someone else.

A man riding a bicycle once instructed him to eat "the product of the cow" and confirms that he is the progeny of the Levites. In Foggia, milk is often used as a medication. It works well. And as for the Levites, they are linked to the priests. So the answer is clear enough. Like the Levites, whose name he has adopted, he must continue in his role as a leader, whereas the healing products of the cow indicate that his strength will most surely return. Immediately he forgets about the idea of choosing an heir for the role of leader.

There's no shortage of concerns, frustration abounds, and no one can shake off their minds that for the men to become Jewish, they must undergo circumcision.

In this far-flung region, the rumbling of anti-Semitism is still weak. When a mafia representative rolls up one day to demand that Donato pay a fine for gathering people together without a permit, the entire community bursts into laughter, and then begins to fume.

"Rotten *camorra!*" they rile, shaking their fists at the mafioso as a warning, "We know how to deal with you!"

Donato hushes everyone and pays, not understanding what the problem is, nor is he entirely sure that this is indeed a mafioso, and he's so fed up with the worries overwhelming him anyhow that who needs another idiot coming with demands? What makes him question whether this is really a mafioso, is that his Italian is barely comprehensible.

One day, Eliezer Tritto returns from school with a long face after being insulted for not crossing himself in prayers that morning. Even then, Donato and his community members don't see the event as racist but as ignorance over who they are now.

To Manduzio, the sparks secretly igniting through his own community are far more troubling. It is the community he has shaped, nurtured and watched over, and like a rebellious child, seeks to follow in others' steps. A conflict forever engraved in his memory revolves around Bonfito, that jovial fellow and a follower of Judaism from the outset, who for some time now has preferred to pray along with a group of people out in the fields. Although Donato will record this in his diary, thinking about how it's what the forefather Yitzhak is known for, it nevertheless divides the small community.

Harsher for Donato to watch are the endless feuds with Francesco, their original reason never having altered despite time moving ahead: the fact that Francesco is desecrating the Shabbat. But it is clear to all that the real grounds for the spats between them is the fierce competition and envy which Francesco harbors. Everything can be turned into a platform for undermining, floating conflicting theories, and voicing criticism. The atmosphere is not pleasant.

On a particularly gloomy day when the sky is one vast gray cloud, Corlone brings Donato a package. Ten books of Torah, and ten books of Tehillim, the psalms recited during prayers and on many other occasions. They are gifts from a Jewish organization: the Keren Kayemet, as it's known in Hebrew, or the Jewish National Fund, as it's called elsewhere. Hope immediately resurfaces. Only Donato is busy closely watching his community members' faces, trying to work out who had contacted this organization, which is primarily geared to easing the passage of Jews worldwide to the Land of Israel. Everyone is sure there's a simple explanation: the Chief Rabbi in Rome must have weighed the pros and cons. Could they have realized that it would be a dreadful mistake to distance your own people rather than accept them warmly?

Something about Rome's handling of their circumstances disturbs Donato. He has trouble putting his finger on it. But something is holding back, or even damaging, the strengthening of ties with the community.

Donato puts the Bibles in a safe place in his home. What criteria will be used to decide who receives them? A riot could break out! For the same reason, he's left the twenty-two Tallit shawls stored in his house. Every so often, the community breaks into a hubbub of demands for what it believes it deserves.

The passage of time doesn't bring Donato reasons to rejoice. Yes, Jewish babies are being born, expanding the initial community of converts. By contrast, some members have left the community, making their way to the Holy Land despite Donato's requests to wait until the San Nicandroan group reaches the size of a raging American river. Why American, some wonder? Sometimes Donato feels that the community's enthusiasm is cooling.

Cerrone has returned to the core group, but that *testa di ferro*, that iron-headed block, as Donato's mind labels Francesco, continues selling ice on Shabbat, dragging about his old wagon which is now coming apart at the seams. In fact, Francesco has ceased lighting the Menorah in the synagogue before Shabbat because, as he explains, he simply doesn't have the time. Rivalries among the converts proliferate.

Working to maintain the community's cohesion, Donato has become more controlling. He resolves disputes within the family through a method entirely his own. He simply orders a specific form of behavior, and has no hesitation about causing the other party to feel guilty. He is willing to continue caring for the ill but not with medications he himself makes, only with prayers and respectful observance of God's laws. No one dares challenge his instructions. But because his instructions work, for the most part, the respect he garners continues to grow.

And he continues to carry, deep inside, the same pure, solid, and authoritative faith.

More often than not, the disputes are minor but have on occasion led to rival community members leaving. Matteo Cataldo is one such example. One of the community's founding members, he took his family and left after a quarrel with Donato. And what did they argue about? An excerpt in the Gospels, from Matthew 28 and Luke 17, which they'd learned as children back in the day: "Where there is a carcass, vultures will gather." But now they knew this verse originated in Job 39. Donato interpreted "carcass" as a concept implying destiny; each of us, Donato explained, shall end where we are destined to be. But Matteo Cataldo claimed that "carcass" means each individual human, utterly contradicting Donato's view. Cataldo's understanding allowed the imagination to run wild across the range from good to evil thoughts.

"You may well be an expert when it comes to Judaism, but surely you don't presume to explain the Gospels to me?"

"That wasn't my intent, but on second thoughts, it would seem not to be such a bad idea."

"Have the two of you gone crazy?" the normally calm Emanuela shouts at the two men so as to be heard over their chatter. Turning to her husband, she has a question. "Why has the Gospel come up today? Don't we have enough to study in the Torah?"

"Quite by chance, Emanuela. We needed a point of comparison for a text that's in the Book of Job and which we both recalled while talking about the Eternal One."

"You, Donato, go and concentrate on the Holy One of Blessed Name. And you, Matteo, let my husband be – can't you see how tired he is? Or I'll send you packing with a shotgun! *Capito?*"

Yes, Matteo got it, loud and clear. Matteo stepped away, turned and left. Neither man said goodbye to the other.

Matteo and his two daughters never came back to the community.

***

Once again, Donato tries to contact Rome, hoping to advance plans for the men's circumcisions. Joy and encouragement need to be infused in the community, which was beginning to feel trampled. An end must come to these situations of strife.

The answer is a burning insult:

"You are not Jewish because, on one hand, you were not born Jews, and on the other, your conversion was never certified."

Why the change in tone? Why this demeaning backing-off? Has David Prato changed his mind?

All hell breaks loose. Donato, furious, asks every community member, even those who cannot read and write, to sign a response letter to Chief Rabbi Prato.

"If our Jewishness has not been validated that is not our fault but the fault of the Rome community which refuses to handle the matter, fearing it may lose some income while, rather, you are causing the loss of souls."

Donato's words hold nothing back.

There is no response from the Rabbinate.

But hope continues stubbornly to beat in the hearts of San Nicandro's Jews.

***

On 27 July 1939, Donato wheels himself to his late father's vineyards, wanting to check their growth. Suddenly he halts as a vision comes to him. He sees himself at the center of a massive plain. A thunderous voice is heard.

"Here is the great empire which will be victorious over Italy! From the north, unfamiliar battalions shall come!"

Donato moves closer to the leader of these charging battalions and calls out.

"Commander, save me, or I shall save you."

The commander smiles. The vision dissipates.

Donato, back in reality, ponders the stunningly clear images he's just seen.

In his diary, Donato interprets the vision: the officer is none other than the leader accepted by the angels and the God of heaven. But what is this great empire, if not the thousand-year-old Reich announced by Hitler?

Not long afterwards, France and England declare war on reckless Germany.

***

Donato sends a message to Rafael Cantoni on 4 April 1940, aiming to maintain contact with him in order not to lose ties with the Jewish community of Rome. Concetta has her doubts.

"The Chief Rabbi wrote that we aren't of the Jewish race. What sort of response do you expect from Rafael?"

"I explained to the Rabbi that even if we weren't born Jewish, we conduct ourselves according to the laws which God gave Israel. I want to remind Cantoni of the many things that God commands us and how the Creator urges us to glorify his eternal name. I don't understand their opposition. They compare us to a gang of lawless non-believing thugs. In the end, they will convert us. One day, I'll go to Rome and the wearer of official robes will not be able to dictate his laws to me!"

Emanuela pipes up. "That's a good joke! What do you mean? When you thought there were no Jews in the world other than us, you didn't need anything more than your love of Judaism and your faith. You were happy. Now that you know there are other Jews, are you about to forego the essence of our lives, our faith, our learning? It's as though I'd stop making minestrone or pasta forever because plenty of others in Italy eat only that, without being willing to acknowledge that my cooking's excellent too. Is there any wisdom in doing that?"

Everyone laughs.

And then Cerrone intervenes. "I have to tell you about an incident. Yesterday I was called to the police station again. Ever since registering my twins in the municipality, they're constantly badgering me. I was asked, 'Are you Jewish or Italian?' I was thinking, 'What kind of rubbish is this?' but something made me want to be careful. So I said that I'm an Italian who worships the one God and rests on the Sabbath as God and the Duce have told us to do. What do you think of that, Donato?"

"I think that's a smart statement, about not working on Shabbat, and that…"

A sharp glance from Emanuela silences her husband. But a moment later, the usual phrases come to the fore.

"But let me remind you that you do work on Shabbat afternoons."

"So what? Are you starting with that again? That's between God and me!"

"And a bad example to others."

"Stop it, both of you! As for the police, those questions sound very odd. I can't put my finger on why they really disturb me," Concetta says.

"Maybe they're scared of us, stupid things!" Emanuela retorts.

"Maybe they wanted more information about us? Cerrone is like a flowing tap. Can't keep a secret. They know that. Let's see what else happens. We need to keep an eye on these things."

Donato keeps his community going. Luckily, he receives frequent visions which help him overcome various obstacles.

One day, a vision shows him leading a large number of hogs. Pigs! Could anything be worse? He concludes that someone in the community is continuing to breach the Torah's commandments. He needs to be more sensitive to the community's doings. Another conflict with Cerrone seems inevitable.

Then he sees himself in a field next to his wife, planting grape vines. One plant is left, but there's no room for it. His wife hoes the wheat between the rows of vines, and the sheaves cover the vineyards. Donato is angered.

Back in reality, he understands that "planting" is the word of God, but God's word has been buried under piles of earth. In his diary, he explains: *Without love of the truth, nothing can occur, and there is no reward for one's work.*

Donato knows this. Donato is exhausted. Yet he decides to implement a powerful action, both personally and communally. He calls the community together and tells them that he wishes to send a delegation of members to Rome, led by Francesco Cerrone.

"Has Donato gone crazy?" Bonfito wonders aloud.

"No, not at all," Marochella responds. Marochella has strong instincts. "He himself can't take such a trip and he's foregoing Cerrone's position. He's both revealing his compassion toward Cerrone but clarifying to Cerrone that no matter what happens, Cerrone is dependent on Donato for all matters related to the community."

One of the women is riled. "Five men? And what, aren't we counted? Didn't we help you, support you, long before our husbands joined in? Are you forbidding us from going to Rome without even consulting us?"

"It's no place for women. It's a long, complex, and exhausting trip."

"Donato? What's this I hear? All this nonsense about women? What would you men do without us, who raise your kids as Jews and pass the laws of our religion down to them?"

"Concetta, I'm begging you, don't add fuel to the fire. I would have asked you to join them but these odd answers we've been getting from Rome make me wary of the community there. That's what my senses are telling me…"

His senses, and his belief that women should not be in protests.

Despite their very just claims.

Concetta, Emanuela, Angela, Alina, and even Rachel are not going to be taken for a ride. In silent comradeship, they dig their heels in, which doesn't cease in causing the San Nicandro men discomfort.

But then an unexpected event flips all their plans.

That year, 1941, in Rodi, a distance of some forty kilometers from San Nicandro or, we might say, on another planet, a young and so far unpretentious lass begins to become well known as a result of effective treatments she provides to a certain group of patients. Her reputation quickly spreads throughout the region. She becomes known as a saint who never disappoints.

Wanting to establish her fame, those around her beseech her to bear prayers and perform a miracle that will touch everyone. She accepts the idea. Sometime later, she announces that she will die in the coming spring, and that her death will mark the end of the war in Italy. She gives a precise date for her demise, which will be the first night of peace, since she will cease to exist at night. In line with a very ancient custom of that region, she asks that families remember to leave their doors open that night because she intends to pass through each home, leave a blessing behind, and take some food for the long journey.

This information races from Rodi to Foggia and quickly spreads everywhere else. The people are already taking up their positions beneath Rosa's windows to ensure that they are as close to her as possible when she joins our Lord Jesus and our Lady the Virgin. Numerous police officers from Foggia travel to Rodi on the night of her announced death. Along the way they see all the homes abandoned, their doors open, as though caused by some supernatural force. What negligence! It's wartime, dammit! Local robbers must be having a field day! Moreover, no one has heard about any declaration of peace. In San Nicandro, doorways are also open, except those of the Jews.

Emanuela questions her husband. "Don't get angry, but I want to ask you something. You've already said that the other religions don't hamper our Jewishness. If so, why shouldn't we open our doors too? That woman does nothing but good and all in all, she's a saint."

"What do you really think she is? Enough, my love. No more silly talk and leave the door shut."

"But come and look, even some of our people have their doors open."

"That's exactly what I don't want to see! Take a walk around the village and tell me which of our people are behaving like superstitious folk."

Emanuela's eyes look to the heavens but she says nothing…and goes out.

A tightly-packed throng is being watched by police regiments. From all corners of the country people come to Rodi, among them entire families seeking benefit from the pre-announced miracle. Shots ring out from pistols and rifles following suspicious sounds or dangerous millings of the crowd. Or are they shooting into the air to declare the end of the war? Slowly the number of shots lessens. As night falls, a nervous silence spreads through the area. Children fall asleep on parents' laps; parents gaze heavenward in expectation. Everyone is praying for Rosa and an easy death so that hers may save them from terrible death and illness.

In the morning, Rosa is beaming with vitality, as though she's just become engaged to a fiancé. Nothing has happened. The food prepared for the event starts to get stale. Doors are still open but the crowd is miserable. All hope is lost.

Some, a small chunk of the people, chuckle at the whole affair.

Some are fuming. Rosa should never have played with their faith.

And then police stride into Rosa's home, arrest her, and incarcerate her in Aversa, near Naples – some three hundred kilometers away.

When the community gathers for prayers, Donato doesn't miss the opportunity to relate to their retrogression. "We, as Jews, have long since stopped believing in magic. It's excellent that none of us opened our doors yesterday. They say there were thefts and plenty of damage…"

Some congregants look down at the floor. Others bury their noses in their Siddurs, their prayer book.

"Now, back to our plans," Donato adds.

He isn't sorry that the ridiculous event took place. It's served to fortify his adherents' faith in God.

***

Without any warning to the Rabbinate in Rome, the delegation readies for its trip. They've got some four hundred kilometers to cover, and meager funds in their pockets to cover their needs. The adventure could be lengthy. But don't they say that faith can shift mountains?

Francesco Cerrone, Bruno Palmiero, Peppino Augelli, Leonardo Tardio and Giuseppe Santelmo are loaded with food. They're accompanied for part of the way by other community members, and then continue on their own to Foggia.

The long trip over four days requires plenty of patience with the various inconveniences. Everywhere they go, people seem deeply troubled, and the atmosphere is somber.

Eventually, the name of the German rabble rouser who was released from prison a few years earlier reaches San Nicandro, too, along with the news that he's already taken control of the government in Berlin. He released criminal offenders doing jail time and recruited them into groups donning uniforms that impart doom and death.

What has this to do with Italy? What endangers this country? The Duce is an ace at manipulation. Yes, he's coerced politics into a single party and is basking in his power, but he's not a creature of prey. Our villagers have just learned that Mussolini's mistress is Jewish! So what's there to fear? This war doesn't really hold any interest for them. And to their joy, an array of good events awaits them: two rides on a bus, a makeshift meal in the home of a farmer they met along the way, a night of better sleep at a cheap inn where Peppino has the innkeepers scratching their heads when he offers to help them wash the dishes.

"Is that because you can't pay?" They are understandably worried.

"Of course we can. Why do you ask?"

Cerrone is making sure everything goes according to plan. The men pray together every day and stay awake in shifts to ensure that their possessions aren't stolen at night.

Arriving in Rome, they make their way to Livio, Concetta's nephew, who wouldn't have dared refuse his aunt's request to host the five crazy men, who were seeking to meet Rome's Chief Rabbi without setting an appointment in advance.

His home isn't large to start with; now it's quite crowded. What he notices is that the men either pray or yell at each other, they either eat or argue, they all read the same book, and they tell him that the sea split into two, and that Jericho fell to the sound of trumpets. He's thinking of going to some other friend and leaving them alone in his house, but their peculiar behavior is so charming that he can't tear himself away.

On the morning of the great day, he helps them dress in the clothes that the wives had ironed stiff as boards but which are now as crushed as rags. He accompanies them to Rome's ancient Great Synagogue on the banks of the Tiber River in what used to be the old ghetto. The dome of the Saint-Pierre Basilica and that of Rome's ancient synagogue seem to gaze nonchalantly at each other. The San Nicandroans are wonderstruck. What a luxurious structure, what impressive surroundings! Benches, not that anyone has time to sit, and shops the size of castles, and people wandering about...

"I'll be back for you in two hours," Livio says before leaving them to their affairs. He's already spotted a small inn offering delicious pork products. That, he thinks, is a good place to wait.

The San Nicandro men, simultaneously nervous yet decisive, go into the synagogue. They have enough time to open their eyes and mouths in astonishment before a very elegantly dressed man approaches them. Hearing what they have to say, it's his turn to be astonished.

"We're not from here, that's to say, no, we're Jews, but we're not from these parts..."

"Have you come to visit Rome? It's not a good time at all. Nor is it possible just to stroll into the Tempiore Maggiore," he says, calling the place of worship by its Italian title.

"Visiting Rome? Oh, no. We have no time to visit Rome. We have left our work in the fields and vineyards, and handling our cattle, and looking after our womenfolk and children, for a reason," the men chuckle, glancing at each other as they simultaneously have the same thought: this man must have been born with a silver spoon in his mouth

"Could you tell the Chief Rabbi that we're here? We're happy to wait patiently. We're in no rush."

"Do you have a meeting set up with him?"

"Oh no. We wanted to surprise him!"

The synagogue's stunned beadle asks them to wait in the corridor and goes up the stairs to the next floor. He passes the secretary's office, the Chief Rabbi's assistant's office, and enters the Chief Rabbi's rooms.

"Five villagers who claim to know you entered the Tempiore and walked all the way up to the dais. They say they've come specially from a place called San Nicandro."

"Five of them? From San Nicandro? You'll have to tell them, very gently, that I can't see them. They're a little odd, but respectable. Don't give them any hope."

The Chief Rabbi's tone is unequivocal but he nonetheless admires what they've done. They've come such a long way! What courage, what faith!

Nonetheless, he can't receive them. He has no alternative.

Confused, the beadle returns to them and conveys the message. The villagers are angry and voice their protestations. They commandeer several benches, as though each is laying claim to his own territory, and unload their tightly-packed bags, which reveal a mix of items.

"Gentlemen, getting angry won't help. You came without requesting a meeting with the honorable Chief Rabbi Zoller. How could you presume that he would receive you? He has…"

"What did you call him?" Francesco interrupts.

"Zoller. Chief Rabbi Zoller. What, aren't you even familiar with his name?"

"We came to see Chief Rabbi Prato, and none other."

"He's no longer Chief Rabbi. He was forced to go into hiding because he encouraged the Jews to return to the land of our forefathers, to the Land of Israel. He helped them as much as he could but as a result, began receiving serious threats to his life and his family. Eventually he joined the Jews who left, benefitting from his own advice. The Rabbi of Trieste, Israel Zoller, has taken his place."

"And who is this Zoller?"

"Do you think someone who has no knowledge of us can scare us?"

"Right, so show us how to reach him. He'll be so proud to meet us."

"Proud and pleased!"

The beadle Issaco sees that these odd but likeable men have no intention of leaving the Tempiore without obtaining more information. He decides to take them to one of the study rooms and tell them about the extraordinary life of Rabbi Israel Zoller. This move means that regular worshippers won't be taken aback by the sight of these villagers who look like they belong to a long-ago era. Jews coming to pray will just think that a study group is seated there.

"Gentlemen, before electing a person to a role as lofty as the Chief Rabbi of Rome, everything needs to be known about him. I was tasked, during a time of upheaval in our community's history, to summarize the life of Israel Zoller for the voters. I am well acquainted with his life, which is rich and unique, having dedicated myself to discovering as much as possible. If I bore you, let me know."

"Continue, sir. Our lives as Jews depend upon him so we must get to know him."

"Israel Zoller was born in Brody, in Ukraine, in 1881. His father owned a silk products factory in Lodz, and his mother comes from a long line of rabbis. He is the youngest of five siblings. His sister loves poetry. The siblings speak several languages and are highly knowledgeable.

"Chief Rabbi Zoller told us how devotedly his mother cared for him, especially when it came to education. When Mrs. Zoller's husband passed away, she dedicated herself to one aspiration: enabling her son to study for the Rabbinate. But, so the Chief Rabbi disclosed to us in all innocence, even though he too wanted to become a rabbi, he felt a deep emptiness inside. He prayed to God to fill it.

"And this is what he said. 'I imagined a voice from the distance calling me. A kind of infinity arrived. I heard it calling me and it was the name that cannot be mentioned; the very essence of the Divine.' Israel Zoller devoted hours to studying Midrash. More than anything else, he began longing for the figure of the Messiah, whose imminent arrival was declared by the prophets.

"From there, he was swept up into reading the Gospels while simultaneously studying our Jewish texts. He wished to compare the Torah and the Gospels. I can't say that this was looked on favorably by others. Far from it!"

"What is Midrash?"

Issaco was taken by surprise. Who are these people, who can rattle off the Ten Commandments and countless other passages of Torah, yet are unaware of the vast depths of Jewish studies contained in the Midrash, and aren't even ashamed at not knowing what the Midrash is?

"That's encouraging!" Cerrone exclaimed.

Palmiero raises an eyebrow. "What's encouraging?"

"That in the end, he isn't so different to us, this Chief Rabbi. He'll understand us clearly, which will make our work so much easier."

"And what did you actually want to ask of him?"

"Are you willing, Mr. Issaco, to continue the story. We'll explain everything later."

Issaco smiles at their fervor. "In 1904, Israel Zoller left his family and never saw them again. It's clear why, so I won't expand on it."

No. Not at all. It absolutely isn't clear to them. But not a word was uttered. This Chief Rabbi had their full attention. They felt sure that his broad horizons would bring him around to supporting them. In any event, they had no intention of leaving without first meeting him.

"He continued his rabbinical studies in Toscana and finally, nine years later, was appointed as Vice to the Rabbi of Trieste, where he went to live with his wife, her mother from Lvov, and their daughter, Dora."

"Vice? That's a new idea. Is that less than a rabbi?"

"Hush already, keep your mouth shut, Palmiero!"

"As far as our Chief Rabbi was concerned, the role in Trieste filled his expectations. It was in the Austro-Hungarian region where German was spoken. At least, that was true until Trieste was annexed to Italy, as you know, in 1918."

No, they had no idea, but they don't say a word.

"Israel Zoller became increasingly close to the Young

Zionists movement. He helped them find places on boats sailing to the shores of the Promised Land. He used to say, 'I am certain that this movement will grow into the center of spiritual and cultural life in Jerusalem. Jerusalem will be a world-influencing center, greater than the Hellenist cosmopolitan, a beacon of justice, as well as a beacon connecting to heaven. Do you understand?"

Nothing. They don't understand a thing, but they nod in unison.

"Following the terrible loss of his first wife, he immersed himself in study of Torah, and work. In 1920 he married again, to Emma Majonica, who bore him a daughter, Miriam. All four family members are now here, in Rome. They are a very modest, tightly connected family."

"You know so much about his personal life! It's as though you're family!"

"Almost. The wife of a rabbi is as important as the Rabbi, for different reasons, of course. A man can never be appointed to this position if his wife hasn't also been spoken with at length."

"That's true with us too. We won't marry without first gathering information about the prospective bride, and finding out whatever we can. That's customary. If you find yourself with a terrible woman, life can become a lava-spewing volcano!"

That makes Issaco smile. Their honesty and straightforwardness touch him. They are uncompromising when it comes to their faith. He is also waiting to learn more. Later, once he's earned their trust.

"Most people here deeply respect him. The only people who have reservations are those who don't like his lectures about Jesus. The Chief Rabbi feels there is no contradiction in learning Torah and learning the Gospels. But not many share his view. I caution him to remain discreet about the matter, but he doesn't seem to understand, saying that his remarks are directed at brotherhood and peace between peoples. Indeed, his every word is worth its weight in gold. No one yawns when he talks. No one is bored. His talks are far too fascinating. He is clever, highly intelligent, and extremely goodhearted."

"Is he suitable?"

"Pardon?"

"Matteo means to ask if you admire him as the Chief Rabbi."

"Yes, I understood that. I certainly am pleased to work with such a unique person. It is a great privilege."

"Well, good, then. So this Chief Rabbi is suitable to us too. Please go and tell him that his story deeply touches us, and that his heart must be gold, and that perhaps we have more in common with him than some might think."

Taken aback, Isacco takes a moment to respond. "Impossible. I'm so sorry. We will need to say our goodbyes today. Make an appointment with the secretariat. I promise you – that's the only way to receive an audience with him."

Furious, the San Nicandroans eventually go. Instead of departing with warm farewells, they depart coldly, which is rare among them.

Outside, Cerrone blows up. "Who are we, in their opinion? Why do they, with their pale skin like lepers, think they're so special? We'll show them who's more Jewish, in the name of..."

"Calm down, Francesco," Giuseppe says quietly but

firmly. "Have we come here to rouse a scandal?"

Peppino huffs. "No, we haven't. That's not how we'll get baptized."

"Circumcision isn't baptism, idiot!"

But Cerrone's still letting off steam. "Let's get our things together and leave. We're not beggars. For years we've done everything we could to be liked by them. Look around you: Where are the Jews? Shouldn't a synagogue be full, as it is back home? Shouldn't they have received us with open arms? Does the Holy Torah not command us to allocate space for the stranger in our midst? Even if we're foreigners in their opinion, they deserve reproach. Let's go home, friends. Our leader is God of Blessed Name, and any rabbi can only be second to God. Let's renew our learning, fix up our synagogue, and as for circumcision, we'll find a doctor to do it. I'll say the prayers while Donato deals with the ceremony. We'll look for information and get the administrative details organized."

Burdened by their bitterness, the four hundred kilometers back are far tougher to travel than the same number to Rome.

As soon as they're home, they receive a letter from Rafael Cantoni who leaves them amazed when he reminds them of their friendship. He doesn't mention their conversion but does say he will send them three young Jews from Florence, the Servi brothers, and Ben-Porat, who wish to join the army and fight. What army? Where? Is Italy fighting? San Nicandroans live parallel to the rest of the world. But Cantoni's faith, and his recommendation of the young Jewish lads, bring unexpected relief to Manduzio's hurting heart.

"He's acknowledging that we exist. He's examining us, and checking that we know how to receive guests the Jewish way. We'll reassure him."

Several days later, three gangly youth turn up in the village. Rucksacks on their backs, their faces show how surprised they are at being sent to this end-of-the-world place in Italy. If they'd been sent to a training camp, they wouldn't have asked a thing, but here, where the villagers are busier with their black goats than with what's happening in the world, they're left scratching their heads. They were told there's a Jewish community here: where is it, then?

They don't ask too many questions.

The sound of metal wheels squealing against the stone path reminds them that they're about to meet a unique character, and that they were instructed to listen to him and his flock. Behind the wheelchair marches a motley lot of men wearing berets and… are they dreaming? Some are wearing a headcover that resembles a *kippah*, a skullcap!

They are accompanied by smiling, curious women.

And suddenly they're surrounded by greetings in Hebrew. The words are familiar, friendly. They are received as members of a Jewish community would be. After eating and drinking, they happily answer questions leveled at them from all sides.

The matter of the war barely gets mentioned around the table.

The young fellows avoid the topic as though it's a superstition. Moreover, they want to know everything about this very special community, about the warmth that these people show as they fill the young men's bags with food before they let them leave the next day for Bari accompanied by a young San Nicandroan. Friendships are formed within those few hours, and promises exchanged.

Donato is pleased. The future soldiers left with satisfied grins on their faces. They'll report to Rafael about the San Nicandro community's value and nature. But against whom, actually, are they setting out to fight?

**

Routine is restored in San Nicandro. The community, and not just its five delegates, still cannot grasp the meaning of the Rome Jewish community's stance. San Nicandro's community is embittered; it fumed and threatened. Exactly what it threatened and against whom, no one quite knows. But the villagers in general are quick to rebel. The Jews of San Nicandro applaud when, at last, Donato announces his decision to insist on his demand that the men are circumcised and that all community members be confirmed as Jews.

The group is well entrenched in its faith and no one is absent at ceremonies. Conflicts frequently flare among the new proselytes about whether it is better to join the younger members who already moved to the Promised Land, or to stay and expand the community here. Several do opt for leaving the village. Others choose to stay for a while longer.

Additionally, the war is disrupting correspondence and complicating every dialogue. No one quite comprehends how they were allies with Hitler in the past, yet now are fighting him. And anyhow, is that even correct? Donato, who occasionally reads the newspaper, claims that it is the truth.

He tells them that matters are even worse than they can imagine. It seems that some kind of civil war is going on in Italy. Since the ceasefire between Italy and the Allied Forces, the Italians must choose: do they support King Vittorio Emmanuele the Third who fled to the southern peninsula, or do they support the Duce, currently holding power? In other words, will they become part of the underground, or the fascist regime?

There, from the heights of their rocky location, San Nicandroans see none of the violence tearing their country to shreds.

For some time now, since 1943, the Germans and Italians are fighting each other. As they customarily do, the Germans conduct extremely bloody acts of revenge lacking any shred of humanity against the Italians, as they are also doing against France and any region they've taken over. The country is suffering. Crime has become the norm, with criminals getting wealthier.

Not much of this war is seen in San Nicandro, Donato ponders. Nothing happens here. Happily, it will all be over soon. But meanwhile the young generation is being murdered for the sake of the homeland, or justice, or some other fraudulent claim.

***

A magical moment is about to occur in the life of the San Nicandroan community, an unforgettable moment, a wonderful blue and white hued moment.

On 31 October 1943, when everyone's busy with their routines, the villagers hear an unidentifiable thundering which quickly grows louder.

Suddenly, from the direction of Foggia, a convoy of jeeps comes into view. In the center, one item stands out. It enthralls the villagers! Every jeep bears a flag on its hood. The flag comprises two blue stripes and a Magen David in the center. The flag of the Land of Israel! The flag of the Jews in the Holy Land!

The villagers' stunned faces look for a moment like those of their cows. Only Concetta and Emanuela, after a brief exchange of glances, dash into their homes and seconds later return, standing outside, waving the same flags. They run toward the jeeps, laughing, stepping close to the vehicles which have no choice but to slow down and then stop.

Now it's the soldiers' turn to be amazed. Within seconds, the dusty village plaza becomes a Tower of Babel: Italian, and the San Nicandroan dialect, French, Hebrew, Polish, English, and even German! But no one's surprised at that.

The soldiers are young and smile a lot. They turn to this bunch of people gathered around someone who appears to be a kind of leader, who is physically disabled, and from whose eyes tears of joy stream down past his broad smile. Honoring this unique situation, the man leans heavily on a walking stick and with tremendous effort, stands. Complete silence salutes his action.

No one in San Nicandro knows of the Jewish Brigade, primarily comprised of volunteers recruited in the Land of Israel but currently controlled by the British Mandate.

No one in San Nicandro is aware of the heroic actions of a smattering of these Jewish fighters who have excelled in countless battles under the direction of their admired leader, General Koenig.

Where have they come from? Where are they headed? What's happening? Questions fly in every direction.

There in San Nicandro's dusty street, the soldiers await their commander because they can't respond without his authorization. He arrives and presents himself: Pinhas Lapid. The San Nicandroans do the same, and first among them, Donato: "I am responsible for this community. I am Avraham Donato Levi. Welcome, Captain. Here are David and Samuel, and Sarah, and this is Emanuela, my wife. These are Yaakov, Yossef and Rivka, and Rachel, my elder daughter."

The soldiers can hardly believe their ears. These Italian villagers, cut off from the world, have names like those of the soldiers' own parents, and bless them the way their parents do, by placing a hand on their head. And the women, all Jewish, hurry to serve food, piling the soldiers' plates high, encouraging them to eat and regain their strength.

"The food is kosher, don't worry," they nod and smile warmly. "Eat, children," they call the young men, "Eat up!"

The brigade is left speechless when Donato, pausing repeatedly as he speaks, explains the community's history to the young men. Captain Lapid, a man of culture and knowledge, easily identifies the Jewish sources on which these villagers have founded their community.

Donato never ceases referring to God's unity, and the unique connection between God and mankind, and how each community member feels this connection in the depths of their soul. The world is being destroyed yet right at this moment, an encompassing link of love, Godliness, and human mutuality is being cemented.

The villagers want to give the brigade's young Jews a gift.

The women wrap up kosher salamis, as well as peaches and loquats. Some of the shy young lasses hand some of the young men ribbons on which they've embroidered the Magen David, and even cloth napkins in blue and white, as mementos.

The brigade's men, for their part, offer chocolate, chewing gum, crackers, pens, and all kinds of bits and pieces. The village children play with the balloons they received from the soldiers, blowing them up or filling them with water to toss out as slingshots. They're too young to know they aren't really balloons but contraceptives. Sometimes the adults forget to explain some aspects of life to the children.

Captain Lapid decides that the brigade will sleep over in San Nicandro that night. "We'll go at first light tomorrow. Tonight, though, we'll celebrate. Men, take this break to assist anyone needing help in bringing a carriage back to the shed, or transporting barrels."

The young men are gung-ho. They kiss the mezuzahs they see carved into the doorposts before entering the San Nicandroans' homes. Today, San Nicandro is part of that ancient kingdom of Israel.

It is the most beautiful night anyone there has experienced for a long time. The young villagers mingle with the soldiers. Everyone's seated around a crackling bonfire, chatting, asking questions, talking about the soldiers in the Holy Land, and whether San Nicandroans would be allowed to fight for the Land of Israel. "Yes, yes, of course! But life there is pretty tough."

"And you think this place is paradise? We'll come, of course we'll come!"

The evening closes with prayers of gratitude to God. The words are different, the melody is different, but nonetheless a harmonious song rises from all present to the Holy One of Blessed Name.

Then the young people scatter. Captain Lapid updates Donato about the war. Lapid realizes that here in this village, there is no real concept of what the war is causing, nor are they updated about Nazi horrors.

"Everywhere around the world, there are scientists who protect racism through false theories based on biology. But these are cruel and dangerous falsehoods which represent Jews as sub-humans who must be exterminated. In Italy, the Italians are forbidden from marrying Jews. Elsewhere the situation is similar: locals are forbidden from marrying Jews. Interlandi was jumping up and down screaming about this, supporting it tirelessly. And not just him, unfortunately."

"Interlandi? Who is that?"

"A reporter, an extreme anti-Semite, a rabid follower of Nazism. He's been active since 1923, if not beforehand. Imagine hating Jews to such a degree that Mussolini himself is the man to soften his venomous comments!"

"But why should anyone hate Jews?"

"Well, see, I'm keeping this article to show to my family and friends, in our kibbutz."

Pinhas pulls out a piece of newspaper showing an article titled "Protecting the Race" by Interlandi, and begins reading.

"It is time for the Italians to openly declare themselves racist. The entire project shaping the current regime in Italy is fundamentally rooted in racism. In the leader's speech, highly frequent references are made to racial concepts. Racism in

Italy must be approached from a purely biological standpoint, without any philosophical or religions connotations."

"But that's ridiculous. And we're here to prove just that. What's the difference between that idiot and us, other than our religion? That's the only thing being attacked. Why involve biology?"

"As a way of avoiding pangs of conscience. Even dictators look for reasonable lines of thinking to justify mass murder. Later they'll present these reasons as justification for their actions."

Donato doesn't understand it at all. Exterminate? Destroy? But why? Sub-human: what can that even mean?

"Did they never read the Torah, these Nazis?" Donato is incredulous.

"No, they didn't. But they defiled it, burned it, urinated on it."

"That's... incomprehensible! Impossible!"

Lapid thinks he may need to be more cautious. Donato is not a young man, and only God knows how greater details of the war might affect him. Donato's face has become very pale, his breathing labored. Nonetheless, he insists that Lapid continue.

So Lapid describes the concentration camps, the ghettos, the deportations, the crushed families, how Jewish women are forced into brothels for Nazi soldiers, and how crematoria chimneys pump out stench and smoke around the clock.

Donato's head has fallen into his hand. He cries openly.

"There's a medicine that allows fleeing from this horror, my friend."

Donato is heartbroken. "Medicine? How is it that here in San Nicandro we saw nothing? Knew nothing?"

"The medicine," Lapid adds softly, "is called Zionism. The land that God gave to his people, which the Israelites lived in until conquered by the Assyrians around 720 BCE, needs to be restored as the Jewish national home, providing us with freedom and the rejuvenation of our homeland, Israel. At last we could be the nation that settles in its own land, after centuries of devastation, pogroms, the Dreyfus trial, following in the footsteps of modern Zionism's proponents in the form of Binyamin Zev Herzl and his Zionist Congress!"

Dreyfus Trial? Herzl? The young soldiers will need to invest great effort in educating the San Nicandro Jewish community. But the community realizes that being involved and being part of the Jewish nation carries significant responsibility. They are an integral part of this people, a fact which was clarified on this blessed evening.

After the soldiers packed up and rolled out of the village, the community felt stimulated, more consolidated, more Jewish than ever before. They had exchanged addresses with the soldiers. Young San Nicandroans planning to go to the Land of Israel now had contacts once their feet would land on Hebrew shores. Several girls insisted on going as soon as possible to the land of their forefathers. Yes, the land of their people. Perhaps the parents would have trouble trying to prove to others the fact of their Jewishness but they, having been born already Jewish, and thrilled about it, would have no trouble, right? The Holy Land awaits them!

In the synagogue, or at the doorway to Donato's home, they studied Torah more intently and the numbers attending his classes grew.

"We'll prove that Jews can't be eradicated from the face of the earth. The Holy One of Blessed Name does not want that!" Donato said aloud, but admonished himself in his thoughts: *I have sinned in my faith in God. Did not God promise the forefather Avraham that he would make him into the father of a great nation numbering as many as the stars in the sky? And yet I was certain that no Jews existed in the world for thousands of years! I must learn with greater focus, advance my understanding more deeply, collect answers. And find a way to obligate the Chief Rabbi to assist us. His silence over these past few years is increasingly wearing me down,* Donato concludes, nodding to himself.

***

When fate decides to smile down on whoever has been chosen, it's like the sun rising on a wonderful spring day.

In 1905, a boy, Enzo, was born to a highly affluent Jewish family in Rome. Enzo Sereni's father, as the personal physician to King Vittorio Emmanuele the Third, enjoyed preferential status. Nonetheless, and despite the Sereni family being well entrenched in Italian society, Enzo was drawn to socialistic and Zionistic ideas from a young age, all the more so as points of comparison to the insufferable fascism driven by Mussolini. Enzo works energetically to support the return to Zion. He does not belittle the comfortable life that he and his childhood friends, or fellow students at university, are privileged to enjoy, but is nonetheless drawn into the swelling wave of Jews promoting the concept of resurrecting a state of Israel. Enzo has one single dream: to emigrate.

Enzo's father is of the view that he should earn his degree before making a move, but in actuality only manages to reach a compromise: Enzo will register for university, but will be allowed to leave after that. Arguments, raised voices – nothing can dissuade Enzo. But perhaps the father, deep inside, actually and quietly agrees with his son's claims. Still, it's his parental duty to insist: "You need a reliable source of livelihood!"

No problem. Enzo registers at the Rome University. Despite his commitments toward various socialist organizations, he lives like a fortunate, blessed young resident of Rome.

But the instant he receives his Doctorate of Philosophy, without a moment's hesitation, young Sereni boards a ship in 1927 and sets sail for the Holy Land, known in those days as the British Mandate.

The future Jewish nation penetrates his heart and soul. To him, the country is simply beauty that has been neglected and requires some touching up. King David's tomb is a filthy mess, as are the gravesites of so many Jewish sages. This Jewish land is thirsty, shows signs of age-old abandonment, and vast swathes of it are devoid of people. It is dotted by swamps. It lacks roads. There doesn't seem to be a point of hope on the horizon. But this is a place that longs to be lived in; this is a place where socialism can be planted. Didn't the pioneers operate similarly, driven by fierce idealism, leaving countries that did all they could to spew them out, and returning to the land of their forefathers? Religious or atheistic, engineers became farmers, musicians grew tomatoes, everyone feeling uplifted by their decision to leave their professions, till the soil, and build up the country despite the obstacles, complexities and constant struggle to survive.

From 1930, and for the next four years, Enzo Sereni travels the USA, aiming to establish avenues of emigration to the Land of Israel. Despite the danger, he joins the Pioneer Movement in Nazi Germany whose objective was to assist families wanting to flee the horror that Germany is becoming.

Enzo closely tracks fascist developments in order to fight against them. He travels from Egypt to Iraq, establishing underground emigration networks. He is arrested by the British who claim he carries false passports. That shocks Sereni: how could they punish him for assisting populations in danger of extermination? He begins a hunger strike. The British release him some time later, and he resumes his fight against fascism.

Enzo joins the Jewish Labor Organization, realizing his ideals by working in the citrus groves around the city of Rehovot. Simultaneously, he is among the founders of Kibbutz Givat Brenner. As a sworn pacifist, he obstinately refuses to carry weapons when on kibbutz guard duty, even during the widespread riots of 1936.

That same Enzo Sereni joins a paratroopers' course in Bari in 1944. He is less than two hundred kilometers from Donato's community. On one of his free evenings, he hears about "new Jews" in San Nicandro. He wants to know more: the next day he sets out for the village.

His arrival without prior warning brings great joy to the town's residents. Enzo presents himself. Corlone, proud of his role as the only postman, dashes off to phone the Bari post office and verify Enzo's credentials, since Donato had recently instructed him, in light of this new war, not to receive strangers with open arms. Not wanting to make the community worry, he does his job gladly.

Corlone returns, beaming.

Enzo explains that he helps Jews in difficult circumstances but the community here doesn't seem to fill that description: they seem happy, and calm. He talks about life in the Holy Land, how working the land is moving it from arid to green, blossoming and satisfying to behold. That is the stunning contrast between the land worked by the Jews, and the dry desolation of the land in the Hashemite Kingdom on the other side of the Jordan River. He describes the joy which the pioneers bring into their lives, the nights of dancing the hora around the bonfire, the young generation which insists on speaking only Hebrew, and how they go out to the fields in song. The villagers are charged by Enzo's descriptions.

Enzo then asks Donato to describe how this community, which seems so committed and steadfast, came about. The further Donato gets into the story, Enzo discovers, the more Enzo admires this man, who may be physically limited, but whose vision is unlimited – he has shaped the community, led it, managed it, and never ceased throughout to teach it and guide it.

"Manduzio, you are a true prophet who has been blessed by divine inspiration. Your outlook is more just and correct than that of any Jew born into a Torah-guided life!"

Donato does not reveal his sheer joy at being recognized at last, not only on the personal level, but chiefly from the perspective of his own, and his fellow community members' Jewishness. This is Donato Manduzio's great day as the spiritual leader of an expanding community which thirsts to join their fellow Jews scattered across the Diaspora. On hearing about Enzo Sereni's activities, the community literally bubbles and fizzes with excitement and once again splits between those wanting to emigrate to the Holy Land, and those who prefer to stay. Tones of voice become stronger. Donato intervenes.

"We'll stay for now, because we haven't completed our work. The Lord of the Universe did not plant a seedling in our land only for us to abandon it too quickly. We must continue with our work, open our community to other new converts and receive authorization to have circumcisions performed. Only then can we plan our emigration."

The two days that Enzo Sereni spends in the company of the San Nicandroans leaves a lasting impression on their minds. The young fellow is extremely intelligent, and shows warmth and friendship. He has a big heart, is very sensitive to the plight of fellow humans and fellow Jews in particular, dedicated to helping the victims of discrimination and war. Every San Nicandroan feels at ease in his company; each feels comfortable asking questions, and Enzo never loses his patience.

Sorrow tingeing his voice, Donato describes the letters sent to various chief rabbis which remain either unanswered or do not help them resolve their needs, and especially the missives sent to the current Chief Rabbi, Zoller, of whom he'd had high expectations.

"I can promise you," Enzo says, "that as soon as my training and my mission in northern Italy is complete, I'll go to Rome myself and won't leave the Chief Rabbi's offices without him at least promising to receive you. Trust me, my brothers."

Enzo is raised aloft like a bridegroom and carried around to whoops of joy.

Enzo needs to return to Bari, where 250 partisans are waiting to continue their training which will enable them to parachute into countless locations across Europe. A mixed multitude of desperate people needs their assistance.

The village turns out in entirety to say their goodbyes, as though he was one of their own sons. They reassure each other that they will meet in the future, and share plans to reunite soon in the Land of Israel, known as the British Mandate. But most of all, they look forward to Enzo's intervention in Rome. From San Nicandro's main plaza, Enzo is accompanied as far as the villagers can allow themselves to go. Last hugs, last wishes of "See you soon!" resound.

Sadly for the community, none of Enzo's plans come to fruition.

On 15 May 1944, Enzo parachutes into northern Italy, intending to contact the underground. Unluckily, he lands in German territory, is captured by German soldiers, and sent to Dachau.

He is murdered there on 18 November 1944.

***

Following years of isolation due to an absence of information about the Jews there, it appears that the San Nicandroan community is about to be bombarded with good news.

It has been quite a while since Sereni had left, of whose death the community has yet to hear, when Corlone brings Donato an unexpected item: a letter from Jerusalem! Donato studies the envelope in detail before opening it. The word "Jerusalem" makes his pulse rush. Is it from one of the young soldiers who'd been to the village? Or a San Nicandroan who's settled there?

It couldn't possibly be Enzo, who had a long list of missions to deal with in Italy, and promised to represent them in Rome and contact Donato before returning to his kibbutz. Odd, though, that he remains silent for so long.

Donato smooths the letter out. A certain Jacques Faitlovitch advises that he will soon be visiting. Who is this man with the family name Donato finds difficult to pronounce? What is his reason for visiting San Nicandro? Who in Jerusalem could possibly have heard of this forlorn village?

A week later Donato receives answers. By chance he is not immersed in study but is carving a log of wood into the form of a Lion of Judah when he notices a man striding toward him like an angel of God. Even before the man is close, Donato notices the visitor's calm demeanor and broad smile.

"Donato Manduzio!"

The words sound more like a pronouncement than an enquiry. The two men have not exchanged a word yet both men, who share identical natures, inherently know each other well.

As their two-hour conversation comes to an end, Donato invites the man to join the community. "Of course you will stay with us over Shabbat. Would you be willing to give the community a lesson after prayers?"

"Gladly!"

The next day Jacques joins the community's Shabbat service and is deeply moved. Donato, on the podium, invites Jacques to join him. The community is anxious to hear what their visitor has to say; they're surprised when he speaks in fluent Italian.

"Friends! As you see, I am from Jerusalem. I bring you greetings from Alfonso Pacifici and your brethren in the Land of Israel."

Villagers gaze at each other with questioning eyes, then turn to Donato. He says nothing but gestures at the speaker, who continues.

"I understand that you're not familiar with the name. I'll tell you briefly who he is and why his name is important. Pacifici was born in Florence, and is Italian, like you. He currently lives not far from my home on the land which the Holy One granted us. At the start of this century, Alfonso moved mountains to spread the knowledge of Judaism in your land through culture, religion, and Zionism. Since 1934, he's been living in the Land of Israel and writes important works there. He learned that I intended to visit you and knowing about your history, asked me to bring you his warmest wishes and support. 'Ask them if they need anything from me,' he insisted."

Happy smiles are seen on the community members' faces. How wonderful that they are recognized by fellow Jews!

"Donato!" Emanuela exclaims, "If the whole world continues coming through our village, you could end up the Chief Rabbi of Rome!"

And why not? Donato wonders. His eyes sparkle.

Cerrone screws his face up in anger at Emanuela

interrupting the guest's speech. In fact, he's right: manners should come before spontaneity, no matter how warmly intended!

"Excuse us for the disruption, our dear Mr. Faitlovitch. But what lured an important person such as yourself to visit this poor, ignorant band of farmers?"

"Ignorant? That's not my impression so far. I came to say how amazed I am at your unique adventures. I came to say that you aren't the only Jews in the world, although you only learned of this recently, as our friend Donato updated me. Let me tell you a little about my life.

"I was born in Lodz, in Poland. That country has been exterminating its entire Jewish population with no end in sight. I studied Ethiopian languages from my esteemed teacher Joseph Halevi, who has traveled broadly and lectured at the École Pratiques des Hautes Études in Paris. He was the first Jew to encounter the Falashas, or as they call themselves, the Beta Israel, the House of Israel. These Jews have lived for centuries in northern Ethiopia. They are not allowed to own land, they are accused of bringing bad luck, they live in abject poverty and danger, and their only wish is to 'return to their home,' the Land of Israel.

"Their wish became a matter which I took a personal interest in because I couldn't stand the thought that any of my brethren, no matter where in the world, would endure the kind of suffering my family experienced in Poland. Some years ago, I brought an extremely talented young Ethiopian Jew by the name of Taamrat Emmanuel to Israel. He studied in Jewish organizations for seven years, including here in Italy, in Florence. Since 1930, he serves as one of King Haile Selassie's advisors.

"Obviously bringing the Beta Israel back to Israel is, especially for people like me, of tremendous importance. I can't share all our adventures with you but some have been quite dangerous, and they are always extremely difficult. What I do want to emphasize is that the Beta Israel uphold Torah commandments just like you do, that's all. They aren't at all familiar with the term 'Jewish' but view themselves as descendants of the Hebrews."

"If so, we're one hundred percent the same," Cerrone, frustrated at always being seated among the regular community and not with the 'senior' members, couldn't hold back.

"Not quite," Faitlovitch answers quietly, grinning. "The Beta Israel are dark-skinned. Very dark."

And Donato immediately interjects. "So what?"

"My friend, I love your answer. Concluding, I repeat: I find your story touching and it's touched the hearts of many. If I can help in some way, don't hesitate to contact me. I admire you and am proud of you all."

As expected, an improvised celebration infuses liveliness into the village for the two days that Faitlovitch stays. Anyone wanting a one-on-one conversation with the guest is invited to sit with him.

On the day Faitlovitch departs, he has gained dozens of devoted friends to whom he has brought the tranquility and surety that they sought; or perhaps he simply restored it.

Some days later, Donato makes a diary entry:

"...he told us wonderful tales, he was amazed when he learned of how we came about, and I told him the details... he has left us with Hebrew books, and after he departed,

sent us copies of the Hebrew-Italian dictionary. He also left four books describing people from Africa who had sent him letters."

As Donato closes the diary, a flash of enlightenment passes through his mind. He fidgets on his wheelchair, slams his palm down on the armrest, and laughs out loud, then just as suddenly behaves normally, as though uncertain of the insight he's just had.

Emanuela, who's never far away, joins him in the doorway. "What is it, Donato? Are you feeling unwell?"

"No, not at all. I just figured it out. I just realized…"

"What? What, Donato? Tell me!"

"Too late. I need to think. But I'm pleased. Firstly, I'll talk to Tritto. I need to read up on some documents. I'll ask him to get them for me as quickly as possible. That way he'll learn a lesson for causing a rift between us."

***

Costentino Tritto and his family, after reintegrating into Donato's community, are looking for opportunities to earn their fellow community members' esteem. Donato reopened the community's doors to them warmly, but the long months of dispute have caused a disconnect between the two men and left its mark. Donato knows how to hold a grudge. The two have very few verbal exchanges. They only smile at the same time when they harmonize in prayers aloud together: one is a baritone, the other a tenor. It's an uplifting pleasure to listen to them. Wanting to reinstate closer ties to his friend, Tritto convinced his cousin Ciro di Salvia to join the community. Ciro readily agrees: since his youth he'd made it clear that he would worship no one but God himself.

Perhaps because Ciro is blind, Donato receives him with more evident enthusiasm than usual. Of Ciro it could be said that he was deeply affiliated with Judaism long before he acquainted himself with its formal framework. He's among those who love God through some internal drive.

Having heard from Captain Lapid about the Talmud and rabbinic literature, Donato begins tightening his ties with Tritto, eventually requesting that the latter find Donato a Talmud on one of his trips to Foggia or Bari.

Two weeks later, Tritto is back with high fever and a neatly wrapped tome. Not wanting Donato to wait for the Talmud, Ciro brings him an abridged version. But it is too abridged for the richness of the Jewish sages' discussions to truly captivate Donato's heart. He does leaf through the book, though. The format of questions and answers, in which everything and its inverse are unraveled, proven, and pedantically confirmed, irritates Donato and upsets his equilibrium.

Captain Lapid described the Talmud as a vital stage in studying Judaism. The Talmud is like a constantly swinging pendulum of investigations, comparisons, and disputes among wise elders. But Donato is convinced that such freedom of thought, and the unusual method for working through a problem, could cause terrible outcomes. He would indeed become inflamed if he realized, by studying the Talmud, that one of its sages, the modest Rabbi Akiva, of brilliant mind, agreed that Bar Kochba was the messiah. Yet when Bar Kochba was killed, Rabbi Akiva was forced to admit a simple fact: no, he was not the messiah. Donato would fume and rail endlessly at such complex yet errone-ous proofs. He would find it a dreadful misuse of valuable time to discuss back and forth and reach no solid conclu-sion. Is the truth not in the hands of God? And God's logic cannot be grasped by mere humans.

"In the end," he said to Lapid, "the book opens up the way to cast doubt. It turns the concept of doubting into a worthwhile trait. How can any doubt be cast, though, after reading the Torah? How can time be wasted on the Talmud?"

"When you read it, Donato, you'll discover a universe of thought and knowledge. From memory, I can recite what my own teacher said about the Talmud: it requires true love of God, and of fellow humans, to study it and im-prove our understanding of Torah; it requires great, finely honed mental skills to understand the issues at hand and how their meaning is extracted, it requires deep humility, being warm toward others, being honest in business, loving justice, trusting your mentor, sharing the other's pain, to en-rich yourself through constant learning, to enjoy.."

"And where is God in all this? He gave his Torah to a nation of farmers, like us, of workers who weren't required to attend schools in order to understand and implement his commandments. I'm sure that studying God's word is suf-ficient for any Jew to fulfill his obligation to God. And you yourself told us that we are good Jews. 'True Jews,' you also called us."

"Yes, Donato. But you need to understand another point which my teacher also explained to me. In fact, everything that the sages present in the Talmud was already spoken by Moses when he conveyed the Torah to the people at Mount

Sinai. The sages held these discussions as a means of emphasizing the Torah's wonders and innovativeness, rather than to reveal new aspects from their own minds. And so they question themselves, they disagree with each other, they try to find ways to prove, or support, or explore. Their discourses and interpretations seek ways of explaining the Torah toward reaching Hashem's truth."

"Hashem?"

"Yes. It literally means 'the name' and is another of the terms used to refer to the Holy One of Blessed Name."

"I didn't find it in the Torah."

"No, that's because it isn't there in a blatant form. It developed later as a way of referring to God without using God's name in vain."

"Are you certain of that?"

Lapid chuckles. "Absolutely certain!"

"Well, never mind that. Why should I break my head to prove the existence of Hashem and his truth, when it's abundantly clear in the Torah?"

Lapid nods quietly. All things, he thought, occur in their right time, and perhaps it's still too soon to convince Donato of the Talmud's immense importance.

And luckily right then, Emanuela appears carrying a *panettone*, a traditional rich bread domed like a bell, fresh and hot from the oven, a bottle of wine, and another chair so that she could sit with them for a while.

***

Donato, having repeatedly read his abridged Talmud, does not alter his original viewpoint one iota vis-à-vis its contents. Could he, even if he wanted to? From the first time he read the Torah of Moses, he gave heart and soul to it, and that Torah has provided him with a unifying set of answers to questions he'd repeatedly pondered but had never voiced. He therefore sees no reason to delve into texts which aim to institutionalize God. He will, however, accept and adopt the reference for God that he hadn't previously known: Hashem. As for the rest, he is highly wary and unconvinced.

"I find numerous points in the Talmud which are not appropriate for the children of the one true God, our Father, since our spirit is feeble," he writes to Captain Lapid.

Worse yet, he views the Talmud as almost a betrayal of Judaism, claiming that it causes distancing from the Torah of Moses.

"After all, who drew the people into sinning if not their leaders?" he questions in his diary.

As time passes, the converts' Jewish children learn to read, write, and think independently, which leads Donato to hearing answers he does not like, and whispers that contradict him.

Wanting to set his unruly adherents straight, he describes a vision he received. "I asked God to shed light on my path of actions, and he showed me my own self in a grove overgrown with thorny bushes. I removed the wild grass and nurtured the beneficial plants. What else is necessary? Does clarity encompass deficiency? God showed me that the Talmud contains both bad and good."

And then Donato makes an announcement: he forbids reading the Talmud in the San Nicandro community! "We have far more worthy tasks to fulfill," he adds.

But some do not agree, especially the military rabbi, Ephraim Auerbach. He arrived the previous night to meet Donato, having heard from Captain Lapid of the community's existence.

Even though Lapid spoke warmly of Donato, Auerbach remains reserved toward him, nor does Donato view him too favorably. Rabbi Auerbach is well known due to his activities and research on Jewish thought and philosophy. He holds a doctorate in literature and Rabbinic studies, and prior to his 1938 emigration to the Holy Land, taught in the great Jewish centers of learning in Breslau and Rome. Therefore a person like Donato, lacking culture and of untamed beliefs, and who therefore arbitrarily boycotts the Talmud, can only bring the Rabbi to anger. He was also told of Donato's miraculous and magical healing activities back in the day.

The day following his arrival, Rabbi Auerbach joins Manduzio at his doorway before Emanuela has managed to show off her talents as a perfect hostess.

"Do you have books on magic?" the Rabbi asks firmly.

"For the Holy Torah given at Sinai not to be defiled, the Creator said: 'Be holy for I am holy.' Is that not so?"

Auerbach is indignant. "So, according to your quote, are you the son of God?"

"No. All of us who behave in accordance with the Holy Torah are God's children and his people."

"I don't believe in visions."

"You are a rabbi because you were born into the world of Torah and your father taught you your people's history. That isn't true for me. I was blind, imprisoned in evil, and didn't know the Creator and the Torah. Had God not grasped my hand, like a father guiding his child, how could I have come to know His ways?"

Rabbi Auerbach is not convinced.

Donato rejects the intellectualist perspective which in his view cheapens the community's mode of birth. Donato detects the Rabbi's anger in this dispute and therefore, in the end, it holds no interest for him. To him, it is like two bucks battling for victory and later demonstrably and pridefully turn their backs to each other.

Once Auerbach has left, Donato tells his adherents that God enlightened him about the Rabbi. He sums up that information.

"He's nothing special. Just another one doing his job. That's how it is. He's a clerk, whereas we are prophets. We have nothing to learn from him. God talks to us without mediators."

"And are you *the* Prophet, Donato Manduzio?" Cerrone slams the question down, his eyes sparking with fury.

Cerrone's twin girls, Ester and Sara, who more than all else love sitting next to Donato and hearing his beautiful stories, are never too far from their father. Angela has tasked them with preventing conflicts between Cerrone and Donato. Energetically, they tug at their father's shirt sleeve, but he's persistent.

"Would you ever renounce something you established even if it's relevance has passed? You didn't conduct an honest discussion with Auerbach as soon as you sensed he opposed your views. With that same approach, you forbid us from going to the Land of Israel now, even though it's also your own most desired wish, but you won't agree until our numbers grow all the way to Foggia, or before we're all recognized, and circumcised in Rome, even if Rome has remained silent for years. Am I mistaken, or are you still waiting for Chief Rabbi Zoller to answer your three letters these past five long years? Nor do you entertain the reasonable idea that in the Holy Land, we'll find someone to circumcise us. All of it amounts not only to a lack of logic but to sheer idiocy!"

Someone calls out "Oy!" in a concerned tone. Donato's students have worried looks on their faces. More stunningly, Donato not only remains silent but his eyes, unbelievably, are streaming tears.

This time Francesco has gone much too far! Donato knows what he's doing: he's the only one who receives messages from God, he lives the way he guides others to live, he devotes himself so wholly to his mission that events like these can churn his heart and stomach.

Cerrone is publicly denounced. The twins are still dragging their furious father away but not before the struggle between proponents and opponents of Aliyah, as emigration to the Holy Land is called, resume their battle. It is a struggle between Manduzio's supporters and his adversaries.

Once again Cerrone, Tritto, and Marochella head the group who Manduzio labels as making his life difficult. Although he continues to actively guide the community, he is exceptionally fatigued. In full view of the community, some complete their plans for Aliyah, which inflames Donato. He sees their actions as a rebellion against God. In his view, the plan to make Aliyah is none other than a refusal to accept God's plan, and everyone knows that these are times when the people of Israel must obey Hashem and stringently follow his instructions.

In his diary, Donato notes the following:

"You have always heard me say what the people of Israel must do. But know that I am not talking to you from a patronizing perspective. Although I am neither a rabbi nor a maestro, and no more than a link in a connecting chain, the Torah from Sinai shaped me and from the Torah's power, I became one of the Creator's children, as all who fulfill his Torah become. Look at me and see: I am no great disciple, but I was called to this through a miracle, just as God called Avraham our forefather. The Creator wanted a light lit, since he had never heard the words of Israel in a desolate place such as this."

That evening Donato cannot fall asleep. The rebellion churns and he fears that matters are beyond his control. If everyone leaves for the Land of Israel, who will ensure the continuation of the work that needs to be carried out here?

In pain he sits up, covers himself with a blanket, and picks up his pen. Not wanting to disturb Emanuela, he draws up a kind of memorandum by the light of a small candle. The document is intended to restore peace in the community. Of course, as he commonly does, he cannot help himself from formatting it like the Ten Commandments. He hopes it will be sufficient.

The Torah is the same as was given at Mount Sinai.

Shabbat is a holy day.

The house of prayer is paid per person and each person has their own chair. All expenses are shared equally.

The key will be deposited with Manduzio.

No one shall write letters of his own accord. All letters

will be written and sent by Manduzio and all incoming letters will be handed to him.

Marochella will read from the Torah, Cerrone will read from the Prophets, and everyone else will read and interpret the Psalms, each on his own turn.

Any interpretation will be offered in the ethos of the Prophets.

Eternal life is the reward for living life according to the Torah.

We were born for the sake of the vision, and through the vision we can implement Torah teachings. Whoever voids the vision will be banished from us and from eternal life.

And that's how everything will be well organized, thinks Manduzio, a moment before falling asleep.

**

The following day the community gathers in the synagogue. Donato appears to want the prayers to finish quickly. What kind of important announcement will he make this time? Usually he loves the prayers and recites them with great respect.

"My friends, although five years ago we waived the idea of being received by the Chief Rabbi of Rome, we must continue to make every effort with our Jewishness. We must weigh returning to Rome and convincing them that we are Jewish. I will join that trip."

Emanuela suddenly jumps up, her eyes gazing heavenward in despair. What's got into her husband? He's exhausted, he's being attacked on all sides, he takes on additional tasks, he never lets himself rest.

As for Concetta, she begins to jibe. "You're not serious, right? Do you want people to fist-fight each other over your honor? Do you feel the need to be thrown into the street like some lowly drunk? No thank you. You'll get no admiration or support from me!"

For the first time, Concetta, who has long since changed her name to Devorah, turns her back on her old-time friend and huffs off home in a cloud of vanity well known to the community.

Why does Donato seem unaffected by her departure? Devorah is a steadfast, active figure in the community. She has donated, and contributed, and given of her time and money. Beyond all that, she is a trustworthy colleague. If she severs ties with Donato, an irreparable rift will split the community.

Nonetheless, Donato does not hurry to call her back, shattering everyone's expectations.

Only the next day, he knocks on her door. He is alone. Devorah opens it but she's still furious.

"Devorah, let me in and I'll explain to you. I only need five minutes to persuade you. Perhaps less."

"And if you don't succeed?"

"It means that God's spirit has left me, and I'll stop."

"Enter."

Ten minutes later, Donato leaves smiling. That evening, Devorah appears for prayers as usual.

***

A brief letter, as polite as the previous correspondence, is sent off to Rome's Chief Rabbi, Israel Zoller, advising that the San Nicandro Jews are on their way.

This time, Donato, like an experienced strategist, chooses his delegation with greater care. This time, there will also be five of them: "Bruno Palmiero, David Spitalieri, who'll help me in my new role as a mobile invalid, and me."

"And the two others?" Emanuela and Devorah ask simultaneously.

"Tritto and Cerrone."

"What? The 'traitors?'" Emanuela almost screeches, surprised at Devorah's silence. "They've insulted you so much, they've caused you sleeplessness, they've been incessantly critical. What's got into you? You've got dozens of faithful people to choose from who love and respect you, yet you want to send two people on this arduous journey who've already harmed your health so much?"

"Your husband's right, Emanuela. When he returns you'll understand. Let him do what needs to be done."

"You… do you know something I don't? And that I as his wife am not allowed to know?"

"No, it's not like that. I know because I was doubting, so he came over to explain. You never doubted him for a second even though you were surprised by him announcing his trip. You believed in him. In any event, you'll know before any of the other villagers."

Emanuela is thrilled at her unique status of being acknowledged as the Prophet's wife and graciously stays silent.

Constantino Tritto and Francesco Cerrone are no less surprised when Donato's choice is revealed. They had worked incredibly hard to establish their own community, and their failure burns so deep that they don't even react in surprise. Each readies himself as best he can, with young David's palpable enthusiasm for his new role in the upcoming trip raising all their spirits.

This time the trip to Rome is less agonizing. The war is over. Well, in Italy, at least. The Duce is nothing but a painful memory. People along the way seem calmer, more confident. Suspicion and silence belong to a distant past. Throughout the long journey, Jews open their homes to the San Nicandroans and host them amply for meals. The San Nicandroans are surprised, and pleased.

This time, too, despite a little hesitation over playing host again, Devorah's nephew Livio waits for them at his home's entrance, pleased to greet them again, knowing that although some of the men are unfamiliar to him they will likely behave similarly to the previous delegation's members.

His home is once again turned upside down. The table is lavished with foods he hasn't encountered before. Who could imagine eating salami made from real beef? Livio didn't even know it existed. And why do they refuse to touch the excellent Piemont region acceglio cheese which he specially went to find for them, pushing it away each time they've eaten meat?

"You shall not cook the kid in its mother's milk," Donato offers by way of explanation. "This prohibition is so important that it appears three times in the Torah, my son, even though the Torah usually doesn't repeat itself!"

"Well, really! But you didn't eat a kid goat or lamb, you ate beef! And anyhow, what's this Torah?" the young man asks.

Having enjoyed a good night of rest, the five men head to Rome's Tempiore Maggiore. As on the previous occasion, Livio guides and accompanies them. In gratitude, Donato invites him to join the group.

"But I'm not Jewish!"

"How do you know?" Donato jokingly answers.

"No, no, I don't think this is my place. In any event, not this time."

"Which means that…?"

"Maybe. I really like your strange salami."

They all laugh. Livio goes off to do some shopping for these good men, so unlike him when it comes to food. On the previous occasion he bought a leg of ham in their honor and they almost fled with screams of horror. This time he seeks the kosher sign on shops before making any purchases.

In the synagogue foyer, Tritto, Cerrone, Palmiero, Manduzio, and Spitalieri quietly wait. Palmiero glances about: he finds the elegant surroundings as impressive as on the previous visit. Without hesitation, he joined Donato, not really understanding the meaning of this unexpected decision. As for Donato, he was gripped by excitement as he entered the grand synagogue. He gazes this way and that, his kippah firmly on his head, his hands on his racing heart.

Palmiero notices the beadle, that tough fellow who, five years earlier, went into great detail about the Chief Rabbi's life. His warm greetings and invitation are surprising. "Please, follow me."

The San Nicandroans rise immediately. David grips Donato's wheelchair and begins moving forward, trying to ensure that the beadle has no time to change his mind.

They climb a marble staircase. Luckily for David and Donato, the stairs are not steep at all, unlike at the Florentine castles. Then they traverse a long, well-lit corridor which ends in a cherrywood door.

"One might think we're walking right to God's throne," Cerrone mutters.

"Shush, you angry fool," Tritto nudges his friend, whispering in fear of Donato's reaction. Is this the time to get incensed again?

Whatever impression is being made on the men's minds, they feel something important is developing, something essential to the existence of the San Nicandro Jews. They can hardly believe it: their plans are advancing, and once again, Donato is the one who's rekindled everyone's hope.

The beadle Issaco knocks on the heavy door, then pushes it open without waiting to be called in. *What a rude chap!* thinks Cerrone.

Facing the door is a large oak desk looking worse for wear, and a table painted purple, surrounded by a semi-circle of chairs readied for the San Nicandroans. The chairs are upholstered in brown leather and hammered studs, and have carved legs.

Chief Rabbi Israel Zoller's face is round, his glasses sit elegantly on his nose, and on his head is a hat that covers his kippah. He walks toward them, smiling. So here he is, the leader of the Jews, who has deflected them year after year.

"Welcome, my friends. May Hashem bless you in all your endeavors. Let us all sit. Issaco, could you ask my daughter to bring us tea?"

The beadle nods, turns and leaves the office.

The San Nicandroans are speechless, all except for Donato, who feels more at ease than the others. "Your respected Chief Rabbi, we have come to meet you and beseech that you include us among the list of registered Jews in Italy. We know that being circumcised is one of the conditions of acceptance as Jews. We have come all the way to receive the permission needed for all our men to enter the covenant with God. I beg you to accept our request. Our loyalty is to God and Judaism. For fifteen years we have prayed for acceptance into the worldwide Jewish community."

"We will discuss this matter, and perhaps set a date."

Donato's four accompanying travelers remain stunned and speechless. The youngest, cap in hand, speaks up.

"What's happening here? With due respect, your honor the Chief Rabbi, our representatives were previously treated like lowly scoundrels. The Rabbinate wrote that we contain not a shred of Jewishness, and that we will never be included among the lists of Jews, and now you're inviting us to a glass of tea? I don't understand a thing."

"David!"

"It's all right, my dear Donato. Your companions are amazed, and why wouldn't they be? I haven't forgotten a thing of the past few years and certainly not the moment when I dismissed you all in a manner that does not accord with Judaism. And you, young David, cover your head. A good Jew does not expose his head before God. Hashem is everywhere, remember. But tell me, Donato – you do not seem surprised by what I have said, unlike your friends. Do you understand the reason behind my stance?"

"Very possibly, Chief Rabbi."

"Ah, here's my daughter. Come, Miriam. You can set the tray down here, thank you."

Miriam hands out cups and saucers, places plates near each, stands the teapot on a coaster, and a plate of small cakes, still warm, next to that. She smiles, greets the group with "Shalom," and leaves.

Donato notes the modest beauty of the dishes on the table. At Don Adriano's, he recalls, there'd been items that were bulky, ostentatious, too flowery, and always cracked.

The Chief Rabbi places his hat on one of the nearby chairs and smooths his kippah on his head. "I am particularly pleased to recite the blessing of renewal before we drink together."

Sheh-heh-khiyanou. Literally, 'who has given us life.' The San Nicandroans are unfamiliar with this blessing. Other than Donato, they are embarrassed.

The Chief Rabbi explains. "This blessing is one we make to show our gratitude to Hashem either in unusual or rare circumstances, or in new situations. We say it each time a festival is celebrated, since each comes once a year. We say it over the first appearance of a seasonal fruit, or a new item of clothing. I will recite it, and by responding 'Amen' you are considered as being included."

The Rabbi recites the blessing in Hebrew, the men respond with amen, and the Rabbi translates to Italian: Blessed are you, Lord our God, King of the universe, for granting us life, for sustaining us, and for enabling us to reach this time.

And with that, the San Nicandroans and the Rabbi delve into conversation.

The men hardly dare touch the cakes. The Rabbi goes first, picking up a slice of honey cake, wanting to make them feel more at ease. He takes a bite, sips some tea, wipes his hands on a serviette, and speaks.

"That year, in 1945, was one of great destruction across a large part of the world. Numerous nations lost countless numbers of their populations, and their countries were left in ruins. The Jews, who have no country to call their own and are not known as a bloodthirsty people, were exterminated on a phenomenal scale."

"Exterminated?" Tritto is skeptical. Murdered? Well, of course, wars are not void of deaths. But according to the Rabbi, the situation with the Jews is on an altogether different scope. Why eradicate a people simply because they exist, not asking anything for themselves, and abiding by the rules of the countries in which they live?

"Millions were killed in horrific ways, my friends. Six million were killed. And before that, their livelihoods and possessions were taken, and families split apart. With one bullet, they would often murder both the mother and the unborn fetus. They set up extermination camps. Unfortunately for the Rome Jewish community specifically, its head, Ugo Foa, did not encourage the Jews to leave the city in 1943 when we'd expected heavy bombing. He simply never believed anything worse than that could happen. These days there is talk of six thousand wounded, and one thousand four hundred dead, in Rome alone after three hours of bombing, and those numbers are not final."

"How is it we knew nothing of this? What a nightmare!"

"Because of the distance. You live so far from the center, and in a location that is so difficult to access, that it inherently protected you and saved you, Mr. Cerrone. You did not know that on September 8th, 1943, the Germans invaded Rome. And that was precisely the time you wanted Rome to acknowledge you as Jews! Listen to what happened right when you wanted a meeting with me.

"On the same day that the Germans entered, their officers ordered us to hand over fifty kilograms of gold by September 28th, 11 AM, and if not, one thousand Jews would be expelled. The Nazis came, looted, tortured, barely collected two million Italian liras, but did take artwork and silver items. The regular soldiers given the task of packing up our things were heard joking about how our ritual vessels, art, and jewelry would assist Germany's war efforts. And that is nothing compared to what occurred on the night between the fifteenth and sixteenth of October.

"That was the night of the greatest roundup of Jews from Rome for deportation to labor and concentration camps. Without going into the horrifying details, children were forcibly torn from their mothers' arms, half-naked people were shoved into cattle trucks at gunpoint, and terrible acts of cruelty were carried out. Sick people barely able to move were locked into rooms without windows or air. Others paid for the bullet that ended their lives."

Israel Zoller described the abysmal events in a quiet tone. He mentioned his predecessor, David Pareto, who fled to the Holy Land because of the threat of fascism, which not only saved his life but brought him the joy of returning to Zion, to the land of his forefathers. After he departed in haste, work with the Jewish community of Rome became unbearable.

Now those returning from their exile must be warmly

received, but how can their lives be made easier when they remain silent, so terrified by what they saw and experienced that no words can release them from those images? Israel Zoller is also collecting these stories of horror from those who do attempt to talk about them and shed light on them, telling the world what really happened, and trying to survive.

The San Nicandroans are as mute as fish on hearing these things, which seem to be taken straight from the halls of hell. Neither Cerrone nor Manduzio notice that they are weeping uncontrollably.

"And that, my friends, is why, when you began corresponding with the previous Chief Rabbi requesting to be registered as Jews, the synagogue's committee head was busy with just one thought: whether you are or are not Jews is not the primary issue. We would not register you as Jews despite you believing that you are, and being willing to cross Italy to prove it, because for years the lists of registered Jews were being manipulated for the sake of arrests, imprisonment, torture, robbery, and murder. Villages, cities, and entire regions currently have no Jews anymore. Entire populations were exterminated as a result of a bloodthirsty dictatorial tyrant's ego, and that of his anti-Semitic assistants.

"In all honesty, we were skeptical, doubtful of you from the start. But you persisted. Your request, the story of the community's birth, the way you have organized your synagogue, and various information that came to us, particularly the fact that you felt sure there were no Jews left in the world other than yourselves, which further strengthened your belief in the need to serve the Holy One, all these taken together with the report lodged by Rafael Cantoni, convinced us of the need to receive you, assist you, adopt you, and bring you into the heart of the Diaspora Jewish community.

"You will no doubt be happy to learn that due to his courage, devotion, and exerted efforts, Rafael Cantoni is the head of the United Jewish Communities in Italy. You no doubt thought he'd abandoned and forgotten you, but the truth is quite the opposite. He admires you, cares about you, and is deeply concerned about your development. I advised him that you were coming today. Unfortunately, he is otherwise occupied, but promised to meet you in San Nicandro as soon as he can free up some time. He would have been tremendously pleased to receive you into the Italian Jewish community right there in San Nicandro, in your own community, but not during the war. And so now, you are welcome here, brethren. May God bless you for granting us the privilege of receiving you today."

A long silence ensued, until Cerrone, crying, fell on Donato's shoulder while Palmiero and Tritto hugged the two of them together, and young David fell on his knees before the Chief Rabbi, quickly kissing the corner of his robe.

"Stand, young man. I'm not the Holy Father!" the Chief Rabbi laughed. "I'm just a regular Jew who, through the help of others, was able to save your lives until the right time came for this next stage. What do you say, Donato? You've understood the circumstances, I hope?"

"At last, your honorable Chief Rabbi, at last. I have lived the past fifteen years in San Nicandro seeking only to love God and uphold his instructions as set out in the Torah. We studied a great deal, we worked a great deal. Sometimes we were split into opposing groups, but then we reunited. We needed you but didn't know of your existence. When we did find out about you, how could we possibly have known of the terrible decrees, of the violence, of the continuous horrors? We barely had information about the war, other than the fact that a few of our lads fought for Italy, but we had no knowledge of European Jewry's fate during this period."

Donato shook his head in disbelief before continuing. "Having never met Jews before, for a long time we were certain that we were the only Jews on the face of the earth. But as soon as we learned that other Jews existed, we found them deflecting us quite forcefully. How could we have begun to imagine that Rafael Cantoni's snub letter to us was formulated to protect and save us? He'd seemed so happy when we hosted him, and we made sure to treat him as one of us, yet shortly after he left, I had no choice but to read his missive out aloud to a very shocked community."

Donato draws that letter from his jacket pocket and reads it out again.

"*Dear Mr. Manduzio,*
In light of the increasingly harsh restrictions imposed by the government on non-Catholic communities, and in light of the unique circumstances that our war of liberation has presented to our weary military, it will be difficult for us, if not impossible, to intercede on your behalf... With all due respect, you are not being judged based on race or religion..."

The words rile Donato yet again. He looks up. "I let Devorah de Leo read the rest, then took up pen and paper and answered in great anger."

"Remember: you esteemed dignitaries among the Hebrews, that even Avraham our forefather was once a son in a family of idol worshippers. Yet he became the father of the Children of Israel, and you are the descendants. How dare you deny us who, like Avraham, were born in darkness and discovered the path to light? Allow me to say to you, sons of noble parents, that we too are descendants of Avraham, Yitzhak, and Yaakov. Although we were not born of Israelites, we uphold the laws that the Holy One instilled in Israel."

"How else could I possibly have answered? After all, God forbids shaming another to his face or behind his back. We felt demeaned, belittled, rejected, and abandoned. Your silence trampled us. I couldn't accept that," Donato explained.

"And how could I ever have imagined that Cantoni, as you have just revealed to us, was under arrest and forbidden to contact us, hence his sudden incomprehensible silence? How could I have imagined that concentration camps exist? Nor had we heard of the camp in Manfredonia no more than fifty kilometers from our hometown! Nonetheless, the various conversations, and particularly those with Faitlovitch of late, have intertwined and I have recently understood that you were indeed deeply concerned and trying to protect us from extreme danger. And then I began gathering information..."

Donato fell silent as though dreaming.

"Are you all right, Donato?"

"I am crying with deep inner joy, Chief Rabbi. Forgive my harshness toward you, whether as thoughts in my mind or words from my lips. I have made many uncomplimentary remarks about you, even crude remarks, if truth be told."

"Donato, for fifteen years you've been waiting to be circumcised. I think God forgave you long since. So who am I to bear a grudge at anything you might have said? Let's prepare for a group ceremony and celebration next April, please God. Let's not cry. My glasses are misting up too!" the Chief Rabbi smiled. "Come, let us say the Kaddish prayer for our brethren who are no longer alive. I'll teach you how to say it before you leave. It is a worthy custom to learn one new thing every day."

"That is exactly what I decided on behalf of our San Nicandro community at the start of our conversion process."

"In that case, you are a worthy inheritor of Talmud!"

Donato says nothing, but thinks that the Talmud issue definitely needs to be examined more thoroughly.

***

San Nicandro is abuzz this Monday, 29th July 1946. Rabbi Ravenna has just arrived in the village, accompanied by Dr. Ascarelli, the "mohel," as a ritual Jewish circumciser is called.

A great day is on the verge of eventuating. For sixteen years, Donato's Jews have waited for this moment. Some express reservations, some rush about, others are restless, but all are impatient, for the Lord commanded and initiated this covenant with his people.

At their meeting some time earlier, Rabbi Zoller said he may be able to join this historic event. The community awaits him with bated breath.

The Rabbinate's delegates arrive in Ferrando's carriage. Ever since Ferrando the tailor fell and broke his neck, his son has served as the wagoner. Neither of these city men imagined that in 1946, parts of Italy would still be so undeveloped that a donkey and carriage would remain the standard mode of transport.

Few laborers can be seen in the fields. But for several hundred meters, they drove past trullos, their windows adorned festively and identically: two blue stripes on either side of a blue Magen David, against the white background. Ascarelli nudges the Rabbi, momentarily halting his greetings. "Look at that, will you? The donkey's wearing a hat embroidered with a Magen David! Isn't this just crazy!"

"I'd actually describe it as eager. You're familiar with this village's history. For sixteen years Donato educated them, led them, guided their religious devotion which developed in stages, and for a fairly large number of those years, the Rabbinate in Rome rejected them rather bluntly and cruelly. They established their belief to the best of their ability. They continued waiting for a response or guidance from Rome, and meanwhile proudly stated their Jewishness in any way they can."

This makes the mohel think about the weighty, unusual task ahead. Over the span of three days, he must circumcise dozens of men. A marathon! He will need the faith and skill of Avraham the forefather, who was required to circumcise the men of his tribe: his own sons, his laborers, and lastly, himself.

Many discussions later in Rome, it was decided that the San Nicandro group circumcision would take place on the fourth, sixth, and eighth of August that year. Until then, the religious and spiritual importance of the act was to be taught again in depth, and practical preparations to be undertaken as a way of reassuring the waiting men.

But beforehand, Rabbi Ravenna needed to fulfill his promise to Israel Zoller: to hand over a letter to Donato.

"Donato, my dearest brother,

Our meeting in Rome brought me one of the greatest joys I have ever experienced as a Chief Rabbi. It is also the last of them. I wished to share a matter with you when you visited, but on one hand, I did not wish to diminish from your happiness, while on the other hand, I was still unsure that certain events which have since developed would indeed come to fruition.

You will certainly pardon me for providing some details about myself. Your opinion is important to me, and you will immediately see why.

In my childhood I longed for knowledge, due to my father's clarifications of the holy books and the way he taught me to pray. He was a brilliant man. My mother, shocked by the suffering others bore, was involved in a great many charitable acts and when her initiatives became greater than her means, she would approach friends, both Jewish and non-Jewish, requesting support for these ventures.

We lived in the Hapsburg kingdom, where all religions existed peacefully side by side with mutual respect, in harmony, without fear and without suspicion of each other.

Questions: I had no end of them. At eight years of age, I wondered what God did before he created the world; and why, in fact, did he bother creating it?

Let me tell you that by the time I reached my bar mitzvah at age thirteen, I felt a terrible internal emptiness and could hear an echo answering my calls that came from far off. I knew without a doubt that God was the speaker. You of all people can certainly understand, Donato...of that I am convinced. After all, did you not experience a similar sensation during your confirmation ceremony as a lad?

One day, as a child, I visited my friend Stanislas. A cross hung on the wall. I seemed to feel Jesus in agony over being crucified on it. The figurine horrified me. Later it reminded me of the 'suffering servant' described in Isaiah 53. That brought me to reading other texts, and in no time I had accessed and then read the Gospels, too. While studying Jewish philosophy and history, I was enthused by the messianic messages from our prophets. Isaiah came to be a close companion.

After that I delved into the Beatitudes, which I compared to our Psalms. I marveled at how reading the Torah led me right to the Gospel, without dichotomy, without rivalry, in a gently reassuring continuity accessible to any person able to read without preconceived notions.

As a rabbi, I was not at all troubled by Jesus and his teachings. On the contrary! Instead of moving toward a hazy horizon, I found myself completely aligned with 'Father, forgive them for they do not know what they are doing' as well as 'Love your enemies, pray for them' as expressed in the books of Luke and Matthew respectively.

I traveled a great deal, I studied while gray gloomy years descended on me, and I did not get on well with the Rabbinic Seminary Director, who was angry at me for raising contradictions to the Torah as taught in the Rabbinic Seminary. But I persisted with my studies for my mother's sake.

I will not belabor you with the details of the next several

years. Mostly, just standard living. Joyous occasions, sorrowful ones. And always asking, exploring, investigating, and questioning.

I lived a life of prayer and unity with God.

While reading the entirety of our holy works, I felt joy and pain mingling. I longed to attain that unachievable unity with God. Even though I studied ceaselessly, I was guided by that unrestrained love which burned in my bones.

Conversion never occurred to me; I was very far from such thoughts. Every evening, I would randomly open a book of the Old or New Testament, and always found something to ponder.

I was already closely familiar with Jesus and his teachings, and I approached them without preconditions, without a sense of betrayal of Torah study.

One day, broken by sorrow and concern for my daughter following my first wife's death, I immersed myself in a highly demanding activity and suddenly felt myself floating up. I put the pen down on the table and as though in a state of ecstasy, called the name of Jesus. I found no rest until, before my eyes, an image appeared, like a very large picture out of its frame and which had propped up in the room's darkest corner. I gazed at it for a long time, not in an emotional way but quietly, tranquilly. I had reached the furthest point I could go in the Old Testament. I wondered…is Jesus not one of my own people? Is he not the manifestation of that same spirit?

He became a permanent part of my inner life and yet I still never thought of converting. I know you can empathize, Donato, and your understanding is very precious to me. Vital, even.

Like you, I ruled out study of Talmud, which goes into the finest details with great scrutiny, meticulousness, and discernment. It holds nothing but diverse approaches by the sages and philosophers to an issue under discussion. In my view, the Jewish soul aspires to comprehend the general principle, to unravel the great mystery of life in all its splendor.

I was appointed as Chief Rabbi and director of the Rabbinic Seminary in 1940, replacing David Pareto at the Rome Tempiore Maggiore, and began my job during a time when the cruel unjust influences of anti-Semitic laws were already evident. The disputes within the community between supporters and opponents of Mussolini were highly vocal, as were disputes with ardent Zionists, all of which made my work very difficult and required extreme delicacy.

The letters you sent me were like songs of praise to truth and commitment.

However, in September 1943, the Germans took the city. Assisting you would have been nothing short of assisting our enemies in bringing about your terrible deaths. I needed to repress any hope you had. You will no doubt admit that I acted with your best interests at heart.

At the time, all my attention was directed toward Jews who were experiencing dreadful suffering. And there were many such Jews. I approached anyone I could for assistance. A Catholic friend with ties to the German Embassy in Rome reported on plans which were taking increasingly clear shape among Nazi leaders relative to the Jewish populations. Instantly I realized that if we do not take action, a blood bath will result, and we would quickly be required to close all synagogues.

I handed down a ruling that people could pray at home rather than attend synagogue. Each person should pray on his own, wherever he is. God is everywhere. He will hear the prayers. We needed to prevent the Jewish population from gathering anywhere or being found in groups. More than anything else, we needed to destroy files and lists held by synagogues. By contrast, you kept insisting that we add your names to the list of Jews!

As of the evening of September 10th, the German military controlled Rome. Since half of Italy was already under German military command, Himmler must have felt that it was high time for the Italians to participate in what they termed 'The Final Solution,' a plan to rid Europe of all Jews. When the Germans attempted to demand fifty kilograms of gold from the Jews, threatening to harm three hundred hostages, headed by me, I ordered the community members to do the best they could. They managed to collect thirty-five kilograms. By hiding in a friend's vehicle, I was transported to the Vatican where I pleaded for assistance with the missing fifteen kilograms.

I was ushered into the office of the Secretary of State, Cardinal Maglione. 'The New Testament cannot abandon the Old!' I said. 'Please, help me. As for repayment of the sum you lend us, I offer myself as collateral, and since I am poor, Jews from around the world will contribute to repay the debt.'

He accepted the offer. However, on returning to the synagogue, I learned that my fellow Jews had managed to collect the required sum of gold. I offered my profound thanks to my Catholic friends.

And then, Donato, October 1944 came. It was Yom Kippur.

I have a soft spot for this unique holiday. I always see my father and mother crying throughout the prayer service on this day, the only day of the year when the High Priest is permitted to enter the Holy of Holies.

That evening we had almost reached the end of the long, ritual prayer service. I admit that it is also fairly exhausting. I felt alone among my friends. I felt a certain embitterment as a result. Suddenly a vision appeared, even though I have trouble describing it as such since what I saw was reality. I could see a great plain, and there on the green grass stood Jesus, wrapped in a white cloak. Above him, the heavens were entirely blue. 'You are here for the last time. From now on, you shall follow me,' he said. 'If that is what must happen, then it shall happen, since it must,' I answered.

Returning home to share the meal that breaks the fast with my family, I said nothing as we ate. Afterwards, when I was alone at last with my wife, I heard her say something that amazed me. 'I don't know if you will believe me, Israel. Today, as you stood before the Ark and the Torah, I seemed to see Jesus at your side! He wore white, and he placed his hand on your head. Just imagine how shocked that left me!'

The next morning my daughter, Miriam, began questioning me. 'Papa, I dreamt about Jesus. He was very tall, wrapped in a robe that was as white as marble. But I can't remember what happened next. How should that be interpreted?'

I understood. I was about to move into a different direction, but one which did not contradict my current path, and right then it all seemed very logical to me. Dear Donato, I know that the essence of converting is responding to God's call. A person does not choose the moment in which he converts to a different religion. One day he is simply converted by accepting that call, and then there is no choice but to obey.

None of my experience was preplanned or prepared in advance. There was only the love, the beloved, and the lover. It was a gesture that grew from love, an experience filtered through love. It all came about because of knowing what love imbues.

I continued for a while to function as Chief Rabbi. Those events did not concern me. I knew the texts of both religions well, one following the other without contradicting each other.

And then I met you and your group. Every word you spoke echoed through my being. So we stand, two brothers on the same path.

Can this situation be acceptable to you?

I am no longer Rome's Chief Rabbi. You will love the Rabbi who now holds that position. He is a good man, honest, and pure.

I was not allowed to be present at your community's mass circumcision soon to take place. That saddened me deeply.

If one day I should come to visit you, that Israel Zoller who is now Eugenio Zolli, seeking your friendship, will you receive me?

Please convey my best wishes and congratulations to your community.

I wish you all the very best, with warmth and peace, my friend."

God expects each person to respect and obey him. God is not concerned over which name he is known by as long as his Torah is honored.

Donato remembers how much he used to love going to Don Adriano to hear what he had to say about God, and how disappointed these messages later made him feel. No, God didn't disappoint him, nor the women's way of looking at the world by including superstitious thoughts and action. The lies disappointed him; the militant viewpoints. Those sickened him to the depths of his soul.

Avraham Levi and Eugenio Zolli are attracted by the same kind of pure love, by the same truths, even though their lives are so very different: polar opposites, one could say.

***

For several days, the community bombards Rome's delegates with questions. Nor do prayer times end without a barrage of questions, which grow ever more finely honed as the community absorbs Torah perspectives from Rabbi Ravenna or Dr. Ascarelli. Both those men are amazed at the community's thirst for knowledge, and its deep devotion. Although Donato has already explained the essence of this divine commandment, and the community is familiar with the reasons for it, the community still wants to know the finest details, and how the ceremony has been conducted for millennia.

"First," Ciro di Salvia asks, "why do we circumcise at eight days of age whereas Muslims, so Donato says, circumcise when they are several years old?"

Rabbi Ravenna hadn't expected that kind of question. He ponders for a few seconds, mentally scrolling through his lectures, on the one hand; and on the other, reviewing the many discussions that had taken place with Imams who maintain friendly relations with the Jewish community.

"I believe, if my memory serves me well, that the Quran does not mention circumcision at all. However, Islamic sages emphasize its importance. If you wish to know why Muslim children are circumcised later, the answer is simple. Avraham, respected by Muslims and known as Ibrahim, circumcised his older son Ishmael along with the rest of his household. At the time Ishmael was thirteen years old. Muslims therefore circumcise before their sons reach maturity, or puberty...not only at the age of thirteen. Sometimes they circumcise much earlier, too. From our 'Kol Yisrael Haverim' delegate working in Persia, which recently renamed itself 'Iran,' we learned that infant boys are circumcised there at birth. The most important thing from their perspective is that the child should be circumcised before maturity sets in, but precisely when is less relevant."

The community had heard of "Kol Yisrael Haverim," meaning "All Israel is Connected." Di Salvia was pleased with the answer: more than all else, he loved learning new things and wanted to continue the conversation but Rabbi Ravenna had plenty of other matters on his mind.

"My friends, what we are planning here soon was traditionally carried out by the child's father in ancient times. But for a long time now, circumcision has become the responsibility of the professional mohel. No doubt Donato taught you about this. The Torah very clearly describes who and how the first circumcised men went about this action in Genesis 17, verses 10 to 12, which I'm sure you know, so you can follow the words with me."

Rabbi Ravenna quoted the Torah. "This is my covenant which you shall keep, between me and you and your seed after you: every male among you shall be circumcised. And you shall be circumcised in the flesh of your foreskin; and it shall be a token of a covenant between me and you. And he that is eight days old shall be circumcised among you, every male throughout your generations who is born in your house, or bought with money from any foreigner who is not of your seed."

"All this you already know. Now I will explain why the milah is conducted on the eighth day, based on a fundamental principle to the Jewish people. It is of even greater importance than keeping Shabbat and kosher."

Whispers flash through the community. They needed so much time to acclimate to the main commandments of keeping Shabbat and kosher that the Rabbi's words send a shiver of shock down people's spines.

"I see that you are indeed good Jews. Dear Donato, your faith and your understanding of the Torah have worked wonders."

"But, your honor the Rabbi, we need further enlightenment from you, because we still aren't clear on why the eighth day was chosen!"

"We'll get to that in a moment. We, the Jews, are closely linked to the number seven. Can you offer examples?"

Answers are tossed out in lively tones. Rabbi Ravenna comes to a stunning realization: that a far greater, holier, more powerful event than he could ever have imagined has taken place here over the past sixteen years. These villagers are nobles. They are all like kohanim, like the priests, delegates of God. Every last one of them!

He doesn't know them closely enough to know who is coming up with answers, but what he hears is a throaty, honest, and pure song.

"The slaves who go out free every seven years!" one says.

"The seven weeks of counting the Omer between Pesach and Shavuot!"

"Seven of each of the pure animals taken aboard the ark in the flood!"

"Seven fat cows and seven lean cows from Pharaoh's dream which Yossef deciphered!"

"Seven years that it took King Solomon to build the Temple!"

"Seven kohanim and seven trumpets and seven rounds which brought about the conquest of Jericho!"

"The seventh fallow year!"

"The seven branches of the menorah!"

"The seven sneezes from the boy who Elisha brought back to life!"

"The leper who immerses six times in the Jordan and on the seventh is purified."

"Seven times a righteous person falls yet rises to overcome!"

"The seven days of mourning and the seven relatives who are mourned."

"Seven days of rejoicing with the bride and groom!"

"Seven days of the week!"

Donato is, frankly, in seventh heaven. He's as surprised as the Rabbi at how his community responds quickly and correctly. In sixteen years, the men, women, and children of his community have learned to read, to listen, to discuss, to understand, and to closely examine. In sixteen years, they have become Jews bubbling with joy and eagerness since they, like Donato, discovered that they have a direct connection to Hashem.

Donato sees how some continue to gain knowledge, seeking it wherever they can. At this very moment, all the arguments and disputes vanished as though they'd never existed. Donato's mission, and the persistence of each and every community member, have brought about their acknowledgment as Jews, and is about to be celebrated with great ceremony.

The Rabbi continues. "May Hashem bless you. You bring great honor to Judaism. I am proud to be here among you."

It's all wonderful but Donato keeps a close eye on the San Nicandroans, making sure none sound wiser or more interesting than he. For that reason, Donato takes command by repeating the question.

"Thank you, Rabbi Ravenna, but indeed, why the eighth day?"

"As you know," the Rabbi begins to explain, "the commandment of carrying out the milah is fundamental to our people's survival. Even if a Jew were deficient in all other commandments, this commandment must be fulfilled because it contributes to our unity. The Torah doesn't tell us to circumcise boys right after their birth, or after the eighth day. It says very precisely: 'and on the eighth day you shall circumcise your foreskin.' Even though the rationale for some of God's laws is barely understood by us, we can search for them in theories relating to medicine.

"Medicine notes that the human blood clotting system activates on the eighth day. As for other matters, you've clearly found many instances of the number seven appearing in Judaism, especially in things relating to nature. Thus we can think of the number eight as being beyond the natural, or supranatural. In other words, it is unique, making it appropriate for the milah which is upheld by every Jewish male. It is a unique number, uniquely chosen. This brings us back to the milah's importance as the most prominent action identifying us as Jews."

Dr. Ascarelli intervenes. After all, he is responsible for the men's good health and the circumcisions' success. "Let me add that the milah is conducted on the eighth day, but only if the child is well, has not dropped in weight, or fallen ill with jaundice as so many infants do. If any of these conditions are observed the milah is postponed. The circumcision removes the foreskin from the penis and exposes the glans. The child barely feels a thing. Sometimes a child will give a cry, and just as often he won't. The child is given a drop of wine from the blessings, falls asleep, and the first time he urinates, it's a sign everything is fine."

Without a doubt, the sounds coming from the community are sighs of relief.

Ester Cerrone, at fourteen years of age, glances at her twin sister Sarah before speaking up clearly. "Rabbi, a few days ago, Don Adriano told Papa that circumcision is not valid and that Catholics forbid it. How can God give a commandment to one group and forbid it to another?"

Old Don Adriano, listening closely from a place where he can see but not be seen, shudders. Some years ago he had still been convinced he held the power to bring these new Jews back to the principles of Christianity. He quickly found out that it was far more complex than he'd thought. They are indeed a stiff-necked people, these Jews!

Rabbi Ravenna, after a meaningful glance at the doctor, rejoins the conversation. "My child, Jesus was circumcised on his eighth day after birth, like any Jewish boy. His real name is Yehoshua. Ever since the fourth century, his milah has been celebrated eight days after his presumed date of birth. Don Adriano can of course testify to this: several churches even exhibited the foreskin to adherents of Christianity, claiming to have kept it ever since his milah. Zehariah, later known as John the Baptist, was also circumcised on the eighth day after his birth. I'd be happy to talk about this with Don Adriano, but I haven't yet been privileged to meet him. I'm certain, though, that he wouldn't deny such facts or their significance."

Don Adriano slinks away quietly into the darkness, leaving his spot near the church door, left ajar. He hopes no one noticed him.

"In any event, you surely know he's not the only one who called us traitors!" Bonfito adds.

"Don't let that upset you. Every conversion is viewed by the group which loses its adherents as a betrayal. In a certain sense, from your fellow villagers perspective, you abandoned them. Last Shabbat, I told you the story about Rabbi Zoller, who converted to Catholicism and was appointed by Pope Pius XII to teach Bible Studies in the Papal Institute. We were horrified at his conversion to Christianity right at the time when our own people needed to grow, get stronger, particularly after being so brutally massacred.

"And it's not as though Zoller wasn't demeaned by the Catholics, who weren't convinced of his sincerity. We mistreated you at the outset although not for the same reasons, of course. I heard Zoller's response to those doubting him.

252

'You, who were born into the Catholic religion do not realize the great fortune you enjoyed of having received the faith and Grace of Christ since childhood. But people like me, who came to it after many years of work, appreciate the magnitude of the gift and feel true joy at being Christian.' Are these not the sentiments which Donato expressed in his letters to Chief Rabbi Sacerdoti, to David Prato, and to Zoller before he became Zolli?"

***

The next day Rabbi Ravenna and Dr. Ascarelli set to work quickly and diligently. They go from house to house, each time being received as though they were messengers from God. They are warmly greeted and blessed by nervous, impatient men and excited, curious women. They hear songs coming from one of the lanes: little girls accompany the Rabbi and mohel but are not allowed to enter the homes.

In certain houses, a grandfather, father, and boys are circumcised one after the other. Tables are laden with festive foods, even though the post-circumcision instructions require complete rest. San Nicandroans presumed this was a simple intervention, probably of very little pain, but the most important order they were given for their own well-being was to stay indoors in their rooms for three full days to prevent infection and ensure that the wound heals properly. They have all promised to follow the rules. No one actually does.

In their keenness, the freshly circumcised men are so joyful that they wander about the plaza greeting each other with whoops of joy. At last! We're Jews!

They are recognized by the Rabbinate and are equal to any Jew in Italy, or America, or anywhere else for that matter. Wanting to show how thrilled they are, they improvise a hora dance, a circle around a bonfire, without any idea how tremendously popular this very type of dance is in the Land of Israel.

The women keep their distance, huddled together off to the side, laughing warmly, trying to imagine what will become of their menfolk without that foreskin. How will the men feel now that something they've always had is gone? How will the women feel?

The Rabbi beams at everyone. He is relieved at how happy the community is, how well they are relating to the event.

On Sunday, the circumcised males will travel to Torre Moletta to immerse in the Adriatic Sea, purifying themselves as the last stage of the circumcision and conversion ceremony. Meanwhile the festivities carry on. The atmosphere is uplifting, inspirational; and tears of delight flow at entering the covenant with God.

It seems that a pinch of the joy felt by the Israelites at Mount Sinai hovers above San Nicandro. Some gaze at the heavens: God is here, they mutter, we feel God here, we breathe God's divinity.

Only Dr. Ascarelli's brow shows worry lines. He is concerned that the new converts are being too active and will begin to feel discomfort. He goes from male to male: raising the chin of a lad to check he hasn't developed fever, glancing at older men and signaling that they should sit down, gesturing to the youngsters dancing round the bonfire.

Donato approaches, laughing. "There's no chance on earth that you'll teach San Nicandroans obedience!

I imagine that it does hurt, though. I'm very sorry that you refused to circumcise me."

"God's laws are as familiar to you as to me, my dear Donato. Your body is too weak to undergo physical interventions, even of the simplest kind. God is first and foremost the protector of life. I know you have learned that even Shabbat is deferred in preference to saving a life. And this principle applies whenever there is risk to a person's life. We wouldn't want to conduct an action that could put you in unnecessary danger. But thinking about it, there's a similarity with the great leader of the Hebrews, Moshe. Having been raised in Pharaoh's home by the Egyptian ruler's daughter, he wasn't circumcised either, as you well know."

"Yes. I do know that. And I know that his wife Zipporah compensated for that in her own way by circumcising their son Gershom."

The doctor smiles. Donato is very learned in matters of the Jewish religion. Donato also loves to have the last word.

The San Nicandroans march toward Torre Moletta, about to embark on the final stage of becoming fully Jewish, focused and thrilled. The sea is quiet, the waves are inviting, but this is no time for play. Each man must fully immerse, accompanied by the Rabbi and the mohel, while pronouncing the benedictions which Donato had taught them.

Arriving at the shore, they turn to face the Rabbi, sparks of joy flashing in their eyes. In a few moments from now, none of them will ever have their Jewishness, their faith, and their closeness to God doubted again. The men wish each other well and enter the water. Their bodies must submerge below the water level: in this way they conduct a ritual shedding of any impurity, uncertainty, or skepticism.

"Do we need to be completely naked?" young David asks with a worried tone.

"Well, you certainly will have nothing to be ashamed of, you *ragazzo*. You're built like that marble David of Michelangelo!"

David is too ashamed to ask Ascarelli who Michelangelo is: perhaps a Jew from the community in Rome?

The Rabbi allows them to leave an item of clothing around their hips, even though Donato is not thrilled at the idea.

"Typical of him to oppose!' Cerrone huffs.

"Enough, Francesco. The doctor forbade Donato from having a circumcision due to his poor physical health. Let him be."

"Of course… and nonetheless, Avraham circumcised himself at ninety-nine. Do you think he was healthier than Donato at that age?"

"Moshe also wasn't circumcised and yet he was the leader of the Jewish people, chosen by God himself. Either you're wicked or you're jealous, or maybe both together," Bonfito says, turning his back on Cerrone and joining the other men in the water, his gaze directed upwards at God.

The joint ritual immersion is an impressive sight. The men leave the water, dry off, dress, and move far away. Then it's the women's turn. The men turn their backs, listening as the women immerse, saying "Amen" when they recite the blessings, never seeing how their hair wafts out across the waves like silken threads. They too come out of the water, dress again, and these new Jews greet each other with charm, beauty, and radiance. The married couples pair off, looking like the couples who hover in the heavens in a Chagall painting. Their eyes shine as brightly as crystal, filled with the love of God.

From the shore, Donato watches with gladness mixed, he's not even sure why, with a touch of bitterness. This group milah and immersion has lifted a heavy load from his shoulders and heart. But Donato knows that even if he managed to bring God into San Nicandro, alone, surrounded by doubters, by villagers whose lives were built on superstitions, the future will see changes and the community will slowly move beyond his control and guidance, just as Moshe was prevented from entering the Land of Israel once his work of getting the nation almost there was complete.

It is March 14th, 1948. Despite his exhaustion, Donato is not ready to give up yet. After being torn between most of the community's desire to travel to Israel, and his steadfast belief that he must stay in San Nicandro, in this same place where Hashem chose to infuse new energy into the Jewish people, he wonders what his role is now.

He has reached a turning point: he agrees that the entire community, including himself, should go to the Holy Land.

In America, there's talk of reinstating a State of Israel in that ancient land which Hashem had set aside for his people. The country will need hard work, a strong will, and unshakable faith. Now is the time. He will call the community together and they will start discussing how to get ready for a journey quite soon.

Dusk falls, the air is pleasant; it is a time when people can relax and let their tension fall away as a night of rest looms. The heavens are busy: stars, moonlight, and auras of rainbow hues. To the community, they are signs of goodness, connecting God and humans.

Donato ponders. Fifty adherents began this adventure with him, and now almost the whole of San Nicandro lives their Judaism in wholesome commitment as recognized Jews. From the day of the immersion, the village has buzzed with plans: traveling; reaching the Holy Land; and joining their fellow Jews fighting a merciless war in which the British are not heroes at all. San Nicandro's residents who have already moved to the Holy Land relate stories of struggles between Jews and Arabs, a result of predominantly British plans concocted the previous November in order to split the land in two.

The clashes are many and violent. For more than twenty years, the Jewish community in the Land of Israel falls under attack. The riots of Hebron in 1929, and the great Arab riots between 1936 to 1939, have stirred deep hatred. The conflict seems more threatening than ever.

Donato would love to meet Ben Gurion, the old lion who the young fighters describe with admiration. Marochella junior, who fought alongside other young men and women and is full of tales worth telling, writes frequently to Donato, aware of the latter's sharp instincts and curiosity, especially when it comes to the Jewish community.

"Ben-Gurion is a short giant of a man who, passing our ranks, turns thoughts into the most unexpected of miracles. A bit like you, dear Donato: you turned San Nicandro into a holy land. You will no doubt be surprised to see how similar San Nicandro is to this unusual Land of Israel.

Yesterday Ben-Gurion announced:
'We do not hope to drive the Arabs out in order to replace
them, nor do we have any such need for that. Our hopes are
based on the idea, judging by our activities in this land, that
the land's vast expanses suffice for both us and the Arabs.'
Donato, I often find myself dreaming of the two of you
meeting each other, while I watch."

Donato smiles. He sees similarities between the warrior and
the prophet, but when it comes to God's plans, the one cannot exist without the other.

Tomorrow, Donato intends to read Marochella's letter
to the community, since it brings news of Jews in various
places worldwide who have just experienced the most unbelievable reality.

Raising his eyes to the heavens, he feels a strong need
to remind his coreligionists about how these divine rules
are far from a burden and actually make life simpler. God's
laws are firm, decisive, and must be upheld daily. They are
not adjustable, nor do they need corrections; their goal is to
support, protect, and guide.

Picking up his pen in an inspired moment, Donato words
a reminder which he titles "The Source of all Things." It is
simultaneously a memorandum to his adherents and words
of gratitude to God. It is a declaration of love for what they
have today and what they will have tomorrow. It is an act of
faith; it is a delicate pearl of beauty.

Gather around, all you heroes of life!
Gather together and praise the Infinite.
He granted us His promise

Which in His book he never ceased upholding.
You revealed Your Holiness to be a scepter of the nation. You
are a maker of laws.
We acknowledge you, Lord of the Universe!
Gather together to beseech the Holy One for he reminds us of
our role through divine vision and His sacred name.
You guided me, You spoke to me.
Grant us what we await.
Thus the storm will be calmed.
Assemble, you faithful, inspiring people.
Assemble to proclaim God's Kingdom.
He will wave the multi-colored flag and the nations' anger
shall subside.
Reveal the Prophets to them.
Lead them to life.
Let them be a light in the darkness, and may every blind
person see.
Assemble, observers of God's law!
Assemble and may God watch over you.
Through vision He told us that in the future the world will
be one nation.
You will gather them in.
You will lead them
You will say, as you said to Moshe:
I shall be that which I am, standing before you!"

On his second reading of the text, the Prophet of San Nicandro feels that he has succeeded in encapsulating that which
cannot truly be summarized, having simultaneously empha-
sized God's role while signaling the path forward.

Enlightened by his multiple readings of each and every verse of Torah, Donato drew and imparted a well-structured yet reassuring manner of teaching. He demonstrated the sweetness of walking with the Lord.

He joins Emanuela, already asleep, clumsily slipping into bed beside her, the words of the Shema Yisrael prayer, *Hear O Israel*, on his lips as he drifts off to sleep.

Tomorrow, Donato will not awaken.

***